to Art & Mark

with warmest wishes

RAYMOND LEPPARD
MUSIC MADE ME

from

Raymond Leppard

Matador
5 Weir Road
Kibworth Beauchamp
Leicester LE8 0LQ, UK
Tel: 0116 279 2277
Email: books@troubador.co.uk
Web: www.troubador.co.uk/matador

ISBN 9781848766327

British Library Cataloguing in Publication Data.
A catalogue record for this book is available from the British Library.

Printed in the UK by MPG Biddles Kings Lynn

Matador is an imprint of Troubador Publishing Ltd

For Jack.

Foreword

CLARENCE HOUSE

I have known Raymond Leppard for many years and, because of this, I was delighted to read his extraordinary recollections of a distinguished life spent in music; a life lived in many different places, working with the world's foremost orchestras and soloists. I recall in particular Raymond's great realization at Glyndebourne in the 1960's and 1970's of the Monteverdi and Cavalli Operas and can vividly recall *The Coronation of Poppea*, among other memorable performances.

When I was an undergraduate at Cambridge in the 1960's, he was a Fellow of Trinity College and University Lecturer in Music and we often used to meet with the Dean of Trinity, The Reverend Harry Williams, who was famous for his memorable sermons in Trinity College Chapel. Raymond's reminiscences of those times make for the most enjoyable reading and evoke many happy memories of a period I find hard to believe was over forty years ago.

Raymond had a long and special friendship with my beloved Grandmother, The Queen Mother. He recalls their first meeting during an air raid in Bath in 1942 when he was a schoolboy. My Grandmother's interest in and love of music led to further encounters. He was first invited to Royal Lodge by my Aunt, Princess Margaret, in 1958 and quite often after that until the Summer visits began at Sandringham.

His friendship with Ruth Fermoy and commitments to the Kings Lynn Festival led to his eventual involvement with *Music in Country Churches*, which was founded by Ruth Fermoy and myself in order to help maintain particularly special rural churches. Every year for the past twenty years there has been a concert in one of Norfolk's treasured Medieval churches and I have lasting memories of Raymond's unbelievably moving performance, with Mstislav Rostropovich, of the *Rococco Variations* by Tchaikovsky and, on another magical occasion, with Maria Pires, of the Mozart *Piano Concerto in B flat*.

He was at the birth of The English Chamber Orchestra, of which I am proud to have been the Patron for over thirty years, and he has performed with them on many occasions. Lately, he has been a most distinguished Director of the Indianapolis Symphony Orchestra, and long may he continue to contribute to the world of music…

I am very pleased to have this opportunity to make a small introductory contribution to this charming volume, written by such a talented musician and inspired Conductor.

Acknowledgments

Following the tradition of recording the image of each Music Director of the Indianapolis Symphony either by sculpture or painting, it was decided to commission a bust of myself from Jeffrey Rouse, who, as a brilliantly successful maxillofacial prosthodontist, had already demonstrated his skills in portraiture. The result can be seen on the cover of this volume and the original is on permanent view in the foyer of the Hilbert Circle Theatre in Indianapolis.

While studying for this strikingly original work, Jeffrey attended most of the rehearsals for Elgar's *The Dream of Gerontius* (see pp. 55-57). He was inspired by the concept of the second part where Gerontius has died and is being taken up by his angel through Purgatory, with its echoes of tempters and devils on earth, towards his final purification and assimilation into the beauty of Paradise (see illustration, p. 121). He created first the illustrative maquette, which is in the possession of Jack Bloom, and later the life-size sculpture, which is beautifully displayed in Christel DeHaan's garden.

Several of the photographs were reproduced with the kind permission of Lady Penn. The photos of 'anima and corpo' on p. 114 were taken by David Hermges.

So many people have encouraged, helped, inspired and advised in the gradual assemblage of this volume. I'm most grateful to them all, but would particularly like to acknowledge Anita Johnson, Una Marchetti, Anne Keynes, Simon Keynes, Ursula Jones, Christopher Slapak, Michael Robertson, Leo de Rothschild, Pauline Gilbertson, Quentin Ballardie, Christel DeHaan, Lady Penn, Marianne Tobias, Veronica Jarnagin and Debo.

PRELUDE

I reckon that, such as I am, apart from the genes, I am an aggregate of what has happened in my life – the people I've come from; the people I've known and worked with; the people I've loved and who have loved me; music and the awe-inspiring visions it has given me from minds so much greater than mine and values that transcend time and never seem to wane.

Part proof of this aggregation is that life, in all its manifestations, seems to have grown fuller, and the more wondrous, the living of it the more enjoyable as I pass through into its ninth decade.

I've never had time for nostalgia. It's a crippling emotion that spawns regret as it seeks out things of the past and, in the process, engenders a sadness that they are no more. Whereas the past, for me, is part of the aggregate and its consideration a grateful recording of how much has been given me by those people, those places, that music. You can only feel gratitude for so much giving, and its recalling is only pleasure with nothing of regret; except, perhaps, for those things we have left undone and those things we ought not to have done. But I dispute the sequitur about there being no health in us for, in spite of these things, the aggregate far surpasses any guilt they might imply.

This collection of images from the past began in letters written to and from a dear, long-loved friend in Cambridge, Anne Keynes, who, I believe, shares my view of nostalgia. The letters often contained phrases like 'Do you remember . . .?', 'What happened when . . .?', 'Have you heard from . . .?' – which prompted lengthy, tho' not always reverential, replies. Then she asked me to write down and extend some of these memories of places, people, happenings at various times since the earliest days – and Music Made Me is the result.

Raymond Leppard, October 2010

OVERTURE: A Brief Calendar of Events

Friends who have been reading some of these 'gobbets of memory', while smiling and being even a little complimentary from time to time, have often said, 'But you don't always explain what you yourself were doing at the time, where you were and why. People can't relate the characters and situations to you unless they know the connection'.

Of course I knew all that – but they had a point and so I decided to attempt a sort of potted *curriculum vitae* with explanations where necessary.

I had already determined that the main interest of the series lay in the events or the personalities themselves, not in any self-promotional way (a characteristic I find and dislike in many similar sets of memoirs); rather, in how these various episodes and happenings have enriched the lives that surrounded them – certainly mine. I have no regrets that they are past, only gratitude that I was lucky and aware enough to have been there and noticed. The list of dates and periods that follows is intended only to let people keep their place if they want to.

From 1927: Born in London, soon lived in Bath. School was jam-packed with activities. We had a remarkable man in charge of music and a fine Headmaster. I slightly fell in love with the biology mistress and briefly thought that, if music didn't work out, I might take up medicine as a career. A scholarship to the Royal Academy of Music and a choral scholarship to Trinity, Cambridge put pay to that idea. Service in the Royal Air Force, which began just as the war ended, put all of it in abeyance. We had a nasty air raid in 1942.

From 1948: After the RAF, I opted to go to Trinity rather than the Royal Academy and, tho' it delayed my professional life for five years, I never regretted it. Apart from the education and a certain maturing, it is there I made my friends for life – Leo, James, several Peters, Brian, John, Malcolm, Neil, Sandy – and so on – their full names will appear later on. They have remained close for sixty years, some for a rather smaller number due to natural attrition.

Other links to connect at this time: I was President of the University Music Club,

15

played viola in CUMS (the Cambridge University Musical Society), sang with the University Madrigal Society (and, later on, conducted them), had piano lessons in London with Solomon, became conductor of the Cambridge Philharmonic Society,. and got a First in the Music Tripos. I then stayed on for two years to write a thesis about 'The Idea of Progress in Music', which I abandoned to get into the music profession in London – couldn't wait any longer.

From 1952: The break with Cambridge caused a rift with my father, fortunately well-mended before he died. It meant I had to make my way on very limited resources, surviving on what I could earn starting out alone in the profession. I had a room in Bina Gardens, a basement flat in Hornton Street and then, as things began to prosper and through the good offices of one of the Peters (Shaffer), I found a flat in Earl's Terrace which became my London base for the next few years. It was an exciting beginning.

In this first time away from Cambridge, while still at Bina Gardens, I started a chamber orchestra, which eventually amalgamated with another to become the English Chamber Orchestra. The ECO has played the larger part in the over 200 CDs (some beginning as LPs) I've made altogether. In all this, Leo de Rothschild, the best of friends, played a major rôle. Knowing him and his family has been among the most important things in my life. I can never thank him enough or express in words how much I admire what he has done for music in England.

From 1957: I was invited to return to Cambridge as a Fellow of Trinity and a University Lecturer in music. For the next ten years I led a double life, lecturing or giving supervisions in one part of the day and rushing down to London, fifty miles away, to rehearse in the other – or vice versa. In between and mostly out of term, various other happenings occurred. I accepted an advisory post at Stratford-on-Avon at the invitation of another Peter (Hall) and wrote music for several productions there and at the Aldwych, their London theatre. In 1959 I conducted Handel's *Samson* at Covent Garden (and later recorded it with Janet Baker and the ECO).

After two summers spent as a répétiteur (one who coaches singers and plays for rehearsal) at Glyndebourne during the Bina Gardens days, management were interested enough to keep an eye on my increasing professional involvement in the music of Monteverdi and Cavalli. Included in a series of concerts at the Victoria and Albert Museum were various scenes from their operas that attracted notice. Ben Britten invited me to realise a one-act opera by Monteverdi, *Il ballo delle Ingrate* for the 1958 Aldeburgh Festival.

That opera was well-received and in the autumn, after a period in Venice unearthing manuscripts, we continued the chamber concerts culminating in a large-scale evening at the Festival Hall comprising two acts of Monteverdi's *L'Orfeo* and extensive scenes from his *Poppea*. Glyndebourne's management came and, as a result, asked me to prepare a realisation of the whole opera to be mounted in 1962. In 1961, just as I had finished the score, the telephone rang in the Earl's Terrace flat where I was pouring a solitary glass of celebratory wine. It was yet another Peter (Brook) from Paris asking if I would enjoy writing the music for the film, *Lord of the Flies* and could I come over to Paris that afternoon. I could and did. That led to more movies and the purchase of a house in Hamilton Terrace next to dear friends Philip and Ursula Jones. After *Alfred the Great*, *Laughter in the Dark*, and *Hotel New Hampshire*, I gave it up. It's a withering, if lucrative business, writing for films.

I shall always be grateful to George Christie and, in memory, Moran Caplat for chancing their arms over *Poppea*. It was quite unknown as an opera and never before professionally performed in the UK. Glyndebourne originally started out as opera in the country in 1934, and has always allowed instinct to influence its decisions. Nevertheless, it was a big risk venturing into such little known operatic territory. *Poppea* was, in the event, a hit and Glyndebourne went on to produce Cavalli's *L'Ormindo* in 1967. Somewhere in the years immediately following the *Poppea* première I conducted *Poppea* in Norway in a production by Joan Cross, as well as Sacchini's *Oedipus at Colonnus* at Drottningholm in Sweden. Life, as they say, was hotting up.

From 1967: What with recordings and concerts, Monteverdi's *L'Orfeo* at Sadlers Wells (another offshoot from the Festival Hall concert), lecturing, supervising and enjoying life at Trinity and London in between, something had to give. After months of to-ing and fro-ing, second thinking and occasionally driving at night after a concert, half asleep, on the wrong side of a dual carriageway (never caught, no crash, thank heaven), I decided to leave Cambridge for a second time.

Poppea and *L'Ormindo* at Glyndebourne were followed by *La Calisto* (Cavalli) in 1970 and *Il Ritorno d'Ulisse in Patria* (Monteverdi) in 1972. They each played for three seasons, *Calisto* for four and *Poppea* was given a new production by Peter Hall in 1984.

That about ended the run on seventeenth-century Italian opera in Sussex, tho' I conducted there the world première of Nick Maw's *The Rising of the Moon* in 1970 and Janacek's *Cunning Little Vixen* in 1975.

There were still two more Cavalli operas I had discovered in Venice and wanted to prepare and perform, *L'Egisto* and *L'Orione*. Santa Fe in New Mexico had already invited me so I took them there. I loved the place – all part of getting to know and feel increasingly happy in America.

The 'authentic' movement (see pp.31-33) was on its clamorous rise in the UK. I was wearied by it and just didn't want to stay and argue – too debilitating. The temptation to migrate grew, symphony by symphony, opera by opera. At Santa Fe in that wonderful opera house standing amid magical New Mexican mountains, I conducted, apart from the two Cavalli operas, *The Mother of Us All* (recorded that, too), *The Rake's Progress*, *Così fan tutte*, *The Magic Flute* and *Don Pasquale*. I loved the place, even bought some land there and nearly built a house but, finally, thought better of it – it was too far from everywhere else.

While still with feet and a house in England and firmly typed for early music, I accepted in 1973 the music directorship of the BBC Northern (Philharmonic), an orchestra I had a great respect and affection for since the early days in Bath. Manchester is a lively city and I hoped the link with a symphony orchestra would allay the effects of a baroque image, however tarnished by the 'authentic-ites'. It didn't and so America became more important. The back-and-forth began to parallel my double life between London and Cambridge, replacing it with one between America and the UK. Those were the Concorde years.

From 1976: I sold the house in Hamilton Terrace and bought a large apartment on Park and 86th in New York. So this last part of life began, possibly the best part, tho' it's all been pretty marvelous.

There was Britten's *Billy Budd* at the Met; Handel's *Alcina* and Gluck's *Alceste* at New York's City Opera; *Poppea* and *Billy Budd* at San Francisco; and a great deal of guest conducting which led to becoming Principal Guest Conductor at St. Louis in 1984. Opera flourished there, too, in that summer and earlier. Some years before, I had conducted Rameau's *Pygmalion* and Rossini's *Comte Ory*. Then there was a rarity, Ambroise Thomas's *Hamlet*, which came off rather well without the original happy ending: *Vive le roi Hamlet* in twenty bars.

Lately, there have been two happy encounters with Chicago Opera Theatre now managed by Brian Dickie, a dear friend who was at Glyndebourne in my years there. We had great times with Rossini's *Il Viaggio a Reims*; Handel's *Giulio Cesare*; Purcell's *Dido and Aeneas*; and Dibdin's *The Padlock*, a charming eighteenth-century ballad opera that I unearthed for a May Week concert at Trinity in the 50's and reworked for Chicago. It does seem that what goes around can sometimes come around quite successfully.

Finally I came to roost as Music Director of the Indianapolis Symphony in 1987. That was for fourteen happy years in a great, blossoming city with lovely people in it, especially one.

As a *curriculum vitae* this is a poor thing, but it might give the curious a point of reference for later if they need it.

It may seem from this enforced list of how I've used my time that most of it has been spent in opera houses. That is not so. At least half of my life has been spent on the concert platform, and I've had long-term relationships with four orchestras.

Concerts only take a few days' rehearsal and one night; operas take many weeks to rehearse and perform so that, in accounting for amounts of time, they only appear to take precedence. I've loved both activities equally.

I. Before It Began

It must have seemed very odd for a second son in such a conventional, equable middle-class family to be making so earnest a fracas over pencilled letters on white piano-keys. It happened the summer when I was six at the rambling old family house in Hove near Brighton where my father's three maiden sisters still lived. Somehow life had left them behind. We went there for some of my early summers, as much for economic as familial reasons I would suppose.

My aunts made a lovely trio – precursors of the Naylor sisters I was to encounter at Cambridge – and they, like the Naylors, played croquet as well. There was no violin but one of them had an upright piano, the only sign of music in the whole family. That aunt was the wild one, a veritable latter-day Mrs. Pankhurst, and her musical taste was limited to the more martial strains of Souza and those military numbers she could associate with the suffragette movement.

That summer, I'm told, I couldn't be kept away from her piano, insisting that my father write the letters of the scale on the keys (in retrospect I'm surprised he knew how). There I would sit for hours driving them all mad making up tunes and generally exploring things and madder still when the penciled marks wore off. Evidently I made a terrible ruction, which no amount of cookies or sweets could abate, until the letters were restored.

I must have impressed or annoyed the family sufficiently for my father to buy a rather tired old Broadwood grand when we got home to Bath, and to begin enquiries about local piano teachers. One was found, a gentle modest little man with a gentle modest little wife who kept a flock of talking budgerigars who flew about the house, chattering away, favouring us occasionally with a visiting card or two. His name, appropriately enough, was Mr. Burge. Looking back, I think he had only a rudimentary knowledge of music and the techniques of piano playing, but he was kind and good with children. We persevered for quite a few weeks, during which he taught me my notes and some simple '*Variations on the Bluebells of Scotland*', graduating to a more advanced volume entitled '*Dainty Maidens,* well fingered', by E. Markham Lee. For some reason I kept that volume, realising only later the dubious significance of its title. Alas, it perished in the flames (*see* pp.84-86), or, more probably, was stolen by one of my less scrupulous friends.

After that began the extraordinary good fortune that has followed me ever since in the way of teachers and colleagues. Their wisdom, enthusiasm, care and skills have enabled me to develop and go on learning as, imperceptibly, I evolved into the profession of music, with its years of encounters with orchestras, singers, composers and directors who have contributed to the making of a life still so amazingly enjoyable.

The first one was Miss Betty Allen, a contemporary with and close friend of Myra Hess. They both had studied with Tobias Matthay, a celebrated teacher of his day. Miss Allen abandoned a soloist's career, I think for family reasons, returning home to Frome. She came up to Bath each week (where we then lived) to give lessons at Milsom's music shop.

She took a great interest in me and I prospered under her guidance, winning a scholarship to the Royal Academy, which I eventually turned down in favour of a choral scholarship to Trinity, Cambridge. She wanted me to become a full-time pianist, but I knew that was not for me. The total devotion to keyboard and its technical skills such a career would demand would have occupied the rest of my life; and that was too heavy a price for me once I'd sensed there were other things in music I had to do as well.

By the time I was called up to the RAF, I was playing at local concerts, sometimes with local orchestras and even the occasional broadcast, all of which made my parents very proud. But it was almost all local, and there were still the years ahead in the RAF. I'm sure I received encouragement from my father because he believed that, once I got up to Cambridge, some more practical sense of a career would take over. If he had known at that time where it was all leading, I'm sure he would have stopped my lessons after Mr. Burge. It was not just the uncertainty and insecurity of the musical profession that alarmed him; he had grave fears that his younger son, whom he loved but didn't really understand, might well stray into the company of all those people he read about in those lesser newspapers: artists.

Otherwise, the years before I was conscripted were full of good things. I fell in love with the girl who played St. Joan in the school's production of Shaw's play; I was seduced by one of the local church organists; I swam in the Roman baths and was taken secretly to see part of the Roman ruins that lie under Bath Abbey. I went to the *Seraglio* at the Theatre Royal conducted by Beecham; sang the solo in Stanford's *Songs of the Sea*; had viola lessons with Mabel Wilson-Ewer; and survived Hitler's bombing raids in 1942. After the first school I attended was evacuated, I went to the Beechen Cliff School where fortune once more attended in the shape of a great music master, Eugene Hanson, and a fine headmaster in Tom Taylor. It was a great school. While my older brother went to the War, I spent much of my time with the five daughters of a brilliant psychiatrist and his caring wife. I cherish the memories of them and loved them – still do.

Most of what happened 'before it began' took place in Bath – the most beautiful city in England – encased, as it is, in its seven hills. Even after Hitler had done his worst, and John Betjeman's fears that the city would soon be carted off by 'developer's lorry' had not come to fruition, it still remains in its honey-coloured elegance, a lovely reminder of more peaceful times when Jane Austen and Beau Nash lived there.

I was so fortunate to have lived there, too.

II. As It Began

When I was a schoolboy in Bath, the broadcasts of the BBC Northern Orchestra were part of my regular musical diet. Already quite a decent pianist, I was learning to play the viola and had an insatiable appetite for the near and far reaches of the orchestral repertoire that the BBC Northern did much to satisfy. Occasionally the BBC Scottish took over but the Northern was my mainstay. Little did I think that, later on, I would be their Music Director for seven years.

After a careful perusal of the Radio Times early in the week, I would set aside times when something new or valuable as repertoire was scheduled. I would find a score and copy out the viola part so that, sitting alone in a little-used room in the house, my manuscript on a music stand, my viola tuned, bow resined and with fingers ready, I could, for example, join in the opening of Borodin's *Second Symphony* (then, for me a rarity) with the Northern strings. It was often quite difficult to keep up with them as they explored what was, to me, new territory; but they were great adventures and when the players outpaced me, I would rush to the score and follow it from that until I thought I could fit in again.

Apart from anything else, this ritual gave me a great respect for those conductors who maintain a basic pulse in a movement, wandering, perhaps, from time to time as the music suggests but, in doing so, always relating their wanderings to the pulse that underlies and integrates the whole. I hated those who, palpably self-indulgent, intent only on making their personal mark on the music, would suddenly, without warning, hold up a section out of context or hasten the music forward like lemmings headed for the cliff edge; enough to make a young violist fall off his chair. It has been a critical maxim ever since.

Many years later, in a pile of discarded books and papers, I came across folder after folder containing rather spindly, hurriedly copied sheets of manuscript, witness to many, many hours spent in that isolated room, radio blazing, learning so much at those first levels of study.

There was a piano in that room, and I particularly remember late into the night of the first Baedeker air-raid on Bath, playing to myself the entire *Scenes of Childhood* by Robert Schumann as if I was giving a concert. Our house was more or less wrecked a few hours later. Looking back, perhaps it was a sort of premonition that innocence of Schumann's sort was soon to be a thing of the past. The raid was one of those mindless bombings, killing more than 400 people, product of Hitler's revenge for some equally mindless raids with which we destroyed so much of Germany.

I've never played a note of those rather sentimental pieces since that night and no longer own a copy. Superstitious perhaps, but you can't be too careful.

I was taught viola by a lady called Mabel Wilson-Ewer, who lived in a lovely house in the Royal Crescent. She was a fine violinist. I knew very little about her past, though she told me she was a Novello by birth and occasionally would say things about her publisher forbears and an uncle who was a musical comedy star. I wish now I'd had the sense and experience to have questioned further.

She took charge of the school orchestra, a doubtful privilege, but, more valuable as far as I was concerned were those times in her lovely drawing room overlooking the city where, after a viola lesson, I would stay for hours as her keyboard partner exploring the great repertoire of music for violin and piano.

Her sudden demise from cancer of the liver was the first shock and sadness of that sort in my life. One week she was quite herself; the next she had turned bright yellow and couldn't play for long; a week later she was dead. I discovered much later that she had left me her entire music library, but her greater legacy was the exposure she gave me to the violin and piano repertoire from Handel to Delius, whose sonatas she loved and played well, reveling in their rhapsodic style. It was as modern as she got, but she opened my mind to worlds I might otherwise have missed.

Living a few doors down the Crescent was Lady Celia Noble, my first introduction to the grander aristocratic world. She was the great granddaughter of Brunel, the pioneer of railways, railway tunnels and iron ships. As a hostess in London before the war, she had a celebrated salon where the Joachim Quartet frequently played. She gave me a copy of Brahms's A major piano quartet signed by Brahms, Joachim and his players, which was, unfortunately, incinerated in my London home many years later. A certain age, a widow, she had retired to Bath and lived in not one but two of the lovely Royal Crescent houses where I gave many mini-recitals to invited grandees who sat on those little gilt chairs that appeared on all such occasions. Her colourful daughter, Lady Jebb, was the wife of our ambassador in Paris, and often during her visits I was commanded to entertain after dinner with some light music while everyone talked. I didn't like that.

Lady Noble was very kind in a lofty sort of way; kinder still to her pride of dachshunds, who followed her everywhere. I made the first of doubtless many subsequent gaffes having tea alone with her beside an open fire in a little withdrawing room she used as a study. Tea was served in china, whose frail delicacy was immediately impressive. It was Sèvres, Lady Noble explained, and had once belonged to Marie Antoinette.

Naturally, I held my cup and saucer with the greatest care. The conversation turned to tea leaves and the fortunes they revealed – quite accurately according to my hostess. 'Swirl the cup round and toss the dregs into the fire'. I swirled and tossed only, to my horror, the cup came away from the handle and shattered itself amid the cinders. There was a moment's silence and then, without hesitation, she said, 'No matter', and went on to talk about a forthcoming recital on the little gilt chairs, which was the reason I was there in the first place. I shiver even now to think of it but, in retrospect, admire her almost royal restraint.

Apart from Mabel Wilson-Ewer, I've been blessed with extraordinary teachers at every stage, even in the earliest years.

At school, the man who showed me the way to several of those other stages and was the strongest influence was Eugene Hanson. After university he had a brief but successful career as a tenor in one of Beecham's early operatic ventures. Involved in a bad accident in Sheffield, he suffered a fractured skull and was unable to sing with intensity anymore. Opera's loss was our gain. Like all fine teachers, he expected more of you than you thought was possible, but you couldn't disappoint and, in that way, you prospered. Eventually the head injury made teaching too much of a strain and he decided, quite abruptly, to leave. He and his gentle wife bought a fruit farm in Worcestershire and, to all intents and purposes, vanished from our lives, returning no calls, answering no letters. He left me his library of opera scores, vocal scores and enough volumes of Lieder, Chansons and English songs to set me off exploring that repertoire.

All this came to an abrupt end when in 1945 I was called up for National Service. The war was virtually over, so a couple of years in the RAF seemed, in prospect, an inordinate waste of time – even more so when, after an intelligence test, I was posted to a course in radar. I've never understood electricity and its power to go in two directions at once. It seems I share the prejudice of Thurber's aunt who viewed empty light sockets with suspicious alarm, convinced that electricity was leaking and doing untold damage. All the same, I passed the monthly tests and emerged qualified (at least, to the RAF) to manage 7K radar sets underground at Trerew in Cornwall, where I spent the next eighteen months.

In retrospect it was a great experience. I had a wonderful time swimming in Crantock Bay during off-duty hours, getting involved in local musical activities. I developed a great affection for the people of Cornwall and the beauty of this remote Kingdom that still had its own language, culture and two different climates: the cruel, rough coastline of the north and the balmy sweetness of the south.

A short way up the northern coast from Crantock was Tintagel, with its castle overlooking the sea where King Arthur held court; and if you were told it wasn't so, then the shades of King Mark, Tristan and Isolde were all about you instead. Standing on the ramparts, it took no stretch of the imagination to believe both legends and sense their presence.

For softer memories there was Fowey, steeply overlooking a lovely, busy river on the south coast and, a little farther south, the fishing village of Mevagissy, where some friends from Bath owned the harbour's Watch House. I particularly remember the vats of boiling water at the harbour wall for cooking the freshly caught lobsters and the reassurance that the loud hissing noises were escaping air and not the anguished cries of the dying creatures. I hope they were right.

The people I met in Cornwall began the forging of links that has persisted throughout life. Thinking about it reminds me of the Old Testament where so-and-so begat so-and-so, who begat so-and-so, and so on.

I went several times to see the Radford sisters, known fondly by their local admirers as Maisie and Crazy. They had done such amazing work before the war, introducing many operas to Cornish listeners for the first time. They even produced Mozart's *Idomeneo* for the first time ever in England, gathering young singers and players from all over with an intelligent enthusiasm that infected everyone about them. Their familial ties to Cambridge were very strong, as I discovered when I got there.

Gerald Knight, director of music at Canterbury Cathedral, often visited. He had acquired the Cornwall habit after having been evacuated with his choir for safety to Truro Cathedral, where the man who taught me so much about music at Trinity, Hubert Middleton, had been Director of Music in the 1920s.

The pianist Moura Lympany was frequently there and, later, often came to play concertos when I was with the BBC Northern. In Cornwall, we would meet and occasionally play duets, but it was mainly a respite for her and a pleasure for me to be in her company. She had an irresistible zest for life, great stories and a wonderful sense of humour.

Now that I find myself moving towards the end of life, I look back with the deepest gratitude to times like those in Cornwall, the people there and those who taught me and showed me so much in Bath. Most of them are no longer with us but I know they played a truly generous and lively part in the assemblage that I now see as myself. The awareness of their cumulative giving makes this wondrous thing called living still more wonderful and enjoyable. I can only hope that along the way I gave back a little in kind for what I received.

III. Early Times at Cambridge, 1

The Music Faculty at Cambridge in my undergraduate days comprised a wonderful variety of highly intelligent, cultivated men, all characters in their individual ways, all passionate about music and the dissemination of its skills and values. The faculty had a new sense of purpose because the Music Tripos, as we then knew it, had only lately been established.

Prior to 1948, the only music degree offered by the University, apart from the rarely awarded doctorate, was the Mus. B. (it did not count as an honours degree, without which no university or collegiate appointment was possible). Music at that time was thought of as belonging to a lower class of study, suitable perhaps for young ladies or 'artistic' men of lesser intellect. The raising of music to the level of a Tripos was largely the work of two men: Hubert Middleton who held a Doctorate in Music and was a Fellow of Trinity and a member of the Faculty; and Robert Rattenbury, Fellow of Trinity and Bursar to the University. They succeeded where people like Walmisley, Sterndale Bennett, Macfarren, Dent, Stanford and many others had failed before them.

The first undergraduates embarking on this new three-year syllabus came up in 1947. I was in the second wave the next year, and we all knew it was important to make a success of it. However, as I recall, the pressure to succeed in no way impeded the excitements and joys of both the music we were studying and performing and all the other activities that lured us away day and night: theatres, concerts, discussions; sports from ping-pong to real tennis and croquet; parties, climbing in and out after college gates were closed. I can't think we slept very much. Certainly at no other time in my life has so much been crammed into eight weeks, which was the length of each of the three terms that comprise the academic year at Cambridge.

Almost all of us were older than past or present undergraduates, which may partly explain why we filled the terms with this crazily intense activity. Blame it on the war, which certainly had made us older and gave us opportunities and experiences we would not otherwise have had coming up directly from school.

We were hungry for learning and the living of life away from the shadows of war. The formalities of university life were welcome – wearing gowns; attending lectures; avoiding late at night the Proctors and their bulldogs (people hired to help police the universities' activities in the city after hours); even the sour little lady in the college buttery who doled out our paltry ration of butter so we could invite people to tea in our rooms. Food rationing was still in effect, but that, too, we coped with. Our first affairs were over and social barriers were much less important than those remembered at school. All these and more were welcome.

It was a wonderful time.

The undergraduate years at Cambridge are always wonderful, but these were spectacularly so, lighting fuses under an amazing array of talent, which thereafter burgeoned and had a widespread effect on the culture of our society. Their names are legion: Peter Hall; Peter Wood; Peter Brook, who was an interacting contemporary at Oxford; Peter Shaffer; his twin, Tony Shaffer; Thom Gunn; Peter Tranchell; Toby Robertson; David Willcocks; Simon Phipps; Julian Slade; Malcolm Burgess; Tony Richardson; Tony Snowdon; and many more.

Then there were the more senior people who looked on, guided, encouraged, dissuaded, took part, persuaded, criticized and praised – people like Donald Beves, Dadie Rylands, 'Pop' Prior, Emily Nicholas, Geoffrey Beaumont, Erika Bach and, particularly in music, Boris Ord. Boris was the only real performer in the Music Faculty until, that is, Thurston (Bob) Dart made his brief and somewhat dubious mark. In any case, Bob's performing ambitions took him, for the most part, outside Cambridge.

Boris developed the chapel choir at Kings until it became world famous. Before the war, he had started a professional life of considerable promise, but Cambridge, and King's especially proved, too attractive. Luckily for Cambridge, Boris (who to our delight was listed on an early HMV label playing continuo as 'Doris Ord') ruled the performers' roost. Apart from King's Chapel, he lectured somewhat infrequently, and conducted CUMS as well as the University Madrigal Society – a small, very select group of some twenty-five singers who met every week of term in some rather remote lecture room in King's, made the occasional record, went to places like Aldeburgh and, most celebrated of all, sang madrigals on the river every year in May Week. This was attended by thousands, and we – I was a tenor in the Society – performed in four or five punts (flat-bottomed boats) strapped together and manned by four of the most attractive punters chosen, of course, by Boris. We sang under King's bridge, where the acoustics and the water made us sound rather well (we were rather good to begin with).

At the end came something none of us taking part will ever forget, nor, I would guess, would the majority of those listening. In the gathering dusk, lanterns lit, we always concluded with Wilbye's wonderful madrigal 'Draw on Sweet Night' as our stalwart punters slowly took us downstream and past the curve of the river by Trinity library, out of sight and nearly out of earshot. People rarely moved 'til it was done.

The madrigal had all the sadness of parting from friends and place, and yet there was the hope of joy and happiness that the beauty of music can bring to such:

> *Draw on sweet night, best friend unto those cares*
>
> *That do arise from painful melancholy;*
>
> *My life so ill, through want of comfort fares,*
>
> *That unto thee I consecrate it wholly.*
>
> *Sweet night draw on. My griefs, when they be told*
>
> *To shades and darkness, find some ease from paining*
>
> *And while thou all in silence dost enfold,*
>
> *I then shall have best time for my complaining.*

No one could fail to be moved by such sentiments.

IV. Early Times
at Cambridge, 2

On a somewhat rickety stage built out over the smooth, well-cared-for lawns of Girton, the chorus, made up of young ladies in swaddling garments and young men in less extensive costumes, did their best to remember their musical lines and personify either the *anima* or *corpo* of Cavalieri's sacred opera, *La Rappresentazione di anima e di corpo*. The production may well have been the only representation of the work since 1600 and was almost certainly the last since 1949 when this all took place.

Looking at photos of these performances (see p. 114), it is difficult to determine who was profane and who sacred. A section of the chorus have their arms raised to the sky, but who's to say whether they were greeting the Second Coming in confident anticipation of resurrection or fending off an avenging God bent on punishing their excess of *corpo* while on earth.

In front of them, on the lawn (some of the photos were clearly taken at rehearsal) is an urgent looking Jill Vlasto, a Fellow of Girton, who directed the staging. Sitting at a harpsichord to one side of the stage, flanked by a small group of string players, is Bob Dart, her ally in this historic project.

This opera production was an effort characteristic of my early years at Cambridge, along with pageants and various productions at the ADC Theatre or the Arts Theatre redolent of that wonderful spirit of exploration that involved all sorts with a lovely enthusiasm and a wicked good humour. We learned so much about a lot of things and had a great time in the process.

I played viola in the Cavalieri performances and various town and gown musicians made up the rest. It was my first year at Trinity. Bob Dart was a newly appointed lecturer destined to play havoc with the established curriculum of music studies only lately determined by the Music Faculty. He was a protégé of E. J. Dent who, though retired as Professor of Music, was in the *di anima e di corpo* photographs. His successor was Paddy Hadley.

Paddy was Professor in my undergraduate days. Not, perhaps, the greatest of scholars, he was a good composer and a much-loved personality. Apart from his composing, I suppose his greatest gift to the fairly small number of people reading music was his ability, scarcely conscious in its application, to broaden our musical horizons. He knew almost all the current English composers and, being part if not wholly Irish, had a particular affinity towards Bax, Moeran, Peter Warlock and, because of the drink, John Ireland. Paddy loved Verdi and arranged chunks of operas to be performed under his eccentric guidance by the musical society of his college, Gonville and Caius, where he was a Fellow.

His supervisions, few and somewhat reluctantly scheduled, were adventurous affairs. Arriving at his rooms at the appointed hour, you may well have been greeted by a sleepy cry from the darkened bedroom where, if you followed the voice, a wooden leg – he had lost the original in the trenches of the First World War – would likely be swaying in the draught (all college bedrooms had a draught). There was Paddy in bed, recovering from the night before, suggesting that you make yourself comfortable in his keeping room while he pulled himself together and eventually tottered out to talk about music and composition. Sometimes, carelessly dressed, he would shock the ladies, but that was an education in itself. Then, looking at your work, he could, and often did, come out with observations and suggestions that really made you sit up and helped you on your way; saying things that frequently came to mind later on, even if they startled at the time.

He lectured hardly at all, but a Professor in Cambridge is obliged to give at least one a year. There was an occasion when, dressed in the magnificent Mus. D. gown, mortar board jauntily set on his head, he was wheeled back from Market Square in a wheelbarrow, having got that far on foot when the wooden leg mechanism had seized up and he was stuck, immobile. A passing undergraduate was given a fiver to fetch the porters at Caius who, probably not for the first time, rescued him in the barrow.

In a peculiar, and I find sympathetic, way, the best of Paddy worthily reflected the Music Faculty's position in the world of academic music. For me, he represented, then and now, the right sort of atmosphere for a young person's induction into the techniques, the mysteries and the power of music.

Alongside that deepening of understanding, the beginning of a quest that never ends, there were explorations into the differing compositional skills that the best practitioners of our art had acquired and applied since the fifteenth century. In their own much more important ways, their quest was the same as ours. It was through our training to understand their differences that we were given the opportunity to hone our own skills and serve our apprenticeship worthily, like David in Wagner's *Die Meistersinger von Nürnberg*, hoping to achieve the ultimate wisdom of the Guild's Master, Sachs.

V. Early Times at Cambridge, 3

Just as the Music Tripos, with its newly conceived curriculum of studies, was burgeoning and providing a remarkable sequence of graduates year by year, there began, with the advent of Bob Dart as an assistant lecturer in 1947, a disturbing undercurrent of would-be reform in the name of scholarship in which words like 'urtext' and 'authenticity' were heard more frequently than before.

Bob was made a full lecturer in 1952 and, by the time I returned as a lecturer in 1957, he had assembled 'round him a number of postgraduate researchers committed to the more arid paths of musicology.

At first a mathematician, Bob, when he turned to music, found the sloppier side of creative music studies intolerable. He put himself and his team to work not only to eliminate the sloppiness but also to set about re-editing many 'incorrect' previous publications like those of the Purcell Society, the English Madrigal School, William Byrd's collected works, and a great deal else besides.

After his election to the Chair of Music in 1962, Bob's enthusiasm for this aspect of musical scholarship knew no bounds. It led him and his cohorts to research the neglected byways of music's past where, I'm sad to say, rarity often counted for more than inherent value. Aspects of aesthetics or anything that had to do with the worth of music were neglected, even abandoned, in favor of textual verification that was rarely accompanied by a study of compositional methods or the standing of its contents among its peers. His rooms in Jesus College became a virtual musicological factory.

Inherent in this was, clearly, a threat to much that was highly valued in the Tripos as originally planned.

The focus on research into music's past sent the scholars of that persuasion scurrying back to a period when there was no intelligible notation of musical sounds. Even the Greeks, who achieved so much, never got 'round to notating their music, tho' they acknowledged its power. There has been a great deal of discussion and altercation about it since the values of antiquity became a matter of concern to the academies in France and London in the seventeenth century.

It didn't take long for the scholars to scan as far back as they could, necessitating a change of emphasis and direction. Soon there was a spate of 'complete editions', at first of acknowledged masters. Bach, Handel, Mozart, and Haydn all had to be re-edited and made as complete as possible. This meant that a considerable amount of their work was brought again to the light that I doubt but they would have wished left in obscurity, a wish I'm certain many today would corroborate as the shelves fill up.

Those major projects achieved, the search was on for unknown lesser lights who might warrant a 'complete edition', or at least merit a few revived masterpieces.

A remarkable manifestation of this later tramp down those barren wastes of musicology came to our library shelves under the title of *Musica Britannica*. Intended as a tribute to England's musical past and dedicated first to King George VI, and later to Queen Elizabeth II, it owed much to the energies of Bob Dart, who acted as its secretary for fifteen years and dominated the Editorial Committee after that until his death.

The first committee couldn't have been more distinguished nor, I'm sure, more full of good intentions: three Professors – one each from Cambridge, Oxford, and Birmingham – together with the Elizabethan scholar Edmund Fellowes and, for good measure, the music critic of the *Times*, Frank Howes. Their declared aspirations were unexceptionable: 'to make available a truly representative survey of the English contribution to music in Europe'.

I wonder what they would think of it now, for they had all been enthusiastic supporters, even advisers, to the Music Tripos as it was formed at Cambridge and Oxford.

To date, its eighty-four volumes have largely confirmed that horrid German quip of England being the land without music.

Unfortunately, after the initial strengths of our fifteenth-century composers like Dunstable, then the Elizabethans and Purcell in the seventeenth century, there was indeed a sad, cavernous gap, remarkable only for its comparative poverty until Elgar in the twentieth century and the great flowering of the present time.

Musicology, concerned only with the past, found that the cavernous gap was their main hunting ground, with the result that, of the eighty-four volumes, barely four or five contain music you are likely to hear outside the occasional University revival – along the lines of Cavalieri's *anima e corpo* that I so much enjoyed in 1949; more a thing to take up, perform and put aside without taking up space in eighty-four volumes. Boyce's *Solomon* or Arne's *Alfred* would have done just as well as the Cavalieri, possibly even with the same sets and costumes.

Bob lasted only two years at Cambridge, frustrated in his attempts to turn the Faculty into a musicological machine and to undo the Tripos. His departure was a great sadness to those who liked and admired him without agreeing with his musical intentions.

He was a fine keyboard player and a hopeful one on the gamba. Of course he had a first-class mind, but he couldn't recruit any of the Faculty, which by this time included George Guest, Peter Tranchell and myself, all home products. We, together with Philip Radcliffe, Robin Orr, Boris Ord, Hubert Middleton and Henry Moule, formed an impenetrable barrier against the sweeping reforms envisaged by the new professor. He minded sufficiently to seize the first chance of escape to the Chair in London, where he could mould a new department as he wished. It was everyone's loss.

VI. Croquet and Pink Knickers

The Misses Naylor – Nellie, Glad and Doll – three daughters of a former Mayor of Cambridge, each in their own way contributed something memorable to the lives of three undergraduates: Philip Higgins, Neil Bramson and me. Collectively they left an indelible impression.

They lived in their late father's house, which had a big garden with a large expanse of carefully kept grass, at the end of which was a large shed with a polished floor, old-fashioned speakers, turntables and mostly 78 rpm long-playing records.

Nellie taught ballroom dancing there, tho' we never saw much evidence of it, perhaps because we were there mostly on Sunday afternoons, when dancing was unlikely to have played much of a part in the Naylor household.

Croquet, however, was another matter. The sisters were demons at croquet and the lawn was meticulously set out with serious hoops and white lines marking the limits. The mallets and balls were of the highest standard tho' the paint was peeling a little. Official rules of the game were strictly maintained and penalties for irregularities emphatically imposed.

Nellie also played the violin. Glad did the housekeeping and Doll cooked.

How it all began I can't remember, but come Spring and the new grass, from then on regularly mowed, we three went out to their rather grand, musty house in Granchester to play croquet and, at tea, consume much of the delicious scones and cakes Doll had been preparing all week.

We made three pairs, different each Sunday, the schedule carefully worked out by Nellie. Perhaps we should have worn boaters, blazers and neckerchiefs as was, doubtless, the custom in earlier Naylor times, but we did make an effort and wore flannels, ties and light linen coats, no head gear. It was as much as we could manage in the way of respecting the seriousness with which the game was played.

Croquet is famous for raising blood pressures when, for example, a ball is coming close to the final hoops and is sent scurrying away by an opponent. We three men remained calm on the whole, but the sisters would appear quite disturbed at particularly tense moments, even occasionally raising their mallets at one another. No rough language was used, but 'Oh Glad!', 'Oh Doll!', or 'Oh Nell!' could be made to sound quite angry and threatening. All, of course, was resolved by teatime, but decorum had been certainly and endearingly tested.

Nellie was better at croquet and, possibly, ballroom dancing than she was at playing the violin. Nevertheless, at one time she played at the back of the first violins in CUMS – the University choral and orchestral society – conducted then by Boris Ord.

I was principal viola and so a close witness to a sad but legendary moment during rehearsals for a performance of Beethoven's *9th Symphony*. Boris detected a flaw in one of those passages in the slow movement that mercilessly expose the first violins. With the rest of us silent, Boris had the first four desks play the offending passage and then the last five, where, by the narrowing-down process, the fault clearly lay. Boris in his cruelest, gravelly voice growled, 'Miss Naylor, stop playing', and suddenly all was well again.

After that Nellie left CUMS and came to play in the Trinity orchestra, where another embarrassment was avoided with no thanks to me.

The Trinity orchestra was a lesser affair made up of those members of the College and their friends who were unlikely to qualify for admission to CUMS but loved to play. Hubert Middleton supervised their weekly meetings. Once a term they gave a concert in one of the large lecture rooms on the east side of Great Court, for which we rather better players came to swell their numbers and support their endeavors.

On this cold Sunday, after a morning rehearsal and rapid return for lunch at my lodging out on St. Barnabas Road, I biked back for the concert rather late, parked at Great Gate and found myself just behind Nellie. As we walked through the gate, I noticed the hemline beneath her coat was uneven.

We were to put our coats and instrument cases in a set of rooms a floor beneath the lecture room. This done, Nellie turned to go up the winding stairs and I saw why the hemline was so uneven. She had tucked the back of her dress into a pair of startlingly pink knickers.

I didn't know what to do. Should I have said, 'Miss Naylor, your knickers are showing'? Could I have tweaked the dress with my bow as I ascended the stairs behind her? Should I have abandoned it all and gone home pretending somehow I'd got the afternoon wrong? To my everlasting shame, I did nothing.

When we arrived at the lecture room, the orchestra was assembled and Nellie had to back her way through the desks to her place and I to mine. The audience saw nothing, but most of the orchestra had a glimpse of a pink flash, and by the time

Hubert Middleton had entered and given a downbeat to Mozart's Overture to *La Clemenza di Tito*, the shakes had set in. The descending scales representing Rome in flames flickered uncertainly rather than sizzled, for it had become difficult to read the music through the tears, and the fires were close to being put out altogether.

Disaster was, thank Heaven, averted when we stood up to the applause of an audience clearly mystified by the obvious levity in the orchestra. A very bright Girton player, Barbara Kellett, picked out the skirt by hand before we sat down, pretending there was some dust or a mark that needed brushing off. Nellie thanked her and, we believe, never knew how close she was to an embarrassment far exceeding, at least in her mind, that caused by Boris.

VII. Further Hazards

The college orchestra at Trinity was something of a free-for-all gathering of college members and friends whose enthusiasm somewhat exceeded their instrumental skills. Meeting once a week, they generally gave a concert in one of the lecture rooms towards the end of each term. They were very happy at their weekly rehearsals with no sign of chagrin that they were not quite up to the level of playing in CUMS, the University orchestra. The reality of contact with the music, even if occasionally distanced by a few notes slipping under the music stands, was sufficient reward and much valued.

Come the final rehearsal and concert, a number of CUMS players joined in to raise the standard a little and make the music-making more enjoyable.

I have already told the story of Nellie Naylor and her sartorially striking introduction to the orchestra after her unfortunate encounter with Boris Ord and Beethoven's 9th in CUMS. Subsequently, she became a loyal member of the Trinity orchestra and was assiduous in her attendance at the weekly rehearsals.

Among other regulars were William and Marjorie Rushton, both very distinguished scientists in their own academic fields and passionate amateur musicians. William, a Fellow of Trinity, played bassoon and Marjorie, his wife, tho' a very competent oboist, preferred to play timpani with the orchestra.

To end one concert, Haydn's *94th Symphony* was programmed. It is known as the 'surprise' symphony on account of a sudden loud chord in the slow movement which was said to have startled the ladies in eighteenth-century London when it was first performed. On this occasion, it lived up to and far surpassed its soubriquet, ably assisted by Marjorie, whose enthusiasm for once got the better of her.

The work ends with a spirited rondo that has a very busy part for the timpani, ending with some twenty-five bars of stellar activity, using, of course, only two notes – 'D' and 'G', dominant and tonic – in patterns familiar to all those who knew their military marches.

Tonic-dominant, dominant-tonic went the ending in various patterns over the twenty-five bars concluding with two bars for the woodwind alone playing a finalising cadence followed by a repetition of this on full orchestra including timps. Then it happened – in perfect time and very loud after the final tonic 'G', Marjorie played on with an extra, cracking dominant 'D' – all by herself.

The shock was like a train accident without injuries. General astonishment rendered everyone silent, followed by ripples of giggles that grew into uproarious laughter and then applause.

There was simply nothing to be done about it. The symphony was forever unfinished. It's rather a wonder Haydn hadn't thought of it himself, for he loved practical jokes.

If we'd had sufficient control of ourselves, we might have played an extra G-major chord so as to end it properly. But it was too late for that. There it was, bold as drumsticks, a dominant 'D' forever and an unfinished rondo.

The look on Marjorie's face was something to treasure.

VIII. Boris Ord

For the young undergraduate in 1948, Boris Ord was the most celebrated and, to some degree, most glamorous member of the Music Faculty.

His choir at King's was already well-known before the war but, on his return after four years with the Royal Air Force, he brought it to new heights with a particular soft-grained sound that made the broadcast Christmas carol service famous around the world. The boys came from the college's choir school, the last in Cambridge where, years before, many of the colleges had schools that supplied young voices for their chapels.

The choirmen at King's were carefully chosen by Boris, who chaired the examiners at the choral scholarship trials. Most colleges offered choral scholarships by way of providing at least some music for their sparsely attended chapels. I put in for Trinity.

The trials had, for me, taken place a couple of years earlier (just before I was conscripted and served in the RAF). I remember we were auditioned in King's Chapel and, afterwards, the finalists were examined singly by Boris in his lovely rooms at the top of Gibb's building. There were ear tests and sight singing, at the end of which Boris asked me why I had put Trinity as my first choice. 'Because I didn't think I would make it to King's,' was my reply. I discovered later that Hubert Middleton, the organist and director of music at Trinity, wouldn't release me and, in retrospect, I'm so very glad.

Wonderful as Boris's choir in King's Chapel was, the demands on the choral scholar's time and loyalty were so considerable that not only were activities outside the college curtailed, but few managed a good degree and still fewer survived their primal glory. I felt the need of the former and had little interest in glory then as now.

Boris, nevertheless, became a good friend, willing to keep his distance. His directing of both CUMS and the University Madrigal Society increased our understanding and involvement in all the music we undertook; it was of the essence that Cambridge had to offer. He gave excellent parties, especially in May Week, when we would often play two pianos in his rooms until dawn. Rather too much was imbibed on those occasions with Boris intermittently handing out digestive biscuits – 'good blotting paper, my dear'.

Only a few weeks after May Week, Long Vac term began and many of us came up for it. After the drab weariness of war and, for most of us, service in the armed forces, we simply loved being at Cambridge and the lively companionship of our fellows. There was certainly work to do and projects to be completed, but they tended to take second place to extra-curricular activities, such as the Cavalieri opera, *anima e corpo* at Girton.

Another regular involvement was with the summer pageants on the lawns behind Gibbs' Building. The subjects for the pageants varied: Royal visits to Cambridge of which there were, over 800 years, enough for several programmes; the Reformation; The Muses in Cambridge, paying tribute to our most notable poets, Milton, Spenser, Gray, Dryden, Rupert Brooke and, with him, the Bloomsbury world that originated with Cambridge people, many of whose descendants still lived there. I believe there was once a proposal for a pageant on evolution because of Darwin, but the Origins proved too sensitive for representation on King's lawns. It also would have been hard to fit in the Puritans. That was one scene that found its way into almost every pageant regardless of subject. It featured the slow, lugubrious procession of Puritans impersonated by Boris Ord, Philip Radcliffe, Donald Beves and, occasionally, Dadie Rylands, all dressed in funereal black with longboat hats or skullcaps, chanting the most miserable of psalms, Bibles in hand.

It was an impressive sight and proved a major attraction.

There was always some dancing for the chorus and, 'tho the music was usually appropriate to the period portrayed, the dancing was always much the same, with a movement forward and backward which became known as the 'Pop Prior Step'. The pageant did very well for a number of years and Mrs. Camille Prior, known to everyone as 'Pop', was involved in dozens of theatrical ventures. She was small, French, and very dynamic. She was married to a senior lecturer, Fellow of King's, who departed this life 'in media res' without anyone we knew ever having seen him. Nor did it seem to halt Pop in her tracks, which covered not only things theatrical but also a flourishing charity for 'fallen women' whom she often took into her house on Silver Street and, in return for certain domestic chores, cared for them until a solution as to their future could be found. Over the years, several returned a second and third time, admonished by Pop for carelessness (she rarely took a moral stance). One of them in my hearing said she was 'awful sorry ma'am ...don't know the name of the feller, but I got his motorbike registration number'. Pop traced him and later took pride in telling that the couple had been happily married for some years after that.

Long Vac meant punting on the Cam, picnic lunches, beer at lunchtime at pubs overlooking the river, trips to Ely, Bury St. Edmunds, and Downham Market, all of which were out of the question in term time. There were many parties and, since college gates still closed at the usual time, there was a great deal more climbing in and out than usual.

To add to the list of distractions, Peter Tranchell had bought a house on Halifax Road, mostly to find a little distance from his college rooms, which were frequently overrun. Privacy apart, the house was, nevertheless, the scene of many fairly wild parties that went on 'til the small hours. The local taxi firms were usually forewarned and you could sometimes hear over their Tannoy system, '...another two for scallywags' road.' The epithet stuck.

The end of Long Vac Term was more a fading away than a stop, a gradual returning to what now seemed a relatively humdrum society from whence we variously came. Cambridge was working its miracle of independence. Tho' we loved the people back in humdrum, we had already begun to enter a new intellectual, social world of our own making that was different from the one we inherited, no matter what that may have been.

The friends we made in this process would become part of life, with friendships more durable than many passionate affairs along the way.

That was a big part of what Cambridge had to offer us all.

IX. Hubert Middleton

The person to whom I owe most for my musical education at Cambridge was Hubert Middleton. He was almost unknown in the professional world; admired and loved in several others. His musical career was characteristic of a rather narrow, older route well-established from the mid-nineteenth century and earlier. As a music student, from school you went to university and from there, if you were among the brightest, you went to a Cathedral as organist and director of music.

After Cambridge, Hubert went to Truro Cathedral, the only one in England built 'round a bend in the road, which makes the nave look rather peculiar. There he improved the choir and met his much younger wife, Dorothy, a sweet person and a perfect support for him. After Truro, he came to Ely Cathedral where he prospered until Trinity invited him to succeed Alan Gray as Organist, Director of Chapel Music and Music Studies in the College where he was also given a Fellowship. At the same time he was offered a Lectureship by the Music Faculty. While at Truro he acquired a rare doctorate in music and loved to appear in the doctorate's gown, a garment of striking peach-coloured damask silk with deep ruby edgings and ribbons. Hubert, a small man, rather portly with fine white hair was, in the ordinary way, no dresser. Seeing see him at University or College functions looking like a peach peacock with a mortar board was a source of much respectful amusement for his pupils.

As a teacher, Hubert had that extraordinary gift of giving you the impression that he thought you much more talented, able and industrious than you knew you were. You loved him and couldn't bear not to live up to his opinion, so you studied and worked like the devil to make sure you did.

Supervisions with him were memorable, mind-stretching hours. Apart from setting standards, without ever letting you know he was doing it, he would assume you were keeping up, even getting ahead. Along the way he would make points, say things that remained with you forever. He had a profound knowledge of sixteenth-century counterpoint, the music of Palestrina and his contemporaries. I remember him stressing the importance of a sensitively controlled relationship between consonance and dissonance and how it applied in essence to all music. As he pointed out, the wilful disregard of this basic principle lies at the root of the fallacy that rendered

Schönberg's twelve-tone system largely unacceptable to the general ear.

Once, when my youthful enthusiasm led me to excess over some composer or other, he gently stopped me in mid-tiresomeness: 'Raymond, you know if music is to become your life, as I'm sure it will, you will have no business to "like" or "dislike" any music. Do you think you "like" breathing?' One day, I complained bitterly about my appalling memory for dates. 'Never mind', he said, 'just know where to look them up. It will take a little longer but you will avoid making mistakes'. Thereafter I ceased to worry about it and now have a large collection of reference books and dictionaries. I wish I could say he was right about the mistakes.

Hubert was known, liked and admired by a remarkably varied collection of distinguished people. I learned later, he used to go alone to Ludwig Wittgenstein's rooms in Neville's Court to discuss philosophic aspects of music. I lived in Trinity during Wittgenstein's last three years and never saw him. He was among the loneliest of men, abandoned for the most part by his fellow Trinity philosophers, Bertrand Russell; G.E. Moore; and C.D. Broad, who did, at least, come up with a witty phrase showing a disinclination to 'follow the eccentric pipings of Wittgenstein's flute'.

Another of Hubert's close friends whom I did meet several times was Sylvia Townsend Warner; poet, novelist and, surprisingly, distinguished music scholar who edited a volume of Tudor church music, one of an important collection published by Oxford University Press. She was an eccentric, characteristic of the liberated, well-educated English woman of the early years of the century. They were the stuff suffragettes were made of, tho' Ms. Townsend Warner was rather more gentle and excellent company.

Zoltán Kodály came to visit Cambridge and stayed with Hubert and Dorothy. A select few of us were invited to meet him, but in his tall, white-bearded way he was inhibitingly silent, coming only partially down to our level when discussing the folk music of Hungary and England. I think he meant to be more collegial but it was beyond him.

There were many more such distinguished people, we gradually discovered, who respected and admired the somewhat self-effacing Hubert, not that his pupils needed to be persuaded to do so. Not the least, we admired the way he bore the burden of the Trinity chapel choir. He inherited a choir devoid of choir school, so the boys had to be garnered in from the highways and byways of Cambridge, mostly the latter. The day for including ladies in the choir had not yet dawned. Talent among the boys was sparse and, once perceived, conserved until they were as tall as the choral scholars and found themselves frequently singing an octave below the notes intended.

Hubert bore this burden manfully but, having had good choirs at both Truro and Ely, the weary, resigned look on his face at practices made us choral scholars very sad.

I realise now that, all that time, he was schooling me to succeed him at Trinity. He knew that I wouldn't be able to cope with those hedgerows, nor would I willingly play the organ (an instrument I've never liked), so he capitalised on the growing awareness among the Fellows that in dismantling the choir school they had done irreparable damage to the chapel's musical standards. Not the most chapel-minded of colleges, it still couldn't bring itself to close the whole thing down, tho' there was, I believe, a certain move in that direction.

Hubert provided an alternative. With the advent of a growing Music Faculty in the University it behooved Trinity to have a successor to Hubert who could teach and supervise studies. So then, why not do away with the hedgerows altogether, have a choir of men only (as Caius had done so successfully a few years before), and appoint an organ scholar with responsibilities for playing the organ and training the men. Then a Fellow could be appointed who would not only supervise music studies and oversee the chapel music, but also bring some elements of non-ecclesiastical music into the college.

I'm convinced Hubert let the highways choir sink to its lowest level in order to achieve this. It was typically kind of him to do so. And it worked. I came back to Trinity when he retired in 1957, and I stayed for ten happy years of Fellowship at the college during which time, sadly, he died. I still mourn him.

Those years were quite differently wonderful from the first five years as an undergraduate and researcher. I had earlier quit my Ph.D. project after two years when the need to make music overpowered the urge to become wise and write about it. There was, too, the underlying hope that a bonding of academic principles with the problems of performance could be achieved with benefit to both.

This was still in my mind when I accepted Trinity's invitation to return. Back as a Don, I led a double life between Cambridge and London where, by then, I had a house. I often drove the fifty miles after a concert to lecture the next morning and returned that same day to London to rehearse in town. It was a newly wonderful and enjoyable life.

Back in Cambridge I was fortunate to find my beloved friends Peter Tranchell and Malcolm Burgess still *in situ*, and the unholy trio pursued their times together with, perhaps, a little more restraint than before.

The University and College were wonderfully generous to me, allowing me to be away for a year in Venice in pursuit of Monteverdi and Cavalli operas. Apart from lecturing, they let me restrict the number of my pupils, and living in splendid rooms in Great Court was but one aspect of a life of hectic luxury.

I could have stayed 'til I died – Peter and Malkie both did. I've lived much longer than either of them and might well have become like the old Fellow of Queens' College who had hung on to his Fellowship and Lectureship longer than he should've. In Hall one evening, piqued by some younger, sly criticism, he said, 'You must understand, I am already an abuse and have every intention of staying 'til I'm a disgrace'.

That wasn't to be my lot and, as the pressures to conduct and play grew, I had to decide again which life would prove the more fulfilling. So I left once more in 1967. Neither then nor at my retreat during the phantom Ph.D. years did I regret the decision; nor do I now. But departing for the second time found me, apart from an abiding gratitude and love for the place and the people there, with one ideal still unfulfilled.

Since my earliest undergraduate days I had believed that an amalgam of the Academic and Professional life in music was not only possible but desirable. The learning of the one would inform the other and the insight of a successfully committed performance would illuminate and direct the scholarship.

The lopsided ways of Bob Dart and the musicologists only served to confirm the need to establish this as a *modus operandi*.

Some of the values of Paddy Hadley, some of the understanding of Hubert Middleton, and some of the flair and informed effects of the performances of Boris Ord were indications to me that intelligent scholarship can enhance performance, indeed give it the strength of license.

I still believe it, but the wave of musicology with its attendant sprites of 'authenticity', 'urtext', and the so-called 'historical evidence' swept the field and stifled my earlier attempts at Cambridge and somewhat in the following years. The restrictions of the wave have denied for many so much of the creative freedom necessary for making the sounds.

If music isn't performed in ways that allow the performer complete, enlightened freedom, then it is nothing.

X. F.A. SIMPSON

Among the most intriguing figures at High Table when I came up in 1948 – one who remained so for all my years at Cambridge, although the adjective gradually changed – was F.A. Simpson, a cleric who had been made a Fellow in the days when a fellowship was for life, no matter how long. A more rigorous retirement age has since been imposed and I shouldn't wonder if the example of Simpson had a good deal to do with it.

He was an Oxford product. Few stories of his earlier years were told, there being quite enough in his time at Trinity to satisfy anyone. While in Oxford he had written the first volume of a definitive study of Louis Napoleon. Trinity thought it had landed a major fish when they offered him a fellowship to complete a second volume and, eventually, contribute to the intellectual life of the College.

He did write a second volume but it was given a cool reception, even some sharp criticism. Thereafter, he wrote no more and virtually did no more for his adopted college, complacently occupying for the next forty or fifty years one of the best sets of rooms in Great Court. Nor did he entertain much, being rarely seen with undergraduates, tho' he liked to look at young people – especially at the swimming place where costumes were not worn. It was known as Parson's Pleasure.

He considered himself an expert horticulturist and, equipped with secateurs, he was prone to indiscriminate pruning on his regular walks about the College and the Fellow's garden, to the despair of the College's staff of gardeners. There were even occasional complaints from neighboring colleges about his snipping activities in their gardens.

Except in the hottest weather, Simpson generally wrapped himself up in several layers for his perambulations, almost always with a very long, grey knitted scarf wrapped 'round his neck, with yards to spare dangling down on either side. This occasionally proved hazardous when crossing a road.

He was prone to stand on the cobblestones outside Great Gate looking increasingly agitated, taking a step or two forward and then back again, ending finally in a lunge across the road, scarf flying, causing a squeal of brakes and the occasional fender bender, to use an American epithet. The windmill effect of arms flailing, scarf flying and high-pitched words of reproach only added to the confusion. He was very rarely clipped and usually, disregarding the chaos left behind, he would then sail happily down the opposite side of Trinity Street on whatever errand he had in mind.

Things happened to Simpson. He complained bitterly (perhaps not without reason) about finding half a mouse in some slices of toast ordered from the kitchens. Dining in Hall he always took the largest helpings of everything that was served in spite of it being a time of rationing. Later in life, he swayed a lot while he was eating and it was reported that, when asked why he did so, he said that it was to remind himself that he was still alive. He had a curious knack of un-cooking the food on his plate, pushing it to and fro so that it appeared to separate into its constituent parts. When he had finished he would sometimes say in a note of despair, 'I can't understand why I have more food now than when I began'. Complaining came naturally to him.

Once, while traveling by train to London in the same compartment, I sat opposite Simpson who was reading a Penguin paperback. The poor paper and flimsy cover must have been distasteful to him, for when he'd finished reading a page he tore it out and, not deigning to crumple it up, put it out of the window where it fluttered away like some forlorn butterfly. It was, of course, amusing but, it equally revealed a lamentable lack of concern for the countryside and the public good not uncharacteristic of the man.

Yet from this man came one of the most moving moments in my first years at Trinity.

John Burnaby, Dean of Chapel at that time, had persuaded Simpson (whom he greatly disliked) to preach in chapel on Remembrance Sunday. It was a foggy November evening and the chapel was full, a rare occurrence, and we choral scholars had the best seats in the house.

I shall never forget the image of that tall, dim figure standing and swaying with the scarf 'round his neck in the Dean's stall opposite the Master's under the organ loft. His subject was the futility of war and the nobility of sacrifice. He particularly referred to the graves of the First World War in France, row upon row of dead Englishmen, many of whose names were inscribed in our chapel on the panels before the altar, the gold lettering glinting in the dim candlelight. Many in the congregation had experienced the horrors of the more recent war and remembrance meant a great deal to them.

That summer Simpson had been to one of those fields of tombstones that testify to the mad folly of war. He may have been searching for a particular stone – perhaps a family member or a lover, he didn't say – but he came across one with the inscription 'Not in vain, my darling, not in vain'. That was his text.

It was a wonderfully moving sermon, made perhaps the more so by the presence of his audience and the fact of these words coming from someone who seemed so removed from emotions like compassion and love. Reiterating his text at the end, barely audible and almost breaking down, he created a moment that none would forget. The silence that followed in that cold, foggy chapel seemed to last for hours.

Simpson left the chapel immediately and returned to his rooms where, by previous arrangement, he dictated his sermon to someone from Cambridge University Press; he had committed it to memory. It was published soon after under the title 'A Last Sermon'. It had something of farewell in it that made him appear more sympathetic than usual.

There was very little small talk at Trinity High Table, as I learned later when privileged to dine there as a Fellow. Men like Housman, Gow, Trevelyan and Russell had set standards for good argument and stinging discussion that were only lowered at your peril.

One such interchange involving Simpson happened later on and I was fortunate enough to be present.

Harry Williams, who succeeded Burnaby as Dean of Chapel, had managed to persuade Simpson some fifteen or so years after the Remembrance Day sermon to preach again in our chapel.

There was great excitement about it and the chapel was packed, this time on a pleasant early summer evening. Being ostensibly in charge of chapel music, I was able to find a seat in the organ loft.

Simpson this time elected to speak from the chancel instead of the Dean's stall, and he chose as his text the parable of the Good Samaritan. It was warm enough for him to wear only the scarf above his clerical suit. As he delivered the sermon, he wandered up and down, bending and swaying with the scarf billowing out behind him.

It wasn't a great sermon and the sense of disappointment was palpable.

After chapel on a Sunday evening, it was customary for the preacher to sit in Hall on the right side of the Master, in this case Lord Adrian. The Dean of Chapel was on his left and, next to him, Burnaby, the former Dean who had come in expressly to hear the sermon. I was one farther down on Simpson's side.

Conversation lagged and didn't get much of a stimulus when Adrian observed, 'Simpson, I thought it was an unusual subject for you to have chosen'.

Everyone within earshot froze, knowing that Simpson wouldn't give sixpence to a beggar. That was the first of several attempts to start things going while Simpson, who clearly knew the sermon hadn't been well received, barely spoke except in monosyllables. Eventually Burnaby observed – somewhat maliciously, I think – 'Simpson, while it was a considerable event for the chapel to have you preach, I thought from the title of the published sermon you gave fifteen years ago – 'A Last Sermon' – you would not preach again'.

A glint came into Simpson's eyes. 'Burnaby, I am surprised that you do not yet know the difference between a definite and indefinite article'. I don't recollect much else being said for the rest of dinner.

It was a sad sequel to one quite remarkable, moving occasion. The sad figure responsible for it had yet to live out his lonely life caught up in his self-concern and fear of ever again seeming as vulnerable as on that November evening in 1949.

XI. 'GRANNY' GOW

Andrew Gow was an old-style Trinity Fellow, a distinguished classicist, and close friend of A. E. Housman who wasn't prone to making friends; nor, for that matter, was 'Granny' Gow. So it was rather surprising that in my second year he began to invite me from time to time for port in his rooms after Hall, usually to meet one or another of his distinguished guests, old friends like Bertrand Russell, who had been a Fellow of the College, and Anthony Blunt. I was so overawed by the former that I can recall nothing but that crow's nose and the shock of white hair. I remember Anthony Blunt was a brilliant talker, but he seemed such a dismissive person, rather arrogant and quite dislikeable. I don't know that Gow liked him very much, but he possessed some lovely Degas bronzes, two of his early paintings and a wonderful Vuillard, all, I think, now in the Fitzwilliam Museum. I suppose that was a bond between them.

Blunt was an active, notorious member of a private society based in King's called *The Apostles* which met primarily for the expounding and exchange of ideas, although dining and drinking, among other things, were not excluded.

Later on I was invited to join that celestial company, but fortunately by then Granny had already invited me to become a member of a smaller, Trinity-based dining club called *The Family*. It had its origins in Stuart days and there was always a toast at our gatherings to the 'Family across the waters'. No revolutionary purpose was intended, as possibly there once had been, but we kept to it. To maintain secrecy, no servants were in the room when the toast was made; a harmless foible and uncharacteristic of our evenings together when the level of conversation and variety of interests discussed were remarkable.

Housman had been a member and, in my time, apart from Gow *The Family* included Lord Adrian, Master of Trinity; Owen Chadwick; and Leslie Martin, who not only had designed the Festival Hall in which I had often conducted, but also produced for our desserts wonderful, rare varieties of apples, some tracing their lineage back to mediaeval times.

Gow was the *pater familias* of *The Family* and saw to it that trivialities were kept to the minimum, tho' wines and the menu were indeed matters for concern. We took turns entertaining and I remember making a splash and ordering Beluga caviar sent up from London as a first course and offering a superb vodka to go with it. My hedonistic tendencies were confirmed by those evenings.

Gow did not tolerate fools nor foolish speech, making no bones about pointing out and correcting either. Yet for all his somewhat forbidding aspect he had the kindest of hearts and a great sense of humour. He didn't pay a great deal of attention to his appearance and, tho' he had no beard, he allowed the facial hair above his cheekbones to grow – 'bugger's grips' he called them, and laughed. I don't think it referred to any past experience.

He once caused a vivid reaction using that word to great effect at a College Council meeting, which was coming dangerously close to putting forward to the Prime Minister the name of someone whom nobody liked as a possible future Master of the College. In a moment's awkward silence bespeaking serious hesitation, Gow, who disliked the man intensely but had contributed nothing so far to the discussion, said quietly, 'Master, I hear he's a bugger'. It was very cruel, but it did the trick and the danger was averted. Such were college politics.

I remember Gow in his rooms rebuking a smut-hunting lady who was writing a book about Housman. She had come to Gow to find some low-down on the early love of Housman's life that, sadly, came to nothing. When the purpose of her visit became clear, Gow was outraged and, turning away from the lady, said, 'I know nothing more than you will find in his poetry. It's all there and only a fool could miss it – and only a fool with a prurient mind would wish to probe further'. She left immediately without a word.

During the war he had volunteered to undertake regular fire-watching duties, which involved sitting up all night and patrolling the roofs of the Wren Library, Neville's Court and as much of Great Court as he could navigate. I don't think he bothered overmuch about New Court or Whewell's, not rating them very high in the preservation list. The image of him in a warden's tin hat lingers on, bringing incredulous smiles.

To while away the small hours in between patrols, Gow wrote letters describing Cambridge at war in endearingly witty, caustic prose. He sent them to dozens of former pupils both at Trinity and Eton who were serving in the armed forces all over the world. The letters were, by insistent demand, eventually collected and published under the simple title of *Letters from Cambridge*. Reading them you sense a man of great heart, great restraint, fine intellect, a mordant wit and an attractive personal modesty.

As my years at Cambridge passed, I got closer to him especially when I discovered that he had fallen in love with Dorothy Tutin.

The first strike of Cupid's arrow had occurred a year or two earlier when he had been introduced to her at a reception after a performance at the Arts Theatre. She had enjoyed his company that evening and invited him to visit her in London. Thereafter he was, as they say, a goner.

Dottie was an important part of the Royal Shakespeare Company at Stratford when Peter Hall took over. He asked me to become Music Advisor and help rearrange the music in the theatre, which was in a sorry state.

To digress a little: From time immemorial, there had always been a small band in the theatre's orchestra pit that played the National Anthem to begin each show and interval music to accompany the clatter of tea trays ordered before the performance and served in the theatre. The band also provided subterranean accompaniment to any song that appeared in the plays and, where called for, the occasional trumpet and drum, all from underneath. The effect was mysterious rather than magical, but the illogicality of it all had passed unnoticed for many years. All was in the charge of Leslie Bridgewater, a wily entrepreneur who controlled most of London Theatre's tea-tray music and guarded his territory jealously.

Peter had other ideas. He extended the stage out beyond the proscenium arch, banishing the pit and its orchestra altogether. We then adopted the policy that the music called for in the plays should happen on stage (or off, if that was Shakespeare's intention). We ended up employing eighteen full-time musicians who played suitable instruments and would appear where necessary on stage. That, and the appointment of a full-time Music Director, put pay to Bridgewater's union-based attempts to stop it. He, after all, employed only five players whom you would hardly wish to see on the stage at any price.

All this entailed many drives from Cambridge to Stratford with, very often, Gow as a delightful traveling companion. I enabled him to attend occasional rehearsals, especially those involving Dottie, after which he might make himself known and perhaps even take her to lunch at the local inn. She was wonderful with him, understanding the situation and gently disentangling herself when an old man's fussing grew tedious and a little possessive. The fondness was quite genuine and he was entirely captivated.

We always stayed at the Shakespeare Inn, which has, in dubious taste, labeled each room after a Shakespearian character. I don't know that there was one for Lady Macbeth, but by the time of the new extension they had run out of principal characters and Gow was amused and tickled to find himself occasionally under the aegis of Peaseblossom or Mustard Seed.

If you're in love, you'll submit to almost any indignity to spend even the shortest time with your beloved. It was lovely to see, and I hope the memories comforted Granny in his last years at the Evelyn nursing home. I had left Cambridge once more and could only rarely come to visit. There he was the model stoic, gruff with the nurses who adored him and relishing any bit of theatrical and college gossip I could bring – or invent.

I'm sure his ending was a peaceful one; it surely deserved to be.

Housman and Gow were, I believe, very similar men, keeping the world at bay with a barrage of thought and thinking and an irresistible virtuosity with words. Some thought that a catastrophic failure of love made Housman retreat from life like a turtle into its shell. Tho' I have no knowledge of it, that may have been the case with Gow.

You have only to read Housman's celebrated lecture, 'The Name and Nature of Poetry – The Leslie Stephen Lecture of 1933', to know that a deeply loveable person was somewhere there.

I fancy that when Granny gave me a first edition of that lecture a few years before I left Cambridge for a second time, it was intended as a gesture of particular friendship, a token of his regard for me, never spoken but greatly valued, if it were so. To my shame, I have only lately read it slowly and with due care. With that now much-thought-of copy of Housman's lecture, he also gave me a copy of Housman's funeral service in Trinity Chapel on May 4, 1936, which he had devised, asking me to make sure the simple Housman lines used for the hymn would also be part of his own funeral service.

The original simple order of service began with Psalm CXXXIX, *Domini probasti*, and then the lesson:

Ecclesiastes (corrected by Granny in my copy for a mistakenly printed Ecclesiasticus) xi,7 – xii 7.

The flaw would have amused both of them, but we made sure the mistake did not appear again. Had it done so, it would surely have been remembered in a hereafter conversation between the two: '"ticus" for "tes" indeed; whatever next?'

It ended with Housman's hymn:

O thou that from thy mansion

Through time and place to roam,

Dost send abroad thy children,

And then dost call them home,

That men and tribes and nations

And all thy hand hath made

May shelter them from sunshine

In thine eternal shade.

We now to peace and darkness

And earth and thee restore

Thy creature that thou madest

And will cast forth no more.

(To the melody by Melchior Vulpius, harmonised by J. S. Bach)

Subsequently, I set the poem to music for the funeral service planned in advance by and for Lady Penn, entitled 'Elegy for Prue'.

XII. Harry Williams

I only got to know Harry Williams when I was back in Cambridge for the second time. We'd met casually quite often in my undergraduate years. Everyone knew about his crippling nervous breakdown and the holding over of his appointment as Dean of Trinity Chapel and Tutor. His recovery and return to full mental health was rightly regarded as a tribute to the powers of the intense psychoanalysis that he undertook and, indeed, often spoke about.

Thereafter he was in full command of himself, highly strung, manipulative, ruthless, self-concerned, formidably intelligent, society loving and opportunity seeking – and taking. This list of characteristics might have added up to a total dislikeability in someone else but, curiously, it made him a most loveable man and wonderful company. He was capable of infinite empathy, possibly because of his self-awareness and endless ability to laugh at himself. He was one of the best tutors Trinity has ever known and, although he didn't have much time for conventional Church of England behaviour, he was a great Dean of Chapel and a superb preacher. The few times when the Chapel was full were when he was in the pulpit. The first volume of his collected sermons called, appropriately enough, *The True Wilderness*, must rank among the more important writings on religion in our time. A latter day Cardinal Newman perhaps. He sang the song of coming to terms with whomsoever you may be, respecting and cultivating the life force within so that it may flourish and bear witness as a manifestation of that force's origin, which most people call God. To him it hardly mattered which one.

I remember talking with Harry about the Newman poem that Elgar set to perhaps his greatest music: *The Dream of Gerontius*. It is an allegory of a man dying then being taken, translated by his angel, on a journey during which he is purged of his human frailties. Eventually there is the promise of becoming one with his maker and returning, so to speak, to the origin of his life force. Both Harry and Newman seemed to believe that we each have our own angelic custodian within ourselves who takes over when our earthly life is done.

Harry knew a great deal about Newman, someone who had been through crises similar to his own and survived. Newman had lost his Anglican faith and spent time in a spiritual wilderness before becoming a Catholic and eventually a Cardinal. I'd recently read a biography and, apart from being impressed by his understanding of Everyman, I was moved by the love he openly expressed for a fellow priest, eventually asking that, when he died, he should be buried next to the priest in a modest grave rather than in the more resplendent tomb of a Cardinal.

To me – and Harry encouraged and confirmed the view – this great poem that Newman wrote about death and the affirmation of life proceeding from it was intended to apply as much to the human span as for the more conventional earth-and-postmortem-heaven vision of most churches. It may be too much to aspire to being translated to Heaven while still on Earth, but we may perhaps be given glimpses of it. I believe they may be sensed in Elgar's masterpiece as well, as at those miraculous moments in music and the arts that literally take our breath away. I'm convinced, as was Harry, that Newman had that double purpose in mind.

Years ago we went on a wonderful trip to Puglia with two American friends from Yale, Elizabeth Cavendish and John Betjeman. Everyone was in great form and, as J.B. wrote of another occasion, 'All of us were bathed the while / in the large moon of Harry's smile'. And so we were for longer than 'the while' in Italy. Harry was a most unusual smiler and a frequent one. His face shone, his mouth widened and the shape J.B. described took form, usually exploding into nearly silent laughter. It was equally visible on the way back out of a laugh and both ways were highly infectious and endearing.

We had all read Norman Douglas's study of the region and were in nothing disappointed. Expectations were even surpassed finding that, perhaps because of the exceedingly dry climate, the Cathedral at Lecce, for example, looked as if it had been built yesterday instead of five hundred years ago. Harry knew a great deal about it and the rest of that part of Italy, complaining intermittently about the Jolly Hotels in which we stayed. John beguiled us with observations on the local customs, people and especially the strange-looking, primitive houses which, because of their primitive construction, looked like casserole lids. They were called trullis and, for months after, John signed all his letters 'yours trulli'. Typical.

Back in Cambridge, I had eventually a lovely set of rooms in Great Court on the first floor by the Chapel. They had formed the college library in the sixteenth century and were immediately above Harry's set. We saw a lot of each other at that time.

On one occasion when Harry was under the weather with a cold, slight fever and, possibly, a slight hangover, I was giving a dinner party in my rooms. There were seven not particularly noisy guests (I rather think Prince Charles was one of them), but there certainly was lively discussion, in the middle of which there came an irate thumping from the ceiling below – Harry's bedroom. The message from below resulted in a hush that rather spoiled the evening even after I'd explained about my downstairs neighbor and his ways. Most of the guests knew Harry and there was even a move to go down and get him to join the party. This I thought inadvisable.

The next morning Harry came up to my rooms still angry (he had a nice line in instant anger that he could summon at will), and said, 'Do you think I would have allowed all that rumpus' (there really hadn't been much) 'knowing you were deathly ill below me?' (he wasn't). I waited a moment and said, 'You know, Harry, I rather think you would've'. Another silence, then the large moon appeared and he burst out laughing saying, 'You're right, I would've'. He was a wonderfully forgiving, loyal friend, and the self-awareness that gave him those great powers of empathy made him a superb tutor and director of studies.

He found fulfillment at Trinity for some years. Then, in his search for, as it were, the conclusion of his purgatory, he retired to Mirfield, the religious community in Yorkshire whose members abandon their personal property and live their lives doing as much for the good of humanity as they can in whatever ways they find possible. For Harry this meant meditation, with occasional ventures out into the wide world and with visitations there from close friends. Even these decreased gradually as he got nearer to that inner peace he had always been seeking.

He died there a happy man, I think; and I hope his angel, like the one that cared for Gerontius, was looking out for him bringing:

> *That calm and joy uprising in thy soul*
>
> *Is first fruit to thee of thy recompense,*
>
> *And heaven begun.*

XIII. MAY WEEK AND PETER TRANCHELL

May Week (always in June) is a Cambridge phenomenon. After the rigours of the Tripos examinations, there is unleashed a pent-up vigour of an amazing intensity, and everyone with a propensity for flourishing flourishes.

One regular feature was the Footlights revue at the Arts Theatre. The Footlights Dramatic Club met regularly in term, usually in black tie. Apart from a certain amount of carousing, the evening's purpose was to try out new revue numbers both for the members' entertainment and the possible inclusion in the May Week revue.

The Club's mastermind in my day was Peter Tranchell, a *rara avis* and a much loved, wonderful friend. Together with Malcolm Burgess, a Russian scholar and a brilliant theatre designer in the Oliver Messel chocolate-box style, we made a sort of unholy trio for most of our years at Cambridge. They are no longer with us, but I think of them often and am endlessly grateful to have been so close and shared so much.

Peter wrote some of the wittiest cabaret lyrics I've ever heard. Some, perhaps, would have to be bowdlerised before they could be published, but hardly ever has skill, wit and tune-writing been bettered. There exists a tape of Peter singing and playing quite a number of them, and I hope something can be preserved from that. One of the best was entitled 'Gerontophilia', a number dealing with the Greek concept of man's attraction to youth in old age and vice-versa. Witty examples were set forth, verse by verse, Ganymede and the like (they revealed Peter's classical background before music took over), the last of which points out that 'we're all in the lap of God' and, after all, 'God's the most ancient of days'.

Good as the revue tunes were, they hardly reflected Peter's skill and originality as a composer. In his more serious music, he favoured a highly chromatic, note-packed, post-Bergian style that didn't please everyone.

His opera, 'The Mayor of Casterbridge', based on Hardy's novel, was performed twice. It appeared, however, just at the time when clinical, twelve-tone, complicated, serial structures were dominating the scene, and music that, perhaps, was overly emotional came to be disregarded.

It deserved a better success than it received; and one day, I believe, when fashions have passed, it will be revived and more widely appreciated.

The disappointment at its reception, and the subsequent failure of Peter's musical based on Max Beerbohm's *Zuleika Dobson*, made him give up all thought of a full-time composing career. Oddly, I think it lightened his soul rather than darkened it, and there followed a series of 'entertainments' written for his beloved Caius chapel choir which gave and still give great pleasure. There was *Murder at the Towers* with the unforgettable lady detective, Miss Bletherby Marge, who, whenever faced with some surprising bit of evidence, just smiled. Others followed: *The Mating Season*; *Aye, Aye, Lucian*; and *Daisy Simpkin*. In 1956 he wrote some excellent music for the *Bacchae* of Euripides, produced in Greek at the Arts Theatre every three years. It bears comparison with the best of a long tradition of compositions by Cambridge composers: Vaughan Williams (*The Wasps*), Walter Leigh (*The Frogs*), Stanford (*The Eumenides* and *Oedipus Tyrannus*), Robin Orr (*Oedipus at Colonnus*).

When Peter Tranchell died, there was a big gap in many people's lives.

I was asked to give the address at a memorial service held in Caius Chapel. It shows, perhaps, something of Peter's character and I include it in this small memoir. The chapel was packed and we had some of Peter's more outrageous settings of psalms and hymns. For a brief time, he seemed back with us and it was a very comfortable feeling.

Address Delivered by Mr. Raymond Leppard

At the Memorial Service for Mr. Peter Tranchell,

12 February 1994

It is said that when anyone you have come to love departs this life they take with them some part of you that never be replaced. And, while I would be hard put to it to defend this view intellectually, I know that it is so. But, being of an optimistic nature, I also know that those to whom you have given something of such significance that you sense its loss, are sure to have left behind as much, if not more, of their own vitality as an enduring gift, a sort of compensation for their departure. The evidence for this is in their constant reappearance – in conversation with others, in remembering what they might have said, how much they would have enjoyed a certain moment, how little they would have approved, how much they would have minded, how they would have reacted in certain situations, or how they would have laughed. It may be a very simple-minded intimation of immortality, but undeniably it happens and it's a great legacy to receive and one, I suspect, that Peter has left to a high percentage of the people here today.

Of course the proposition would have intrigued him greatly, but he, almost certainly, would have conceived it in a quite different way, perhaps twisting the tail of some wild existentialist theory that would have revealed a profound knowledge of Sartre's philosophy. Or, perhaps, he might have recalled the evidence of some good, trustworthy soul – a former bedmaker, perhaps – who had been reported in the

Cambridge Daily News as receiving regular visits from her deceased parrot, bringing words of wisdom from Parrot Heaven. Peter had a flexibility and virtuosity of mind that led him into flights of fancy, be it in words or music, that were uniquely his and usually supported by the most amazing background of classical, mythological, historical, astrological, literary, theological and scientific knowledge. Sometimes, they were prompted by pure frivolity that was as infectious as it was inventive. Which route he took depended on the time, the company and the occasion. You could rarely anticipate it, and it was often surprising but always appropriate to the situation as he saw it, if not always as everyone else did.

Most of his close friends received, from time to time, long and elaborate letters which many of us, I'm sure, have kept. Recently I came across his side of an exchange we had some years ago about the origin of the Sarabande – that dignified dance that occurs frequently in the suites of Bach and his contemporaries.

There must have been a portentousness in some performance he had heard, for the first letter begins with the delighted discovery that in 1583 Philip the Second of Spain banned the dance on account of its obscenity, which of course, as Peter said, accounted for its subsequent popularity throughout Europe. On looking it up in a Spanish etymological dictionary, he found it was claimed that *Zarabanda*, though of uncertain origin, probably originated in Spain. In a poetic dictionary by Giovane di Segovia of 1495, Peter discovered that *Zara* was the Quenchua (Peruvian) word for corn; a word that was later ousted for the most part by the Haitian word *mahiz* – maize. *Banda*, it appeared, not only means a band of people as in posse or an orchestra, but also a band, as in headband or strip. Thus *Zara-banda* may have meant a strip off a corn on the cob. What then if stripping a band of foliage off a corn on the cob were cognate with the dance of stripping the willow? And, as Peter pointed out, we all know what that leads to.

Moreover, as the argument progressed over several weeks of correspondence about other things, he observed that the willow wand, like the corncob, after being stripped has a somewhat phallic appearance, not unlike the *Thyrsis* carried at Greek Bacchanals, which was a pine cone stuck on the end of a reed or wand. So it might be that the Spaniards brought back the *Zarabanda* from Peru having learnt it from the Indians. As a folk dance it was fast in tempo, wild and lewd in steps and movement. In addition the lyrics were disgusting. Peter concluded: 'So that's that. My next quest is the origin of that equally wild dance, the Chaconne'. Unfortunately I can find no trace of this project in subsequent correspondence.

His capacity for intellectual adventure was endless – and fearless. It was just as true of the more extreme days of his youth as in later years when he focused so much on this University, this College, this Chapel, and the young people who came into his care here. This concern with humanity entailed the forsaking of ambitions as a full-time composer; and some of us regret that, for he had great gifts and the ability to realise them. He wrote music in a style that was already old-fashioned, but its lack of more general acceptance did not worry or sour him. I believe that one day works like the *Mayor of Casterbridge* will be heard again and their true value appreciated. Of course the entertainments he wrote for Cambridge will frequently reappear; there is a durability about Miss Bletherby Marge, the smiling female detective, that will ensure her survival. It was all Cambridge's gain. I think Cambridge in its self-concerned way did not always sufficiently realise it.

How can one describe Peter? He was infinitely kind, a wonderful friend, relentless in his assaults on mediocrity and shabbiness, generous to a fault. He could not tolerate fools, but was endlessly caring and tender towards those who could not help their folly.

There's an interesting scrap of paper that Johnny West, who is one of his executors, has shown me, on which Peter had scribbled some lines, presumably for an entry into a musical *Who's Who*. The first part about achievement and biography is a muddled confusion of condensed and amended information, but at the end, there, without a moment's correction or hesitation comes an addendum, as if in answer to a concluding question:

> *When asked recently how he would like to be remembered, he replied, 'for a bright mind, a lively ear, a sharp tongue, an accurate hand, a generous heart, a job well done and the right road pointed to' –*

a reference, surely, to the concern he had that those he cared for followed well their own star.

Among the most gifted people I've known I have discerned two distinct types. There are those who achieve by absorbing the vitality of others. You come away from their company drained, even if you continue to admire them. The others seem to flourish by giving, and time spent with them is life-enhancing. Peter was one of those.

When a dear, much-loved, long-loved mutual friend died he wrote a wonderfully careful letter, as much to assuage my sadness as his own. It will serve, if I can get through it, to express <u>our</u> sadness at losing <u>him</u>.

My dear, it is a horrid, wretched business. I knew in advance and had, so to speak, steeled myself. But shock is one thing, the other thing, which is far worse (and incurable), is the gnawing sense of loss of a super true friend – a sense which all of us close to him cannot escape.

Alas and Alack.

Only the other day I happened to read those lines of Fitzgerald's <u>Omar</u> <u>Khayam</u> *– they're meaningless of course, but they struck a chord:*

There was a Door to which I found no Key;

There was a Veil past which I could not see.

Some little Talk awhile of ME and THEE

There seem'd, – and then no more of THEE and ME.

Ah, well. Be seeing you,

Love,

Peter.

XIV. An Unforgettable Birthday Present

Because of overcrowding in postwar Cambridge, I was unable to find rooms in Trinity College for my first year. Knowing so little about university life, I consulted the list of alternative lodgings in the town and, being of an optimistic nature, tried to assuage any disappointment with the hope that Lady Fortune would come to my aid. She did.

Earlier that year – 1948 – I had attended a strange but wonderful gathering of music practitioners at something called Music Camp, founded some years earlier by Bernard Robinson, a scientist at, I think, London University. It brought together, in a very large field in Berkshire with a very large barn, some hundred or more singers and players for a week of music-making for the love of it.

The campers – we put up tents and slept in them – were mostly university people, but there was always a smattering of young professionals like Dennis Brain, Colin Davis, Susie Rosza and students from the various music schools who came for the experience.

There was a set programme for the week: works like *The Seasons*, *Oedipus Rex*, *Faust*, madrigals, Bach motets were rehearsed in the mornings in the barn. In the afternoon there was chamber music – everywhere, quartets here, octets there, clarinet quintets galore, the players sorting out their own groups. In the evening there was usually a brief rehearsal and then, after supper, the entertainers in their midst provided the late evening diversions. There was something different each night – party pieces, recital pieces, cabaret songs, musical quizzes, with everyone sitting 'round about the barn under blankets drinking hot toddies or hot chocolate. It was a heady diet for a young man just out of the Air Force.

In that first music camp I met Erika Bach who was a fine violinist, a most remarkable person who inspired deep admiration and affection from her friends. Camping wasn't quite her thing but she made the best of it having had many less comfortable experiences fleeing from Nazi Germany with her distinguished scientist husband, Stefi, who was given a Fellowship at Fitzwilliam House, Cambridge.

When she heard I was coming up for the next Michaelmas Term without, as yet, any lodgings, she offered me a room in their capacious house in St. Barnabas Road, not far from the station. I was right about Lady Fortune.

They and their daughter, Irene, couldn't have been more welcoming. What's more, there was a lovely Bechstein in the sitting room, where a great deal of house music went on with drinks, coffee and people sitting about. I imagine it was much like the musical evenings in Bavaria where Erika's father had been a famous judge and their house a haven for artists until all except Erika were carried off to the gas chamber. She and Stefi escaped and made their way to England.

A regular guest at Barnabas Road was Paul Hirsch, another escapee, with his wife, Olga, and his famous collection of music manuscripts packed into crates labeled 'household goods', now in the British Museum. He played the viola, hesitatingly, but so loved it that he was occasionally included in a string quintet with me playing the other viola to help him in and out – he was a poor counter of empty bars. I remember a particularly risky shot at the Dvorak string quintet and the hilariously different versions of the ostinato rhythms played on second viola in the scherzo. There was a joyous, triumphant call for schnappes at the end, Paul ecstatic at having survived.

Partly through the Bachs at Barnabas Road, partly through the University Music Club, a focal point for much music making, I met three good friends and, since two of them played violin and the other cello, we started a string quartet together.

Our first violin was Martin Chadwick, youngest brother of Henry and Owen, who was, at this time, undecided whether to follow his brothers' example and become ordained or to follow what I believed was his stronger impulse to become a professional violinist. He was a pupil of Adila Fachiri, eccentric sister of the still more eccentric Jelly d'Aranyi, both of whom played a part in Martin's musical ambitions and provided an amusing periphery to our quartet's activities.

Thinking back, I believe now he'd left it too late. There comes a time early on when an incipient virtuoso needs the innocent audacity of youth to dare trust his fingers to take him to the extreme limits of technical prowess, without which he cannot succeed.

Our second violin was John Anderson who, with his inseparable brother Robert (who played cello), lived in their parents' house in Hornton Street, Kensington, whose rented basement was my home in London for a while. The house opposite had belonged to Charles Villiers Stanford, erstwhile Professor of Music in Cambridge and a predecessor of mine at Trinity as Director of Chapel Music. To his chagrin, he was never made a Fellow. These cross connections in life never cease to amaze and amuse me.

Our cellist was Ki Bunting, by far the most talented player of us all. He should have had a fine virtuoso career, but he was so tied up with the complications of his childhood and the tragic death of a beloved brother that he made everything more complex than it was. Such are the involutions of the human spirit. Ki more or less gave up performing and became a much-valued teacher at Yehudi Menuhin's music school which was founded originally to nurture exceptionally gifted young performers, many of whom, sad to relate, were destined for the same frustrations and failures.

But, at this earlier time, we met regularly and joyfully explored together the amazing chamber music of Haydn, Mozart, Beethoven and many other later composers.

If nothing else, it showed to me the wonders that had been wrought with four equal string voices in what we euphemistically call the 'Classical' period, when Haydn brought the writing of string quartets to an unprecedented level equaled only by Beethoven and Mozart.

Like the symphony, the quartet later became for composers almost forbidden, or, at best, dangerously exposed territory to be traversed with inhibiting caution. Brahms and Schumann weren't particularly good at it, and each composed only three. Mendelssohn fared somewhat better and composed a few more than that, none quite topnotch. Neither Liszt nor Wagner even tried. Dovrak wrote his best one in America but was happier when he could compose for larger combinations. Tchaikovsky was fairly hopeless at it. Sibelius, Ravel, Debussy, Elgar, and César Franck produced only one quartet each. They are played from time to time but there is always the sense that, as with those composers who have a ninth symphony to compose, a shadow from former times puts a damper on things. It needed classically inclined and disciplined minds like those of Bartók and Shostakovich for the medium to come into its own again.

For three years during term we played regularly and in that time two extraordinary, truly memorable things happened to me.

Paul Hirsch had known Richard Strauss in Germany before the war. They were good friends and used to play a card game called Skat together.

A few years after the war, Strauss came to England to conduct in London, the appeal of his music overriding the considerable prejudice, warranted or not, as to his condoning Hitler's anti-Semitic policies. He came to Cambridge for one night to see his old friend, and the old friend was generous-minded enough to invite me to take tea with the Great Man. The Great Man was kind and indulgent rather than condescending. All the same, Germans tend to be aware of their status and he seemed aloof. I remember mostly spilling some milk on a carpet and Olga Hirsch rushing off for a damp cloth and kneeling, to everyone's embarrassment, especially mine, as she scrubbed the spot. She was known to be excessively house-proud.

The second happening was on my birthday in the last summer the quartet played together, for some concerts during the Long Vac. Paul invited us to a party and asked us if we would play Mozart's G-Major quartet (K. 385) to begin the evening. It was one we loved to play and knew almost by heart.

The evening arrived and I noticed their large drawing room had been partitioned off by sliding panels. The guests arrived and, having put our instrument cases down somewhere, Paul announced that we would play K. 385. The panels opened, there were four stands arranged for us and, as we moved to take our places, Paul said, 'You won't need your parts' – nor did we. On our stands were indeed the notes of K. 385 but in Mozart's own hand, and we played the whole quartet from them.

That was a birthday present to remember.

XV. Bloomsbury
in Cambridge

Bloomsbury had its roots in Cambridge. Names like Clive and Vanessa Bell, her sister Virginia and Leonard Woolf, Roger Fry and the Hogarth Press were known to all of us coming up in the late 1940s. When we arrived at Cambridge, the air was still thick with memories redolent of an earlier, enviable time before the war, a time of artistic originality and intellectual freedom, of a group of people who discovered themselves and were unafraid to be themselves and live unconventional lives of social and sexual liberty that had released, we thought, the creativity that could produce *Mrs. Dalloway*, Duncan Grant, Ninette de Valois, Carrington, Lytton Strachey, Rupert Brooke, Ethel Smyth, the Cornfords, and Gwen Raverat. Goodness, their influence was everywhere and we were going to spend some years where it all began. It was very exciting.

What's more, these 'artistic' people, seemingly rare birds from our humdrum, service-disciplined viewpoint, were significant, accepted members of the larger society. You couldn't say that Maynard Keynes wasn't an important national figure, and there he was, gay as a cricket and yet married to a famous Russian dancer, star of the Diaghilev ballet.

The glamour of it was, at first, irresistible coming out from under the grey drabness of wartime England. Now was no time for the sad melancholy that pervaded the country. It was said 'we won the war and lost the peace', and so it seemed. There was food rationing, a shortage of almost everything. Mr. Churchill had been put out of office and modest little Mr. Attlee (who, indeed, according to Mr. Churchill, had a great deal to be modest about) was Prime Minister. The unions were gaining power and the whole economic prospect was looking grim. Small wonder we breathed in with relish the Bloomsbury airs that still lingered in our new environment.

All the protagonists had gone, or almost all, and memories spoken and published, perhaps to excess, became exaggerated and wearisome in the telling. Inevitably, after a while we reacted against Bloomsbury and questioned their reputations. 'Was Rupert Brooke really such a great poet?' We doubted it and for a while listened to Leavis who certainly did not think so. Very soon we tired of Leavis and his vitriolic condemnation of anything he didn't approve of. Rather, we relaxed into the ways of Cambridge, letting the dust of that dispute settle in our minds while we explored on our own, finding out our own values influenced by this and that discovery, accompanied by our close friends with whom everything was discussed at length into the small hours.

But Bloomsbury hadn't finished with us, or at least some of us – the more fortunate ones.

We came to realize that several of them were still living, creative, free-thinking and very bright and active participants in the world they inhabited. Plenty to learn from them – and they, willing to give.

Dadie Rylands was one. He had been one of the most handsome men of his generation, a great breaker of hearts, mostly male. He spent some time with the Woolfs and the Hogarth Press; but he was brighter than that and returned as a Fellow to King's under the aegis of Maynard Keynes who never allowed a broken heart to influence his judgement.

I didn't have much contact with him until we devised together the opening of the Purcell Room at the Festival Hall in London. Dadie was already well-known for his planning of such programmes as *The Seven Ages of Man* for John Gielgud and was an obvious choice for the Purcell Room's celebratory beginning. We had Flora Robson reading wonderfully, among other things, Adam's discovery of Eve from *Paradise Lost*, and there was a lot of Purcell's theatre music. Eventually I made a cabaret evening out of it all, which we played at the Aldeburgh Festival and, later, with the New York Philharmonic at Avery Fisher Hall. Some of it was rather salacious, as we restored the original texts to the songs and catches that had suffered bowdlerization.

Dadie was a joy to work with. He knew his Shakespeare, all of it, and had a compendium-like knowledge of all seventeenth- and eighteenth-century literature. He listened to music, and the problems of finding a suitable balance between the sounds of words and music were solved equably and, I think, very successfully.

On another occasion we both were involved in the celebration of Sybil Thorndike's 90th birthday. She was a much-loved figure in the theatre, and for all her colleagues in the profession to wish her a happy birthday, the programme had to be performed after the London theatres were closed for the night.

Someone observed that had someone let off a bomb in the one theatre that stayed open for this event, the whole of London's theatre talent would have vanished, for if they weren't on stage they were in the auditorium. It was packed when we began at midnight.

The first half was a brief ballet with Nureyev and Fonteyn dancing to recorded music. Then, after a brief interval, the stage was set up in a semicircle peopled by actors such as Larry Olivier, Wendy Hiller and Edith Evans. Sybil had asked me to play some Bach on the harpsichord, which was placed at the apex of the horseshoe of chairs. Dadie planned the rest.

We had an afternoon rehearsal at which Wendy Hiller gave a spiffing performance of her piece from memory. She wasn't much liked, so her rather self-conscious performance, standing without script, made many of the other performers uncomfortable as they got up and fumbled with papers to read the beginnings and then the ends of their pieces.

Edith was to deliver a frightening piece from Mrs. Siddons's journals, the account of her studying the part of Lady Macbeth in an attic of the lovely little eighteenth-century theatre in Richmond (Yorkshire). (Newly restored, we had opened the theatre a year or two before, with Dadie as master of ceremonies.)

As the story goes, after a performance with her husband of some eighteenth-century comedy, Mrs. Siddons had retired by herself to an upstairs room to learn for the first time the murderous Macbeth lines. She so scared herself that she rushed down the back stairs to where her husband lay fast asleep; she hurled herself onto the bed, shaking with fear.

At the afternoon rehearsal, Edith gave a poor, faltering reading and was clearly upset with herself and the occasion. I heard her mutter 'They'll never do this for me, you know. Never!' The rehearsal over, there were drinks in the wings for old friends to greet one another. Not Edith. I could hear her still on stage complaining in her best Lady Bracknell voice to Binkie Beaumont, the all-important theatre manager who had coordinated it all, 'It's no good, Binkie, no good at all. I can't do it, no, I can't do it. I'm getting very old and live in the country now. I can't do it'.

We let Binkie 'manage', which he did, and when she came to perform that night, the reading (from memory) was electrifying. We were all with her in that candle-lit attic dismayed by what Lady Macbeth was saying and the rush down those stairs.

Wendy Hiller didn't do half as well as at the rehearsal, which was very gratifying to Edith.

Another memory of that evening was at the end, when the 90-year-old Sybil, now badly crippled with arthritis, was wheeled through the pass-door towards the stage where she was to take a birthday salutation. 'Get me up', she said, 'I'm not going on in this thing'. And, as improbable as it seemed, she stood up and walked on stage without benefit of stick or chair. It was the epitome of acting courage. That was when Edith turned to me at the back of the stage and said again, only louder this time, 'They'll never do it for me', and they didn't. Poor woman, she was a hard one to love.

Apart from these episodes, the influence of Dadie on the amazing incipient theatrical talent that came up to Cambridge in those early years was an essential component of their development. Be it by compliance or opposition – and it didn't matter which – his knowledge and interpretation of Shakespeare and theatre in general had to be encountered and reckoned with. Peter Hall, Peter Wood, John Barton, Toby Robertson, Julian Slade and more all flourished in that atmosphere. Dadie's tutelage attracted major talents from Oxford, such as Tony Richardson, John Dexter, and Peter Brook, among others, who interacted constantly and increased the theatrical voltage.

After I left Cambridge for a second time, I mostly saw Dadie at Glyndebourne and was sad to find he had rather given up on things. He was proud, I think, of the achievements of the postwar generation in the theatre, but they had flown the nest; any comparable new talents hadn't yet shown and his energies had somehow run out. This still handsome man, without great achievements of his own and who had such influence, giving so much in a remarkable unselfish way – the perfect Cambridge Don – now seemed to regard himself as a spent force. And so, I believe, it continued to the end.

Another figure of Bloomsbury whom I encountered mostly through Sussex and Glyndebourne was Duncan Grant. He used to come with Rhoda Birley, widow of Sir Oswald the painter, whose hair always looked like a stork's nest in danger of total collapse. Quiet and gentle, Duncan was the preeminent painter of the Bloomsbury group, a man incredibly handsome in his younger days who rivaled Dadie in the way of breaking hearts. After traveling all over Europe in search of something, he finally settled in Sussex at Charleston, in a big house near Glyndebourne that harboured Vanessa, Clive and, from time to time, most of the Bloomsbury people. Virginia Woolf lived a mile or so away at Rodmell, from which house she walked in despair down a lane into the river with rocks in her pockets. Even closer was Tilton, the pretty Georgian house that Maynard and Lydia bought which, somehow, separated them from the rest. A few square miles encompassed the Bloomsbury spirit in its last years but it was now increasingly divided and death made it more so.

Finally Duncan was left and Ruth Fermoy, grandmother of Princess Diana, who started the King's Lynn Festival, invited him to have a show in the Fermoy Gallery, a beautiful space Ruth had created some years earlier. It was to be quite an event with Queen Elizabeth The Queen Mother attending the opening. Ruth was a Lady in Waiting and Queen Elizabeth was a patron of the Festival, lending one or two drawings.

The night before, Duncan, now nearing 90 and, tho' a little doddery, still a beautiful man, came to Ruth's house at Hillington for dinner accompanied by his agent and various of his circle. Asked what he would like to drink before dinner, he said, 'a dry martini'. 'With gin?' 'Yes, please'. It went down quite rapidly, conversation prospered. 'What about a refill?' 'Yes, please'. Conversation prospered still more and we went into dinner whereupon Duncan, upright in his place, fell fast asleep. I was sitting next to him and was once more struck by the beauty of his skin and looks. Ruth, on the other side, told the butler to ignore the sleeper and proceed with dinner for the seven or eight other guests. After, perhaps thirty minutes, Duncan stirred and we all watched. Without opening his eyes, his right hand advanced to where a wine glass would have been (his place had been quietly cleared), lifted the imaginary glass to his lips, showed every sign of appreciation and carefully placed the phantom glass back in its place. He did it only once but it was a magical moment of placid enjoyment, that delighted and amused everyone else as well.

We finished dinner and they all left for the hotel in Lynn bearing Duncan, slowly walking in his sleep to the car. The next morning he was charming to Queen Elizabeth, who bought an oil of Westminster Abbey. I extravagantly bought a self-portrait of him in his 30s, which he had allowed to be sold. It still hangs in my sitting room to remind me of a moving Bloomsbury moment, and of a talent that never lost its innocent vision no matter what complications of life assailed him.

The last Bloomsbury figure whom I was fortunate enough to encounter was the widow of Maynard Keynes, Lydia Lopokova. The Arts Theatre in Cambridge had been built for her to act in after her days with the Diaghilev ballet were over. She wasn't in the least grand about it. Indeed, I don't think I've ever met a less pretentious, less self-concerned person – or a more opinionated one. She had something to say about everything and everyone without let or hindrance. About herself and the Arts Theatre she was quite clear. She wasn't an actress. Her command of the English language in both pronunciation and grammar was quite personal, and a translation of Ibsen, her first and only attempt at acting, proved insuperable so she never acted again. She kept her dressing room in the house opposite the Arts stage entrance above the Arts Cinema, which I occasionally visited in addition to her Gordon Square home in London.

The house at Tilton near Firle in Sussex was another matter; a beautiful, simple eighteenth century house, a rectory perhaps in earlier days. Inside it looked as if it were getting ready for a jumble sale with boxes everywhere and postcards from Picasso or Stravinsky on the mantelpiece and, staggeringly, two beautiful Cézannes: a smaller one of fruit on a dish; the other a vivid dark country image with a black man on the move – fleeing from something, as I recall. It's now so long ago; Lydia is no more and Tilton belongs to someone else, but the image of that house when she was there and the friendliness of it all amid the chaos is still vivid, never to be forgotten.

She was frequently at Glyndebourne and, tho' well received by John Christie, Lydia was inclined to criticize, and he didn't care for that too much ('damned Russians!').

You would have thought that because of Maynard, King's College and Gordon Square there would have been a sense of Bloomsbury in Sussex, with constant visiting between Rodmell, Charleston, and Tilton, but it was not so. While Maynard was still alive, the households separated and stayed that way. Lydia didn't much like Duncan or his paintings – and almost certainly must have said so. It was her way, and perhaps she was somewhere a little jealous of Maynard's earlier obsession with him.

The first time I visited Tilton was during rehearsals for Monteverdi's *L'Incoronazione di Poppea* in 1962. There was a message to come to lunch on a rehearsal-free day and stay the night. Driving up to the front door, I was met by a man, husband of the couple who looked after Lydia, her ways and the house. He took my case and said, 'Lady Keynes is out in the garden, weeding, and she said to go through and call her'. I went through and out into the long garden, at the far end of which I could see a bobbing straw hat and waved at it. It waved back and began the return walk to the house. As the hat on this diminutive figure got nearer, it was quite plain that, apart from a pair of sandals and the hat, she hadn't a stitch on. Almost immediately, it didn't matter one iota except to observe that this little brown body was in perfect proportion and still beautiful to look at. 'Go and help yourself to a drink, Raymond, and I'll go and put something on for lunch'.

That was the first of many visits to Tilton, and I came to be very fond of that free spirit who had made a unique life work so well and with such a sense of the joy of living. She had a remarkable self-awareness. I once asked her if she had ever danced *The Firebird*. The question came after her telling me of a visit she had lately paid to Karsavina, who created the rôle and was still living in straitened circumstances (alleviated, I believe, by Lydia) in London. 'Oh, no', said Lydia without a trace of rancour, 'I could never have danced that. You see the Firebird was a princess and Karsavina is a lady. I am a peasant'. It was a lovely example of her candid honesty.[1]

Once she tried to make a 'wedding' as she called it, between Ninette de Valois and me so that I would bring 'good rhythm' to the ballet orchestra at Covent Garden – something she detected to be missing when she attended performances there. It was a weird idea. I would never have entered the world of ballet but there was no gainsaying an invitation to lunch with her and Dame Ninette at a small restaurant near Gordon Square in London. It was all quite friendly and noncommittal when Lydia, who must have caught a bug, was sick all over the Dame, who behaved with characteristic competence. We got our matchmaker carefully and safely back to Gordon Square, where I left them. That was the end of such talks, and I confess to a considerable feeling of relief as well as inadequacy in the situation. At least Bloomsbury was looking after its own.

What with phantom wine glasses, tired old Fellows of King's College and messy lunches, it seems that I've encountered only the tail end of Bloomsbury from which to look back at them and their achievements. Their best work was done and now it seems that how they came to do it was more important than what they did. Rupert Brooke wasn't that great a poet, Duncan Grant was no Monet, and the tensely crammed prose of Virginia Woolf has been overshadowed by the McEwans, Muriel Sparks and Saul Bellows of our own time. What I find totally admirable was that within the confines of their aesthetics, they worked, created, set examples of endeavour and honesty of purpose that were so badly needed to loosen the artistic and social structures that surrounded them. In that, they were totally successful and admirable.

So we were right to have been excited at the prospect of breathing the Bloomsbury air when we arrived at Cambridge after all.

---

1   That wasn't true; she had danced it but her memory seems to have wished she hadn't, such was her respect for Karasavina.

XVI. Starting out in the Profession

For a few years after my first departure from Cambridge, playing piano and harpsichord for the Philharmonia Orchestra contributed significantly to my feeling of independence – apart from helping to pay the rent.

My parents had strongly disapproved of my quitting the secure groves of academe for the uncertain, wild, possibly amoral world of professional music. It was indeed uncertain, though I never found it wild or amoral, but I was determined to prove myself. How could I have continued telling and instructing people about music – which, after all, is nothing 'til it sounds – until I was sure I, myself, could make it sound in the wide, professional world.

The tangled web of how I came to be counted a regular keyboard player with the Philharmonia had a lot to do with Ursula Jones, who worked for the orchestra, and her celebrated trumpeter husband, Philip, whom I had come to know well. They became very close friends, indeed neighbours, for I eventually bought the house next to theirs in Hamilton Terrace.

The orchestra had begun its life as a recording instrument for EMI, recruited and managed by the redoubtable Walter Legge. He hired as principals the best in their field: Manoug Parikian, concertmaster; Gareth Morris, flute; Sidney Sutcliffe, oboe; Dennis Brain, horn; to name a few. The, so to speak, rank and file (an objectionable Musicians' Union phrase clearly of Army origin) players were hardly less gifted than their principals. It was, perhaps, the finest and best paid orchestra the world had ever seen.

My first encounter (Bartók and the Hawaiian conductor) I describe elsewhere. It was a nerve-wracking experience but, once passed, I was accepted as a worthy colleague and made welcome. Apart from learning a great deal of music from the inside as a player, I was able to observe and, I hope, profit from the array of celebrated conductors who came in the next two or three years to record with the orchestra, their merits and failings made palpably clear from the front.

At first there was Herbert von Karajan. Nobody liked him. When he died there was hardly a note of regret in any of the obituaries. That was sad but, while there was much to admire in the music he made, there wasn't much to like in the man himself.

In those days, however, he was a star and Walter liked stars. For Karajan the association with EMI and the orchestra, arguably the best in Europe, was an opportunity to shed unpleasant Nazi associations that clouded his reputation elsewhere. I believe, too, he saw a way to ride this particularly splendid horse into America. He had already tried to bring the Berlin Philharmonic to Carnegie Hall, a venture that was picketed so heavily that the visit was cancelled. This time, it would be different.

Karajan was among the last of the Führer conductors, redolent of their nineteenth-century forbears, mostly German, whose word was absolute in matters of hiring and firing and all things musical. Karajan personified this, and the English orchestra put up with it for quite some time, laughing at the more tiresome manifestations and appreciating his very considerable musical skills. Occasionally, he would overstep the mark as when he called the entire orchestra for a three-hour rehearsal but then kept them waiting until the last ten minutes while he rehearsed a Mozart Divertimento using just twenty players. He then played a movement from Respighi's *Pines of Rome* for full orchestra; presumably to make the point that he was in control.

It didn't sit well with the players and eventually, after several such indignities imposed with almost sadistic, repressive intent, there was a major rupture at the end of the American tour. He never again conducted the orchestra in public.

After him came Otto Klemperer, a giant of a man, father of Werner, the German Colonel Klink in *Hogan's Heroes*, and in some ways resembling him. He struck up a new fashion in the interpretation of Classical music by playing things very slowly. Slow Beethoven à la Klemperer caught on and for some years was all the rage. Like Shakespeare, Beethoven is hard to ruin, and it was true that you had a clear picture of the composer's striving intellect as his masterpieces trundled slowly by under Klemperer's direction. Somehow, like an imposed speed limit observed, it became interesting to follow the music's argument that way. The mills of God are known to grind but slowly.

He carried with him the authority of a formidable pre-war German career and was now mellowed by ill health enough to be perceived sympathetically by the orchestra and admired. The English love a ruin.

I played very little for him but have a bizarre memory of a Handel *Concerto Grosso* (Opus 6, no. 11) recording. He knew nothing of Handel's notational conventions, especially the one that allowed consistency in playing dotted rhythms not immediately clear in the manuscript. As a result we spent hours, with some sixty-eight string players rehearsing to near distraction the pointed misshapen rhythms against the surrounding dotted ones. The result was ludicrous and, if you were to find the record, it should serve as an example of how not to play that music. In my experience, it was surpassed only by the recording of Fürtwangler playing the opening of Bach's *Third Orchestral Suite* with the Berlin Philharmonic where the trumpets, possibly doubled and certainly exhausted, play Bach's brilliantly light, supple opening as if the gods were making a slow, noisy progress to Valhalla via Leipzig.

Klemperer went on to record the *St. Matthew Passion* and I declined an invitation to take part. George Malcolm, a wonderful player and a good friend, took it on. He told me afterwards it had been a nightmarish experience. Klemperer forbad any spread chords from the harpsichord, an instrument he clearly didn't like, and there came a wonderful moment, George told me, when he shouted in his guttural German accent, 'Cembalo, I can still hear you'.

When Klemperer became too infirm to conduct any more, Walter tried out a number of internationally known people who might succeed him.

Sawallisch was very able but was soon committed elsewhere. Menotti's boyfriend wasn't much thought of. Paul Hindemith came only to conduct for a recording of his own music, a delightful, smiling avuncular person who, having been a distinguished violist in earlier days, established an immediate accord with the players. As a composer he was a superb craftsman and, when the inspiration matched the skills, his music became very impressive and is now unduly neglected – works like the 1940 *Cello Concerto*, *Mathis der Maler* and the *Concerto for wind, harp and orchestra*.

Carl Orff came to conduct the recording of his *Die Klüge*, a comic opera version of Carmina Burana. Walter's wife, Elizabeth Schwarzkopf, sang the title rôle, and the cast, otherwise all male, clowned around and rather leavened the lump of an irritable, unsmiling composer whose conducting skills were of the bandmaster variety.

The best of the post-German era, Carlo Maria Giulini, was a clear possibility but only stayed a while before going to America. Everyone liked him, and I played the elaborate piano parts of *Petroushka* and Shostakovich's *First Symphony* when he recorded them with the orchestra.

They were jolly times, saddened only in memory of the sudden death of Dennis Brain, one of the greatest of horn players. At about that time, just before the chamber orchestra I had formed amalgamated with the Goldsborough Orchestra to become the English Chamber Orchestra, we gave a concert in the Wigmore Hall in which Dennis played the *Second Horn Concerto* by Richard Strauss, a phenomenally difficult work. In the morning rehearsal, there was something astray and I stopped the orchestra. I went over to Dennis standing in front of a music stand which, on inspection, turned out to be holding the latest car magazine, no sign of the Strauss at all. He played it faultlessly then from memory and in the evening concert.

After an Edinburgh Festival Concert a few weeks after this, Dennis had decided to drive down to London and asked if I would like a lift. I had other plans and declined. A few miles from home he fell asleep and drove fast into a tree.

We had a recording session in the Kingsway Hall the next morning; but as the orchestra assembled, bleary-eyed from the sleeper, there was a strange atmosphere. No one seemed to know why, until Walter appeared and told us Dennis had died that morning, a few miles from home. It was such a bleak moment. Of course, there was no recording – no first horn any more; Dennis seemed irreplaceable.

Before I had to leave the Philharmonia for lack of time, Walter, who had taken a shine to me, offered me several unimportant concerts with the orchestra. I recorded with them *Peter and the Wolf* with Richard Baker narrating and Ben Britten's *Young Person's Guide to the Orchestra*, and received a nice note from Ben when it came out.

They were a few very valuable years and I shall always be grateful to Ursula and the orchestra, and to Walter for giving them to me.

XVII. Earl's Terrace, 1

Earl's Terrace (Kensington High Street going west just past the Earl's Court Road) must be one of the oldest parts of Kensington. It forms the north side of Edwarde's Square, whose southern side was replaced early in the twentieth century by some rather grand artists' studios, among the most famous of whose tenants was Annigoni. His portraits have a glossy beauty that, to me, rarely seems to convey the character of the person portrayed, however striking they first appear.

The sides of the square are made up of little, smart houses joined in terrace form, quite pretty and mostly inhabited by second-level well-to-do's – the sort of men who, in earlier times, as second sons would have been given a living and served as heroes in almost any Trollope novel.

Earl's Terrace, a long row of tall, six-story houses was quite different. It was said that the square, with both its north and the now-vanished south terraces, was built by a French architect dispatched by Napoleon to prepare living quarters for his army's officers' families when he occupied England. There was supposed to be an underground tunnel connecting the north terrace with Holland House, now a ruin, but then the secret headquarters of a group of people sympathetic to the ideals of the French Revolution and the subsequent domination of Europe by Napoleon. After I came to live there, we made several attempts to find it but never did. Molly, our Irish housekeeper, hinted darkly that she knew where it was but wasn't telling. For Molly simple facts were usually dull and needed an injection of Irish imagination to make them palatable, so we rather doubted her veracity over the matter of the tunnel.

Before Molly and Earl's Terrace there was a gap between leaving Cambridge in mid-Ph.D. and finding that Kensington haven.

Having decided to abandon the world of academic music in Cambridge, much against my parents' wishes, I was determined to make a go of it as a professional musician without their support, and it was clear I had to live in London and make do with what little income I could muster at the beginning of things. I survived briefly in some rather dire places: a single room in Bina Gardens, a basement flat in Hornton Street, and then I was lucky enough to meet up with Peter Shaffer, an old

Trinity friend. His father's real estate firm owned several of the Earl's Terrace houses, and he, Peter, had a delightful flat on the ground floor of Number 18. The second floor had just become vacant and, having passed the scrutiny of Shaffer père – a real character with a lovely north-country accent – I moved in and a new, wonderfully enjoyable chapter of life began.

Earl's Terrace had its own, almost collegial personality enhanced by the fact that it did not face directly on to the perpetually busy Kensington High Street, but was set back from the noise and bustle of it, isolated by a strip of land planted with trees and shrubs and its own road. Somehow the iron railings, presumably Victorian in origin, had missed the wartime railing scourge for munitions; they enhanced the look and seclusion of the Terrace.

It well suited some Russians. Their embassy had bought three houses and built high walls around their part of the garden. They came and went like wraiths, never speaking, going quietly into their cars with heads down and out of them more slowly, cautiously when it was dark.

Number 18, like its Shaffer-owned neighbours, was home to some remarkable people. There was a gentle banker above me and, above him Brian Epstein who managed the Beatles. Below Peter, two down from me, lived the redoubtable Molly O'Daley. She and her sister kept house for all of those owned by Peter's father's company. They had the run of the basements. Molly had the vitality of a Callas (her sister had hardly any) and came from some dim, impoverished Irish village. She had a badly disfigured face, evidently the result of being dropped as a child by a drunken father into the red-hot ashes of a peat fire and left there. An early, primitive attempt at a skin graft could hardly have been called successful, but it never seemed to bother her and so it didn't bother anyone else after a while. She was never still, nor was she very efficient, but somehow things got done, and she won our often-exasperated affections as we watched the lowering levels on our bottles of whiskey. It may have been conditioned by her early years of drab poverty in Ireland but, honest as the day, she could never tell the truth; it was just too dull for her.

If the laundry hadn't been picked up, 'Why, sure I was just coming to get it and wasn't there a terrible crash in the High Street and we had to rush out and help'. Then, later in the day, 'Oh, Raymond, I'm so terribly sorry about your laundry. I'll see to it tomorrow (she didn't), but you know that Mrs...., well, she had a bad heart attack this afternoon and we had to ring for an ambulance'. And, still later, 'Those Russians, you know... they... '.

The residents of Number 18 used to compare notes as we passed by on the stairs. Molly was quite a unifier.

When I came to the Terrace, Peter had just had a great success with his first play, *Five Finger Exercise*, a social comedy with darker undertones. The setting was a weekend cottage, a family of four, and a visiting young German with whom they all react in differing ways.

There was a lovely story of John Perry, partner of theatre manager Binkie Beaumont, who, on reading the play said, 'But, my dear, you *have* to have a maid; you can't manage a weekend in the country without one; otherwise it would be wash, wash, wash, dry, dry, dry all the time and nobody would get anything done'. Dramatic license would have to cover the washing and drying. It had to be pointed out to John that people with six fingers were very rare.

The opinionated mother of the weekend family – and the least likeable member of it – was closely modeled on Peter's mother who expressed delight at her replication, which greatly amused his friends at the first-night party. It's a remarkable play and the first of many still more remarkable to come.

At about this time, I had been giving a series of concerts at the Victoria and Albert Museum. These frequently included the later madrigals of Monteverdi that used smaller combinations than the earlier, more customary five voices. They were wonderful examples of the then new concertante style, declamatory and overtly emotional, accompanied by a continuo of harpsichord, or lute, or organ with cello, and sometimes other instruments. It was the world of seventeenth-century opera and I was captivated by it.

I had already 'realised'[2] the one-act opera *Il Ballo delle Ingrate* for Ben Britten at Aldeburgh, and it may well have gone further with Ben and Peter had not Glyndebourne offered me the chance to 'realise' Monteverdi's last great opera, *L'incoronazione di Poppea*. This caused a rift with Aldeburgh which I much regretted, but Ben bore a grudge against Glyndebourne and anyone who worked there became *persona non grata* at Aldeburgh. Eventually reparations were made but, for the time being, it was a matter of casting your die for one place or the other.

The Victoria and Albert concerts culminated in a Festival Hall evening of Monteverdi: Acts One and Two of *L'Orfeo* and extended scenes from *Poppea*, the success of which triggered Glyndebourne's invitation. I had already spent two wonderfully instructive seasons in Sussex as répétiteur and I suppose they'd had a chance to assess my potential. I so much admired the sense of standard, the extent of rehearsal and the commitment of everyone there. As a way to prepare and perform opera, it could hardly be bettered.

2   I should here explain what this use of the word 'realisation' implies.

All the earlier seventeenth-century operas were written almost entirely on two staves, one for the voice and one for the bass line with occasional figures to help indicate the harmonies. Occasionally there would be a sinfonia or ritornello to be played by strings written out in five or three parts, but the main burden of accompanying the singers on stage was borne by the continuo players. We know what instruments were there (harpsichords, lutes of all sorts, harp and organ), for they got paid and there are account books, but we don't know what they played. Over weeks of rehearsal, supervised by the composer, a sort of semi-permanent improvisation was built up which would endure for the number of performances.

Presently, we don't have the luxury of such extended rehearsal time, and players are no longer used to improvising from a single bass line, so someone has to imagine what might have been; hence, 'realise' the composer's intentions and write them down.

I had nearly completed the 'realisation' of *Poppea* by the time I came to Earl's Terrace, where Peter Shaffer was full of excitement over producing a film script of William Golding's novel, *The Lord of the Flies*, for the Hollywood mogul Sam Spiegel. Peter Brook was also involved and the to-ing and fro-ing in Earl's Terrace was quite remarkable. Somehow and sometimes I was drawn into the hubbub and discussions.

The redoubtable Mr. Spiegel proved to be a very jumpy individual, prone to flashes of unwelcome inspiration, such as the need for sex in the film and, therefore, the inclusion of a girls' school among those who crashed on the remote desert island. On being denied this, he threw a tantrum and lay on the floor in Peter's flat making strange groaning noises by way of a major sulk. One of his minions, clearly unmoved by this not unaccustomed behaviour, put his head 'round the door, looked down, shook his head and said, 'Sick, sick, Mr. Spiegel', which didn't help matters.

Eventually, Peter Brook bought the film rights of the novel from Mr. Spiegel, made a script for the most part out of direct quotations from the book itself and spent a summer on a Caribbean island with mostly embassy children, a camera crew and the minimum of staff. The kids enacted the novel stage by stage in an amazingly powerful way, starting in school uniforms looking neat with hair clipped and brushed, then gradually becoming more and more ragged and wild. It was an inspired way to film the story, letting the moral of it all speak for itself.

In the early autumn of 1961 I had just put the last notes to the concluding duet of *Poppea*, the manuscript ready to be collected by Fabers for copying and printing, when the telephone rang. It was Peter Brook in Paris. 'What are you doing, Ray?' 'Just finished *Poppea* for Glyndebourne'. 'Would you be free to come and write the music for *The Lord of the Flies*; I've nearly finished cutting it and it's good'. 'Yes'. 'Could you be here this evening for a showing of the film?' 'Yes'. And I was. Earl's Terrace was like that.

A long weekend in Paris with endless showings of the newly cut film followed, during which Peter and I came to conclusions as to where and what music could heighten the impact of the gradual disintegration of well-behaved English schoolboys marooned on a desert island into violent, almost cannibalistic savages. So much for the lasting power of Western civilisation.

I had the idea of having them sing, in flash-back before they set out on their disastrous plane journey, a *Kyrie eleison* in their school chapel, which then turned into a march as their society crumbled and '*Kyrie, Kyrie*' became 'Kill the pig, Kill the pig'.

Apart from the children's choir, I wrote music for six players. It was all recorded in one day at the Aldwych Theatre, then in the hands of the Stratford-on-Avon Shakespeare Theatre with which we were both associated. The image of the children, all offspring of the lately formed English Chamber Orchestra, marching up and down the aisles chanting 'Kill the pig' is forever imprinted on my mind. It was all so improbable but it worked, and the film became something of a cult flick still played in way-out cinemas.

I occasionally get a royalty cheque for ten dollars from the original promoter. The whole recording cost something over two hundred pounds.

Also, I still get letters from provincial clergymen who, I suppose, have just seen the film, asking for copies of the original *Kyrie*. The family of William Golding asked me to add a *Christe Eleison* to be sung at his memorial service.

All that from Earl's Terrace – but there was more.

XVIII. Earl's Terrace, 2

Apart from so many other moments of importance, the Terrace had still one major part to play in my life, something for which I will always be grateful. In particular, I think of Peter Shaffer's kindness in letting me come back to his ground floor flat while he was away in America. I had the whole of *Il Ritorno d'Ulisse* to rework and nowhere to go. My house in Hamilton Terrace went up in flames and with it 400 pages of score, the first version of the opera. It had to be reworked and ready for the next summer at Glyndebourne, 1972.

Soon after my return to Cambridge, I had left Earl's Terrace and bought the house in Hamilton Terrace, St. John's Wood, next door to close friends, Philip and Ursula Jones. Philip was a superb trumpeter who, apart from founding his own celebrated brass ensemble, usually played principal trumpet with the English Chamber Orchestra. Ursula was one of the founding directors of the orchestra, which came about as an amalgam between the chamber orchestra that I had started in London and the longer-established Goldsborough Orchestra, whose founder had lately died.

There were multiple, sometimes heated discussions about the name this amalgamation of the two should adopt – the year we were in, the sort of music we would play, the place we were or weren't at, a composer's name. But, finally, Ian Hunter of the Holt agency came up with The English Chamber Orchestra. At first it seemed a mite pretentious but it soon earned its title; it became and still is one of the country's finest ensembles. My close alliance with them over many years is among the most valued parts of my musical life. It was at its best in those days when we recorded all the instrumental music of Handel and Bach and explored many other different musical avenues working with artists like Janet Baker, Gerard Souzay, Arthur Grumiaux, Hugh Cuenod, Rampal, von Stade, Elly Ameling and Ileana Cotrubas. Great as they were, for the majority of our recordings at that time, the star was the orchestra itself. Quentin Ballardie, who took on the job as general manager, devoted his life to the orchestra of which he was part founder and, for some years, principal viola. He had an extraordinary gift for discovering extremely talented young players. I can't speak highly enough of their skills at that time, their musicality and sensitivity, their feeling for ensemble and sound. It was a unique band of musicians and a privilege to be with them.

I had got to know Ursula much earlier on when she was working for Walter Legge and the Philharmonia Orchestra. She hired me at the last minute to play the tricky, elaborate piano part in Bartók's *Music for Strings, Percussion and Celesta* at a Festival Hall concert conducted by a little-known Hawaiian conductor who, we heard, was rich enough to have hired the orchestra for a London début. He was handsome as well as rich but, as it turned out, rather deficient in conducting skills.

The Bartók is a difficult piece. I had known it only as a casual listener and had to learn it, as luck would have it, over a weekend staying at Exbury, my friend Leo de Rothschild's country house.

Leo: How does one describe so valued a friendship as his? We've known one another since we both came up to Cambridge in 1948, and the depth of the relationship that evolved since those early days is beyond calculating. William Johnson Cory's poem about Heraclitus says much of it:

> *They told me, Heraclitus, they told me you were dead,*
>
> *They brought me bitter news to hear and bitter tears to shed.*
>
> *I wept as I remember'd how often you and I*
>
> *Had tired the sun with talking and sent him down the sky.*

> *And now that thou art lying, my dear old Carian guest,*
>
> *A handful of grey ashes, long, long ago at rest,*
>
> *Still are thy pleasant voices, thy nightingales, awake;*
>
> *For Death, he taketh all away, but them he cannot take.*

– except that neither of us is dead – as yet. Leo and his family allowed me in and have supported, encouraged, guided much of my life and been tolerant of my many willful divergences.

At any rate, having studied the Bartók amid the weekend delights at Exbury, I came well prepared to the first rehearsal. The difficulties of the score were made more so by the young conductor and I found myself watching the orchestra's brilliant concertmaster, Manoug Parikian. Catching his eye, we managed to sort things out in our various departments eventually, enabling a moderately uneventful performance which left the Hawaiian pleased as punch while we all exchanged sighs of relief that disaster had been averted.

After this initiation by fire, there followed several years of intermittent enjoyment playing the piano parts in works like *The Firebird* and *Petroushka* under some of the most interesting and instructive musicians of the day: Karajan, Klemperer, Cantelli, Hindemith, Giulini. Even Toscanini came to conduct the orchestra in a Brahms series at the Festival Hall. Of course I wasn't needed – there being no pianos in Brahm's orchestral scores – but it was fascinating to watch this legend in rehearsal. By that time America must have allowed him full reign of his egocentric, almost lunatic, ill-mannered behavior, something the English orchestra found tiresome, close to unacceptable. The concerts were, of course, sold out but the performances were not that well received. The music was kept on high tension but lacked gravitas and the pace was too frenetic for this Londoner's taste.

What with playing from time to time with the Philharmonia, giving concerts with my small ensemble, the ECO, Glyndebourne, travelling to Venice for research and to Aix en Provence for festival and much else, the to-ing and fro-ing to Cambridge became rather testing. I loved both lives and felt passionately about combining scholarship with practical music-making. Driving fifty miles in a fast car after a concert for a lecture and some supervisions the next day and back that evening for rehearsals the next morning were easy enough in the first years, and there were the long vacations between terms for getting about and abroad. So it continued for ten years until, finding myself more than once on the wrong side of a motor way in the middle of the night, I knew I had to come to a decision and leaving Cambridge once more became inevitable. That was in 1967.

In 1962 *Poppea* had been a success at Glyndebourne. For the first time in their history, an opera was repeated for three years running. It was, in the first place, courageous of them to have taken on unknown early seventeenth-century Italian opera. George Christie and Moran Caplat were, I believe, the prime movers. Apart from the staple diet of Mozart, they had given Rossini a very good, successful run under Vittoria Gui who had a wonderful, almost classical sense of the style.

It was time for change; Monteverdi was new for them and a risk, but they judged it exactly. There followed two operas by Monteverdi's pupil, Cavalli, *L'Ormindo* and *La Calisto* (I had been spending quite some time researching at the Marciana in Venice) and then back to Monteverdi finally for *Il Ritorno d'Ulisse*. They were all very well received by both audience and the critics, too, until the 'authentic' movement caught their attention and my way of presenting those operas went out of fashion – perhaps not forever.

Il Ritorno had loomed over them all. It's a majestic work. The journey of Ulysses back from Troy to his beloved, constant Penelope, hampered by some of the gods determined to destroy him, but guarded and defended by Minerva who loved him, is wonderfully told in the libretto and set to some of the finest music Monteverdi ever wrote.

Plans had begun with a view to putting it in the 1972 season. I had finished the score early, in 1971. Leaving it on top of my new, uninsured Steinway, I left London to go to Whitehaven for a concert at the lovely little theatre Miki Sekers had built onto his house close by the sea and the mills where his wonderful silks and satins were produced. Returning Sunday, I arrived in the early evening at Hamilton Terrace in time to shower, change and put my music case in the L-shaped music room on the first floor before leaving for dinner with friends at Marian Harewood's house in Orme Square. I noticed an odd, musty smell but thought it must be some flowers too long in their vase. It wasn't.

Earlier in the year I had converted from oil to gas central heating; various thermostats were placed about the house, notably, as the firemen later identified, one on the wooden shutters in the music room. The shutters had been in place since the Terrace was built in 1800. Sitting at my desk during the summer, I had looked at that thermostat and wondered why it was there; even noted there was a dent in it and, stupidly, did nothing about it. Una Marchetti, who looked after so much of my affairs, had kindly turned on the heating (the weather had turned very cold). Unfortunately, my leaving the music room door open created a through draught that kindled the faulty thermostat into flames.

Hamilton Terrace is a quiet, wide street lined with trees on either side. Though it looks like a terrace, the houses are separated inside, one from the other, by at least the width of a brick; this because of a building law in force since the Great Fire of London in the seventeenth century. It saved the houses either side. My neighbors to the west later remembered that it was getting rather warm in their sitting room, but they knew nothing of the fire until the fire engines arrived. On the other side, Philip was fast asleep and didn't stir until Ursula, arriving home late, rushed upstairs and woke him.

The fire was first noticed by two charming maiden sisters who lived opposite. They called the fire brigade and then called Una. She didn't know where I was and telephoned everywhere, even including Kensington Palace, but eventually found me as I was leaving Orme Square after a delightful evening. There was nothing to be done once the valiant firemen had quenched the fire. Tall houses when they catch alight tend to act like a funnel so there was very little left. I found one leg of the Steinway and a few scraps of the *Ulisse* manuscript.

Oddly, the shock of it escaped me. The next day, there was a live broadcast of a lunch-time concert at St. John's, Smith Square which, I believe, went well. I remember that everyone seemed more distressed than I was. A few days later there was a grander concert at Westminster Abbey, where we performed Cavalli's great *Messa Concertata*, which I had found in Venice. I enjoyed that too. I think I must have come to a resolution that 'There it is, no one got hurt so we'd better get on with things as best we may, cleaning up the mess as soon as possible'.

After the two concerts, the main thought was to rework *Ulisse* and I think the gods – perhaps Minerva, who looked after Ulysses so well – was looking out for me. Peter Shaffer offered me his flat at Number 18 Earl's Terrace (he was attending rehearsals of *Equus* in its New York production), then a call came from Ben Britten at Aldeburgh kindly offering me his copy of the microfilm of *Ulisse*, which I gladly accepted.

So I shut up professional shop and went back to Molly and No. 18 Earl's Terrace for some of the strangest and, in some ways, the most rewarding months of my life.

Days and nights became blurred for I never went out, staying for most of the time in pajamas and dressing gown. I worked on the score for as long as I could, microfilm projected on a screen, plate by plate. There was neither night nor day in the darkened room. I would have something to eat and drink, go back to bed for a few hours, then wash, shave and shower, before starting the cycle again. Fabers, the publishers, sent someone to the house every evening to collect the day's manuscripts and so gradually and, in chronological order, the four hundred pages were re-worked.

I thought and lived the opera with almost no interruption, hardly seeing anyone – Molly excepted *en passant*, but only for a minute or two's comic relief and perhaps a swig of whiskey.

The strength of the melodic lines with the marvelous harmonic structure of the bass line took me through the whole opera:

Through the huge opening soliloquy of Penelope, nearly at her breaking point after twenty years of waiting.

Through the landing of Ulysses on Ithaca after the gods had destroyed the Phaeacians boat in which he was returning.

Through the recognition by his old faithful shepherd, Eumete.

Through the transporting of his son, Telemachus, from Sparta by Minerva through the air.

Through the sending of Telemachus to give hope to his mother assailed by the three avaricious princely suitors.

Through the arrival of Ulysses disguised as a beggar, abused by the suitors.

Through the competition as to who can draw Ulysses's great bow and win Penelope's hand and, with it, Ithaca.

Through the ensuing slaughter which finally leaves Penelope and her husband alone.

And then comes the inspired final scene where Penelope (like so many war-widows reacting to their returning men) suddenly doesn't want him: He has been away too long and she has closed her heart.

So he has to woo her all over again with wonderful words and music so that their reunion becomes less of a love duet than a hymn to constancy.

I shall never forget that on the first night, Ben Luxon, a superb Ulysses, broke down and wept during that final duet. Janet Baker had to hold him to get through it. Then on the last night of that season, it was Janet who broke down, tears plashing on the stage with Ben holding her. I could see this from the conductor's desk and needed someone to hold me – even now as I write this.

Each performance was as the undertaking of a long, arduous journey. We all felt it, I believe, though in some ways it was a joyous, thrilling one as well. The cast was superb. John Bury's extraordinary sets made brilliantly clear the war in the heavens between the gods intent on Ulysses' destruction, as well as those who would shield him and see him safely back on Ithaca. Above all, binding it together, was Peter Hall's restrained, inspired direction, true to the text and a most remarkable manifestation of theatrical genius. All those combined in a wonderful blend of music- making, singing, acting and total theatre.

Earl's Terrace had done its magic again, if that is not too presumptuous an assumption.

I've not set foot in it ever since but, driving past, I always smile and gratefully remember.

XIX. ALICE THROUGH THE LOOKING GLASS

In those early days in London after the first break with Cambridge and the rift on that account with my family at Bath, I was, understandably, rather anxious about my finances. There was rent to pay even for such modest accommodations as a room in Bina Gardens or a basement flat (a step up the social scale) in Hornton Street.

Various adventures occupied much of those earlier years and one of the first was to take on the musical direction of a production of *Alice Through the Looking Glass*. The wonderful Lewis Carroll story (so much more adult than *Alice in Wonderland*) had been adapted rather skillfully by the mother of a Cambridge friend, Toby Robertson, who directed it. I was very largely responsible for the music, though some of the tunes came from Vivian Ellis, an aging musical comedy composer. Vivian was best known for writing the signature tune for a film about the Coronation Scot, that wonderful, revolutionary, streamlined blue train that ran daily from Euston to Glasgow with, at that time, unparalleled speed. The composer's self-esteem far exceeded his talents, so I had to score, edit, rewrite and compose most of the music for a small orchestra of about ten players.

The management who employed all, actors and musicians alike, proved dishonest and eventually swindled most of us out of a considerable amount of salary dues. Nevertheless, in the days of rehearsing and early performances we did not know this, and it was an intriguing and lively time; a great experience for someone just entering the big, wide professional world of theatre.

Margaret Rutherford played the White Queen. It was a brilliant piece of casting. I first met her several years before at Stratford, where her nurse in *Romeo and Juliet* was a revelation of how such a wonderfully warmhearted, fussy, caring soul could be brought to life. It seems someone had discovered her in one of the provincial repertory companies where she had worked all her acting career.

Late in life she had married an actor, Stringer Davies, who gave the impression of having strolled absent-mindedly into the profession quite by chance, liked it there and stayed. He was perfectly happy looking after Margaret and playing small parts beside her. With us he played a rabbit or something like it. Margaret took all her parts very seriously, studying, asking directors and colleagues about them. But whatever she did (Miss Prism, Miss Marples, Mme Arkarty in *Blithe Spirit* or the endless stream of headmistresses of girls' schools often supported by Joyce Grenfell as the games mistress), whatever she undertook, it always came out as Margaret Rutherford, adorable as such and a perfect living White Queen.

Her opposite number as the Red Queen was Binnie Hale, equally well cast. A fading music-hall star, sister to the more famous Sonnie Hale, she had a mordant wit that suited the part. She took great delight in finding others' weaknesses and getting people to laugh about them. Hard to forget is the glee with which she came one morning to an early rehearsal bearing a page out of the current issue of 'Spotlight', the professional actors' year book. It had a full-page photo of Margaret's husband and bore a simple message: 'Have you thought of Stringer Davies?' Well, of course no one had until he became a reality with Margaret in rehearsal. It was not kind, but there was a more likeable side to her character that was evident from time to time. She considered the whole production beneath her reputation and fame, even if it was work (which she needed). It's hard for some to climb down the celebrity ladder and, it must be said, she made a poor job of it.

Much the same might have been said of our White Knight, Michael Denison, who had been young stars together with his wife, Dulce Gray, in earlier days. Though Michael was still handsome and charming, the years had taken their toll, and his quixotic interpretation of Lewis Carroll's hopelessly muddled old knight came more naturally to him than, perhaps, he would have admitted. He had about him a lovely air of old sports cars, silk neck scarves with open-necked shirts, and he was as good-natured as the character he was playing.

Then there was an acridly amusing American 'queen', doyen of many racy reviews, Wally Crisham, who played a lily or two along Alice's journey. He was fun.

Alice, herself, was played by a rather petulant, pretty young actress whom stardom had passed by. She had begun in a big way with the young Richard Attenborough in Graham Greene's *Brighton Rock*, but nothing more had come of it, leaving a rather resentful Alice, talented but not quite the eager, enthusiastic girl that Carroll had imagined. Like Binnie Hale, she rather minded her involvement in something not quite first-rate and under a shady management.

It was, nevertheless, an enjoyable time and wonderful experience. We rehearsed a while in London and then on to Brighton for a week before the opening, not at the best theatre but at its slightly sleazy neighbour down the street, now closed and probably demolished. Backstage was redolent of former, vaudeville times, and its dusty chaos occasioned torrents of discontent from Binnie who had 'never' (high voice) seen anything like it. Of course she had, but it was more evidence of fading stardom and she resented it.

Margaret accepted all with Girl Guide enthusiasm and determination to make the best of it. She had, after all, a part that suited her like a glove plus a good-natured Rabbit who had barely one line to speak, but looked after her so well.

For me the atmosphere of an old vaudeville theatre enhanced the otherwise drab surroundings, which became an apt symbol for determining and encouraging the present end of my pursuing the *Idea of Progress* in the previous two years at Cambridge. Nothing much had been done to it since 1914 and in no way could it be said to have progressed since then.

When a theatre company spends some weeks together away from home, living in 'digs' (theatre lodgings), a certain 'hothouse' atmosphere prevails, some of it enjoyable, some of it petty and rather grubby. The digs are often in areas you wouldn't ordinarily choose to live in. Walking back to my digs late one night, I was knocked out by some hooligans who were robbing an old man. I still bear the scar, but at least they ran off with little harm else, and the old boy picked himself up and went off with a policeman. Altogether, it was an instructive as well as mostly enjoyable time.

The performances went well. Indeed, we transferred for a few weeks to the Prince's Theatre in London at the end of the Brighton run. We had good houses, doubtless the better-known names in the cast ensured this, and there were sufficient unexpected episodes, especially in Brighton, to keep us all amused.

There was one lady in Brighton who turned up at every Wednesday matinée, always taking the same stage box by herself. Halfway through the show, or thereabouts, she emptied a bag of coins onto the floor of her box, creating a remarkable clinking, clattering sound; she then spent much of the second half picking them up. The ushers knew her and, amused, just let her get on with it. I imagine she tipped them well and probably left some coins on the floor. At least we all got to know what day it was.

A nice moment in the play came when Alice rowed the White Queen, who at this point has been transformed into a knitting sheep, across the stage. The boat was pulled across on pulleys by stage hands. As Alice rowed, they sang together the Eton Boating Song 'pull, pull, together'. On one occasion something went wrong with the pulleys or someone pulled too hard too suddenly, for, in mid-river, they and the boat disappeared from sight behind the footlights. We went on playing in the pit until Margaret's head appeared above the footlights, sheep's wig somewhat askew. With those celebrated jowls a-quiver, she shouted in that wonderful, quavering voice of hers 'SPLASH', just as the stage manager called for a blackout. The audience loved it, thinking it was a regular part of the show. Indeed there was a suggestion, rapidly quashed, that we repeat it at every performance. There's no doubt Margaret saved the day.

XX. A Rude Story

When I was at school, Diana Dors was the most glamorous of our English film stars, almost as glamorous as America's Jayne Mansfield, whom she closely resembled: dazzling near-white, blonde hair and a very shapely figure, which was always well delineated by her costumes, sequins glittering in all the right places.

We all had cuttings about her and saw her films. Some even had signed photos in their lockers, for which you had to send away. On the screen, no matter how tense the situation, she would move from one mesmerizing pose to another without very much happening in between. The magazines reported that she had always wished to be considered for her acting abilities but had few opportunities to show them. We didn't mind much about that.

An opportunity occurred later on at Stratford-on-Avon where, in an inspired moment of casting, she was offered the small part of Audrey in *As You Like It* – a wonderful production with Vanessa Redgrave as Rosalind. Audrey is the good-natured country girl who bears life's vicissitudes with fortitude and an endearing good nature.

She was wonderful in the part and won every heart in the audience and, backstage, in the company. Her voice was nothing like the one heard in the cinema, a low-pitched, languorous blonde-bombshell of a voice. Instead, without being common, it sounded like that of an ordinary Londoner, with some inflections in it that singled her out from the rest. She was unspoilt, unpretentious company with a predilection for the rude.

Perhaps it was the last element that prompted her to tell the story about herself. She came from Farnham, a market town in Surrey, where her family name was Fluck. So she was born Diana Fluck, which, of course, she changed.

At the height of her fame she had been asked to open a fête planned to raise money to restore the Farnham church tower. There was great excitement when she accepted and huge crowds assembled for the opening ceremony to see their very own film star. She was to be introduced by the new, young vicar, enthusiastic and, understandably, very nervous.

With every seat on the platform filled and the National Anthem played, the vicar stepped forward to face the crowds, saying what a signal honour it was to have so great and celebrated an artist among them once more and for such a cause. '...but of course you all know her so much better than I, a newcomer, can possibly claim. After all you saw her grow up and knew her by her family name as Diana . . .'. Here he hesitated; a second or two felt like an hour. 'You know and love her as Diana . . .' The choice had to be made – 'as Diana . . .' – and he got it wrong – 'as Diana Clunt'.

I wish so much there had been a film of the vicar's face when he realised his gaffe. Diana Dors was delighted and loved to tell the tale.

Later on, her blonde bombshell days over, she played the mother of a working-class cockney family in a television sitcom series that became very popular. Eventually the mother developed cancer. Perhaps it was written that way because Diana Dors herself developed cancer; her decline and eventual demise from the dreaded disease were played, step by step, with moving sincerity by the actress herself: Method acting at its best.

It was a brave, touching farewell to a life lived as fully as she knew how, her dreams of becoming a fine actress eventually fulfilled.

XXI. Hazards of a Traveling Orchestra

In 1970 I took the English Chamber Orchestra to Osaka for concerts in the last days of Expo. My memory of them is rather hazy: long journeys, limited recovery time, and the time change all took their toll. But they must have gone well to judge from the wildly flattering press we received, tho' we know the Japanese are obscuringly polite, and who's to say the translation of their subtle, complex language was accurate. I do remember the amazing queues of young people after each concert holding records to be signed and, for sure, the ECO never gave a bad concert in those days.

Memory caught up with actuality in the days following Osaka. We were engaged to play two concerts on the southern Japanese island of Kyushu in the towns of Kumamoto and Kagoshima. The island was as bucolic and rusticated as Osaka was skyscrapered and European.

We flew there in a chartered plane, tired and dressed in the most casual clothes, by this time crumpled and none too clean. So we left the plane looking like a party of Worzel Gummages, only to be met on the tarmac by a diminutive figure in immaculate Edwardian morning dress standing by a very old, shining Rolls-Royce, silk top hat doffed as we descended the skyway staircase from the plane. It transpired he was the Mayor of Kumamoto. This was explained by another diminutive figure in a dark suit who acted as his translator, tho', as he explained proudly, the Mayor was looking forward to a conversation in English, which he had been studying for the occasion.

Ursula Jones, our guardian, organising angel of the tour, myself, our soloist Bob Tear, tenor, and, if memory serves, our first flute, Richard Adeney, were ushered into the wonderfully commodious, museum-quality Rolls Royce. The Mayor sat up front beside the driver, top hat firmly in place, doffed only as a prelude to each strand of conversation. It was, clearly, an important symbol of office, like the heavy gold chain that dangled forward each time he bowed, a frequent sign of courteous welcome. We couldn't keep up with the bowing and there grew a sense of unreal levity as it showed no sign of abating.

The orchestra was shown into a somewhat ramshackle bus that followed the Rolls at a respectful distance.

The ride into town was fairly long and after several repetitions of reciprocal expressions of goodwill and esteem, the smiles and bows lapsed into a somewhat embarrassed silence. Then, the Mayor who, having clearly studied an English phrase book and now run out of small talk, took off his top hat and read from a piece of paper that, tho' we would be staying at the best hotel in Kumamoto, the concert would take place in the next town which was Kagoshima. There was a bow and, again, silence until, hoping to bridge the gap, I foolishly said, 'Mr. Mayor, so you do *not* have a large enough concert hall in Kumamoto?' After a brief pause he replied, 'Yes'.

Of course he was right, but it didn't sound it. In the silence that followed, no one knew what to say. A suppressed giggle from Ursula started one of the most embarrassing pew-shakings I've ever experienced, made worse by our determination not to cause offense. I'm afraid we failed.

I have no memory of those concerts either, but I hope we redeemed ourselves somewhat with the gift of music.

The hotel in Kumamoto was situated high above a lake, in the centre of which was a conically shaped island. It was not large but the wisps of smoke curling out from its summit gave it a somewhat sinister aspect: a live mini-volcano we surmised, correctly as it turned out.

In the morning of our leaving, we came down to breakfast set out in a long room overlooking the lake and found all the hotel staff crowding the windows in a state of great, high-pitched excitement. The volcano had erupted. Rocks and lava were shooting up into the air and rolling down the sides of the cone, at the foot of which was a spa where rheumatoid-arthritic patients, immersed in sulphuric water, bathed away their hurts. The boat traffic between the base of the cone and the lakeside was so engrossing that some of us nearly missed the call to the plane returning us to the mainland. I believe the spa patrons, like we, managed their escape safely and in good time.

We were originally scheduled to return via India with concerts in Delhi and Bangalore, but the British Council, who had arranged the tour, suddenly re-routed us through Winnipeg. The Queen had lately been there to celebrate the city's quarto centenary and had been nearly eaten alive by blackfly. We were to add to the festivities – or, at least, lessen the insect buzz.

So makeshift were the arrangements that the day after a concert in Winnipeg, we were put into coaches and trundled off on a two-hour journey to a small town, Brandon, which has a large university. Unfortunately, that performance coincided with the Vice-Chancellor's annual welcoming address at the beginning of the academic year to the whole university, our potential audience.

As a result, we played to a nearly empty hall with only a group of elderly ladies commandeered from a nearby retirement home. They sat in the front rows – about forty of them – good souls, slightly over the hill and quite unaccustomed to concerts. They applauded every movement and broke into every silence with high-pitched appreciative comments.

The first half of our programme ended with Britten's *Les Illuminations*, and I ventured to explain that this lovely sequence of songs would be best heard without applause after each one. The ladies, after some discussion, nodded their approval.

The atmosphere was already unreal and veering towards the hysterical when Bob Tear, a prankster by nature, produced a set of plastic party vampire teeth he had acquired somewhere and slipped them into his mouth whenever he could turn and leer at the orchestra during the purely instrumental bits.

Things were getting close to out of hand when, at the end of the fifth song, 'Marine', a dazzling virtuoso piece, the solo voice sings *tourbillons de lumière*, ending on a sustained high A. 'Flashes of light' wasn't it. As the ladies rose to their feet to applaud, their leader let out a shriek that could have awakened the dead.

It was too much for us, too. The ensuing interlude for orchestra alone had very little to do with the notes Ben had written, after which we tottered to our two coaches without waiting for any further applause or illumination.

Back in England the wonders of Osaka, Kumamoto and Canada faded. But you only have to say 'Brandon' to any musician who was with us on the tour and there's no doubt that the little old ladies had left an indelible impression.

XXII. The Doyenne
of Sadler's Wells

Lilian Baylis, a passionate populist, became manager of the Old Vic Theatre in Waterloo Road just before 1900. Both she and opera flourished and, after the formation of an associated ballet company, in 1931 she moved both to the Sadler's Wells Theatre in Rosebery Avenue, site of a rather spurious seventeenth-century watering place. It continued to prosper under her aegis and its name later became known over all the world.

Miss Baylis, in those earlier days, was an ardent protagonist of opera for the people, and 'Opera in English' became the watchword. Indeed, no opera was performed there in a foreign language until they commissioned me to prepare a version of Monteverdi's *Orfeo* in 1964. I had the devil of a time persuading the Sadler's Wells board to break with their tradition. You could almost hear Miss Baylis groaning in her grave as they deliberated.

My argument was, nevertheless, correct and won the day. The main thrust and intention of Monteverdi's writing in the style of *Le Nuove Musiche* was to enhance the meaning of the text, to make it more vivid by using every syllable of every word in heightened declamation, giving it an intensity reflecting its own rhythm that could not be rivaled by the spoken or written word. It was simply not possible to make any English translation fit the notes of the Italian vocal line without making one or the other ridiculous or ruinously altered. Before a number of the Board, we performed a scene in both languages and the case was made.

The opera, in its original Italian, succeeded without any public protests nor yet a moan from the ghost of Miss Baylis. It was always said she favoured simple logic in things, so perhaps she was won over, too. There were lovely sets and costumes from Yolande Sonnabend, and it was simply and well-directed by Frank Hauser, another Oxbridge product. We had a wonderful Orfeo in Johnny Wakefield and an unforgettable Messenger in Patricia Kern, both among the unsung great artists of postwar opera in England.

Another was Joan Cross who was a star in the company before the war. She played Ellen Orford in Britten's *Peter Grimes*, perhaps his greatest work. I was lucky enough to have been present at the first performance in 1945.

Together with Anne Wood, Joan started the Opera School and I was brought in to conduct a *Figaro* and an *Albert Herring* (Britten) in which, one night, she took over from a sick youngster and sang the part that was written for, and possibly about her – Lady Billows. The voice wasn't what it had been, but there she was, Lady B. to a tee.

Reminiscing one day, Joan told of an occasion in the 1930s at Sadler's Wells when she was taken ill the day before a *Magic Flute* performance.

Lilian Baylis was still very much in charge. She lived in a small flat at the top of the theatre and watched over everything with a glassy eye. (In fact her eyes weren't quite straight and they gave her a somewhat forbidding aspect.) She often cooked her supper backstage on a gas ring, from whence the smell and sound of sizzling sausages and bacon frequently wafted through to the audience.

Joan had given warning that she wouldn't be able to manage the next Pamina (her character in *Magic Flute*) in good time for the understudy to be prepared. She was a young novice soprano new to the company.

At the end of Act I, the young lady came off, flushed with the relief at getting through it, only to be met by Miss Baylis on the move, frying pan in hand. Lilian looked at her, still on the move, and said, 'Well, dear, 'ad yer chance'. Her cockney accent was imitated everywhere even as late as my time with the company, long after her demise. A short silence and the frying pan with sausages sizzling moved on accompanied by a voice from over the shoulder, '...and missed it'. Poor girl, I don't think she was ever heard of again.

Sadler's Wells is no more. They moved to the Coliseum Theatre, larger and much more accessible in the centre of London's Theatre District. Even the name was changed but – '*plus ça change, plus c'est exactement la même chose*' – it still is an excellent opera company. Lilian Baylis would have been pleased; some say they can still smell the sausages and bacon.

XXIII. IT'S ONLY OPERA

In 1962 *Poppea*, to use a vulgar phrase, hit the jackpot at Glyndebourne and was repeated in three successive seasons – a record, I think, or at least one equal to the most successful of their *Figaro* productions.

As a result, in the late 1960s, I was invited, along with the distinguished German director, Günther Rennert, to perform it again with the San Francisco Opera; tho' with different sets, different cast, different costumes.

Production rehearsals began in a building a few blocks away from the main Opera House, whose stage was heavily occupied with the last full-blown dress rehearsals of the opera due to open a week or two before ours – lighting, makeup, costumes and all.

The opera was *La Traviata*, with Joan Sutherland and Luciano Pavarotti in the starring rôles. Joan's husband, Richard Bonynge, was conducting (he was known in the profession as Boing-Boing after the Mr. McGoo character). A young English director was in charge of production, or as much in charge as was available with major stars who had performed their rôles a million times already and weren't overly sympathetic to appeals for deeper penetration of the psyches their characters might reveal in performance.

The sets, inherited from an earlier, experimental production, were based on a floor-cloth of weird, black rubber lily pads. The cloth stretched from back to front on a rather steeply raked stage irrespective of whether the scene was out in the country or in Violetta's salon.

Günther was anxious to see how the Verdi was coming on, so after an afternoon rehearsal of *Poppea* down the road we both sneaked into the back of the stalls as discreetly as possible.

We really needn't have troubled about being discreet. There was, of course, no audience but at the bottom of the stalls above the orchestra pit there was quite a crowd of people talking rather loudly.

We caught a glimpse of Joan as she exited into the wings in her own costume for Violetta, which she had insisted on wearing after trying on the one designed in the lily pad days. It was a flamboyant affair in pinks and blues, with feathers and a sort of mobcap with lace hangings intended, we supposed, to make her look a little less tall.

More striking and noisier, however, was Pavarotti's struggle to rise to his feet from a kneeling position, presumably after beseeching Violetta for some favour or other, which she had declined before her exit. Once down, and being considerably overweight, the celebrated tenor just couldn't get up by himself. No one was near to assist until the young English director rushed onstage to help and got some fairly instructive, sharp words for his trouble.

This, of course, stopped the music, and amid the noise of production staff, house staff and the general manager, was heard clearly the voice of Boing-Boing complaining in rather strident terms his discontent with everything. 'Why should Leppard and the Monteverdi lot have so much more orchestral and stage time when the Verdi needs it and it is being neglected'.

At this point, we thought it politic to leave. As we made our way through the pass door to backstage, we encountered Joan in the wings, looking splendid, listening to the caterwauling noises coming up from the pit.

She came to greet us and I introduced Günther, who had never met her – pleasant smiles all 'round – Joan is one of the best-natured of singers. For want of something better to say, I remarked, 'It seems they're having a bit of trouble in the theatre'. 'Oh, don't worry about that, Ray', she answered in that inimitable Australian twang. 'After all, it's only opera'.

Good answer, I thought.

XXIV. TOM GOFF

He became one of the great harpsichord makers of our time, tho' he only made fourteen of them. I count myself very fortunate to own one he made for me and still more fortunate to have known and counted him a friend for many years.

With his Hanoverian nose and aspect there was no doubting the legend that Tom was descended from that part of the late eighteenth-century Georgian Royal Family whose susceptibility to the charms of beautiful actresses was known, acknowledged and celebrated. He was recognised as a relation and received by the older present-day royals and greeted as a cousin which, in the biological sense, he almost certainly was. Mrs. Jordan was, I believe, the actress in question and the Royal protector, William IV.

Tom lived in a big house, 49 Pont Street, which he shared with his mother, Lady Cecilie Goff, a small, lively lady with a strange cockney accent who, apart from writing two volumes devoted to the family history at Grimsthorpe, was a considerable needlewoman. She embroidered the spectacular curtains in the drawing room that were much admired by Queen Mary, an expert in those matters. I rather think they were accepted by the Victoria and Albert Museum as worthy of inclusion in its historic collection of distinguished needlework.

Tom was a great reminiscer and teller of stories – he had a particularly strong line in haunted houses – and was persuaded by his friends to put some of them on tapes, which have subsequently disappeared. Even so, he was reluctant to reveal much of his own earlier life. He spoke of 'deviling' with a law firm after Oxford – which work he found very tedious – and he went to Canada during the war, a member of the Lieutenant Governor's staff. Sometime before that, he had studied the making of clavichords, working with Herbert Lambert in Bath. Lambert was Photographer Royal according to his widow, a rather tough, pretentious lady active in Bath musical circles when I was growing up there (tho' I do not know that there is or was such a court appointment). Herbert Howells composed a delightful series of 'fancies' published as *Lambert's Clavichord*.

Eventually Tom's career in the Diplomatic Service lost its appeal and he began to devote himself entirely to the making of harpsichords, clavichords and, eventually, because of Julian Bream, lutes. He teamed up with a skillful, cheerful, rather small cabinetmaker called Cobby, and their workshop occupied the top two floors of 49 Pont Street.

With a butler, Marchant (whose wife cooked and kept the house in order), Tom settled down happily to making his lovely instruments. He used as his model the harpsichords of Jacob Kirckman, 'the first harpsichord maker of the time', according to Fanny Burney, doubtless quoting her father, Charles, who certainly knew.

In his day Kirckman used every sort of modern 'improvement' made available through the latest advances in eighteenth-century scientific research: the Venetian Swell, a device for raising and lowering the lid by means of a pedal which gave a certain control over crescendos and diminuendos; the separation of single rows of strings like the 4' and 16', buff or lute or harp also by means of pedals which gave an even greater variety of sound. All these Tom incorporated in his harpsichords (except the Venetian Swell which tended to clatter), and added some more of his own. Most of his seven pedals had half-hitches which controlled subtle dynamic changes and enabled most remarkable colouration of the sound. This involved the most delicate setting of the plectra, the whole made more easily regulated by being built around a metal frame that, unlike the wooden frames of the eighteenth century, remained stable through all changes of humidity and temperature.

Of course all the purists, with their commitment to a quarrelsome 'authenticity', which advocated narrow keyboards (the very devil to play accurately for those of us who had also had to play on the wider piano spacing of the keys), lower pitch (which made everything sound flat), and pedal-less purity (which necessitated frantic lunging at hand-controlled stops just above the keyboards). One of them, with uncharacteristic wit, suggested that if Tom went on like this he would invent the piano.

The sound, the look, the stability of his instruments are unequaled, and in his lifetime they were used extensively for recordings and concerts in preference to most others.

Tom was much encouraged by a friend of his whom he greatly admired, Violet Gordon-Woodhouse, who, before the war, had become something of a cult figure among the musical enthusiasts of the higher levels of London society. She was, evidently, a good harpsichordist and a great presenter of the music she loved. She rarely played in public, but her recitals in drawing rooms became celebrated. In this way she established the harpsichord in London society where the Dolmetchs, with their 'knit-your-own-violin' philosophy celebrating the home-spun life, couldn't.

Once a year Tom took the Festival Hall to put on a concert with four of his harpsichords placed along the front of the stage in echelon. Behind them sat a small orchestra, at first the Boyd Neel and, later on, the English Chamber Orchestra. It was a wonderfully impressive sight and an evening of musical delights that came to be known affectionately as the Annual Harpsichord Jamboree.

There was, of course, the question of repertoire. J.S. Bach had arranged Vivaldi's *Concerto for four violins* for exactly this combination. He also had written two more concertos for three, and a further two for two harpsichords for concerts in Leipzig. They are all delightful works but, in aggregate, not quite long enough for a whole evening. So Bob Dart arranged another Vivaldi for us, George Malcolm set brilliantly some variations by Mozart that had originally been composed for a violin and viola, and I re-composed a concerto for harpsichord and piano by C.P.E. Bach for our combination and a slightly larger orchestra. We recorded most of these later on and the sound now brings back memories of lively music-making and visions of Tom endlessly fussing about the tuning and regulation of his instruments, but looking so very proud, pleased and paternal when all went well.

We had a fine group of soloists. Eileen Joyce, the celebrated pianist, played with us several times; George Malcolm, Denis Vaughan, Geoffrey Parsons and Bob Dart were more regularly members of the group. Eileen had met Tom socially and asked to see his harpsichords, greatly admired them and asked to play at a Jamboree. Her husband, a rather grand theatrical manager, brought another person he represented, Ginger Rogers, to one of the rehearsals, which caused quite a stir. As I recall, there was little of Fred Astaire about her, which rather disappointed, but instead a rather small, vivacious, ginger-haired lady with freckles and a ready smile. You'd never have thought of 'puttin' on your top hat' to dance with her.

Tom was a bachelor and I doubt he ever put serious pen to paper, so to speak, in the way of an intense relationship. Friendship and loyalty of and to his friends were extremely important and, with some of them, paramount.

He helped in the discovery of Julian Bream's extraordinary talent, eventually making lutes for him and, from the first, seeing that he met and played for people who could advance his career. Not that such a talent can be stopped, but, especially at the beginning, a protecting, encouraging person like Tom, with all his contacts, can only have assisted the gifted, cheeky young cockney on his way to being the mature artist he became.

Tom loved to give dinner parties. I remember one where, after the first course, Charlotte Bonham-Carter got up and left the dining room. We thought she'd received an unexpected call of nature and waited – and waited – and waited – until Tom asked Marchant if anything was wrong. 'No, sir, Lady Charlotte put on her coat and left'.

Thinking it a little odd, we went on with dinner and then to the drawing room, where I was asked to play. Halfway through a Haydn sonata the door burst open and Charlotte rushed in saying, 'Goodness, I'm so glad not to have missed the music. You see, I'd accepted two more dinner invitations for this evening and managed to spend a little time with each of them. Such fun'.

It was said of her that she never missed the foyers of any theatrical or operatic first night, but rarely attended any of the performances.

On another occasion Queen Elizabeth (The Queen Mother) with Ruth Fermoy in waiting, Lady Cecilie, Riette Lamington, David McKenna and his wife were gathered in the drawing room with the lovely curtains for some music. Queen Elizabeth and Ruth sat together on a huge pouffe. The rest settled where they could.

David, one of Tom's oldest and most valued friends, was a modest tenor but also quite senior in the management of British Railways, at that time on strike. There were no trains to anywhere. Tom asked him to sing and me to accompany, and as luck would have it, David chose to begin with a touching Handel arioso which, in translation, came out as 'Where ére you walk'.

There were straight faces on the pouffe for about thirty seconds after which, seeing the irony of the train strike, there followed a choked giggle on the part of Queen Elizabeth, echoed by Ruth, which started wave after wave of pew-shaking all over the room. I could hardly play for crying.

Dear David never knew, I'm glad to say.

Tom was a man with all the inherited complications and connections of a very long-established aristocratic family which, with all its twists and turns either side of the blanket, became known for its eccentricities. Tom didn't escape them, but the genes came together in him to make a highly intelligent, driven sort of person. He had a strong determination to succeed and achieve his goals with a certainty of purpose that enabled him, with charm and easy confidence, to overcome difficulties and opposition. Occasionally, when things weren't going well or people let him down, you sensed the darkening of shadows beneath the warm, confident personality that usually prevailed. One such darkening eventually completely overtook him, and in 1979 he committed suicide by jumping from his lofty workshop window at the back of the house to the concrete yard floor beneath. It was not done, I believe, from any sense of failure but from an intense wave of depression brought on by some dreadful imagined despair. It was an appalling shock to all his friends.

XXV. ORCHESTRAL HAPPENINGS

Musicians love telling amusing stories about each other, not always complimentary. I thought a few, at not all of which was I present, might leaven the lumps, should there be some.

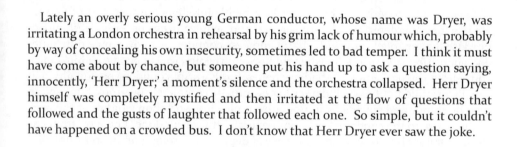

Lately an overly serious young German conductor, whose name was Dryer, was irritating a London orchestra in rehearsal by his grim lack of humour which, probably by way of concealing his own insecurity, sometimes led to bad temper. I think it must have come about by chance, but someone put his hand up to ask a question saying, innocently, 'Herr Dryer;' a moment's silence and the orchestra collapsed. Herr Dryer himself was completely mystified and then irritated at the flow of questions that followed and the gusts of laughter that followed each one. So simple, but it couldn't have happened on a crowded bus. I don't know that Herr Dryer ever saw the joke.

Another incident to which I was privy happened with the Philharmonia orchestra, many years ago, in a concert to mark the arrival of a refugee composer/conductor from one of those countries that Russia was prone to overrun at that time. The concert was at the Festival Hall, attended by our Government, several of the overrun ones and, I think, a Royal or two.

It was to begin with a Nocturne composed by the conductor himself. The rehearsals had not been going too well and the orchestra was restless to say the least.

The piece began with a very soft, interminable side-drum roll in which the player was directed to start at the rim on one side of the drum and make his way slowly to the other side.

It seemed to us that an unconscionable amount of rehearsal time was being spent on this opening roll. The restlessness grew to such an extent that Manoug Parikian, the concertmaster at that time, addressed the orchestra in the Green room, just before going onto the platform, admonishing us to behave – it was an important concert of international significance and we must be good.

Duly chastened, we went on stage. The conductor entered to storms of patriotic applause. He raised his baton, shut his eyes and signaled, with an expression of one who has suffered much, that the side drum should begin his roll.

The drummer was about halfway across when the principal Double Bass, a delightfully witty Scot, gently extended his right arm, palm upwards, and looked up in a worried way towards the ceiling – surely so new a roof in our wonderful new concert hall couldn't already be leaking?

I was once conducting Walton's *1st Symphony* with the BBC Northern (now Philharmonic) in Leeds Town Hall. It had gone particularly well and you could sense it. This happens sometimes in a good performance; difficult to define beyond the fact that everyone involved, including the audience, knows it when it occurs. There's a thrilling sense of something achieved together, and the time has flown by unnoticed.

We came to the end of the last movement which, like Sibelius's *5th Symphony*, ends with a chain of explosive chords separated by fairly long silences in which the underlying pulse of the movement is felt but not heard.

After the first loud, staccato chord, there was the silence – broken only by a single voice shouting loudly, 'Bravo'. The second chord arrived cutting him short, but the silence after that was broken by a high-pitched and astonished 'Oh!' The third chord was followed by a sad little voice calling out, 'Sorry'.

All on stage were hopelessly stricken. I really don't remember how or even if we ever finished the symphony. And it was a live broadcast.

There was a celebrated occasion with John Pritchard and the Liverpool Philharmonic in the Newcastle City Hall where the seating on stage is steeply tiered, with doors high up on either side leading inside to a spiral staircase. I was not present but it's a story worth telling. They were touring the North of England with one of John's favourite works, *The Fantastic Symphony* of Berlioz. At the end of the last movement, the *Witches Sabbath*, the *Dies Irae* plainsong sounds out on tubular bells. John, having a strong theatrical sense, always amplified the bells, which were larger than usual, made especially for this movement.

In Newcastle there was no room for the bells on the stage, crowded to such an extent that they had to be hung, suspended over the well of the staircase leading up to the high platform doors. The microphones for their amplification were hung alongside the top of the bells.

Unfortunately, the head of percussion – not the brightest person on two legs – had failed to realise that in the cramped space you could only play the bells if the doors leading to the platform were closed. And if you closed the doors you couldn't see the conductor.

This concert was one of several on the tour so there was no rehearsal.

It was going splendidly until, at the end of the *Witches Sabbath*, the first great *Dies Irae* moment arrived. John stepped forward and gave a magnificent gesture – to absolutely no effect. The doors were closed. Clearly annoyed he set off at a faster pace whispering to the inside player, the first desk of violins, to go up and see what was wrong. Soon the second statement of the Dies Irae went past unnoticed and John was getting even more annoyed and still faster.

The inside player on the first desk squeezed past in front of the leader and promptly got his fly-buttons caught in the neck of the concertmaster's violin (as luck would have it, it was a lady). Extricating himself, flustered and embarrassed, he dashed up the side steps of the platform, flung open the doors and shouted straight into the microphones – echoing all over a packed auditorium – 'What the f-----g hell do you think you're doing?!'

That got into the papers – somewhat bowdlerized.

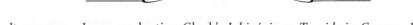

It was 1979. I was conducting Gluck's *Iphigénie en Tauride* in Geneva. It had an excellent cast: Rachel Yaker, Eric Tappy, Robert Massard, and Rudolf Constantin; brilliant sets by Robert Aeschlimann; and it was staged by Erhard Fischer.

Weeks of rehearsal were coming to an end and we still hadn't seen or heard the *Dea ex Machina*, as Diana who, when all looks blackest and human sacrifice inevitable, comes in the last bars of the opera to save the situation.

'Scythians', she cries, 'stop'. And they do. (We were performing the opera in its original French: '*Scythes! Arrêtez*').

Diana has very few lines to sing so her absence hadn't been a problem even though this was the final dress rehearsal.

We knew she was coming from Rumania or one of those Balkan countries that keep on changing names. We knew she was a close friend of the Opera's Intendant and was going to sing a larger rôle later in the season, possibly Tosca. We knew she was flying in that morning to have a costume fitting and meet with one of the répétiteurs to make sure she knew her lines. But we wondered if she spoke French.

The rehearsal was going extremely well, and the final confrontation of the opposing forces, Scythians and Greeks, was especially tense and exciting.

Exactly on cue the vision of Diana, spear held high, appeared brilliantly lit, standing on a temple-like structure that moved forward, her ample form glittering in a silver costume.

I cued her first little phrase, but it didn't happen. Then she remembered and at the top of her considerable voice addressed the invading solders . . .

'Sh i i i i i i i i...T!'

It was clear that she certainly didn't speak French – or English come to that – and was quite unaware of the effect she was having. But the Scythians – the Scythes – certainly stopped in their tracks, everyone stopped, and we didn't get to the end of the Act; at least not that time.

In the early days of the English Chamber Orchestra we gave a concert in St. Pancras Town Hall, a mediocre building compared to the great early twentieth-century railway station across the road, called after the same Saint. It is a multipurpose modern building with one of those large, multipurpose spaces within it seating about a thousand people, designed equally, and optimistically for meetings, plays, concerts, lectures and, of course, mayoral pronouncements. Even with the dubiously variable acoustics, the place has never fully achieved any one of its intended purposes. Moreover, it had fixed, tip-up seats, cinema-style (I suppose that was one more intended purpose) to make passing along the line easier and, as it turned out, dangerous.

One of the works we were playing at this concert was Vaughan Williams's *The Lark Ascending* for violin solo and orchestra, now frequently performed but, at that time, virtually unknown. V.W. himself had agreed to attend and we felt honoured that he would do so. I knew him through Cambridge. He had been at Trinity and, through the Wedgewood family (his mother's) was related to the Cambridge dynasty of Darwins, Keynes, Adrians, Trevelyans and Cornfords.

The Lark was to ascend immediately after the interval, during which V.W. chatted amicably with many of his old friends in the audience. He was a genial friendly man, rather stout, even rotund. Since his hearing was poor and he disliked wearing one of those hearing aids, he carried with him a hunting horn (one he had inherited from the Lake Hunt[3] of which he was a founding member when at Trinity). This, applied

---

3   The Lake Hunt was devised in the years after the First World War by a group of Trinity men, including G.M. Trevelyan, G.E. Moore and Vaughan Williams. Over a period of three or four days they went to a large farmhouse, owned by Trevelyan, at a place called Seatoller not far from Keswick in Borrowdale. There, after a good breakfast, two of the party – there were usually about eight – were chosen as hares by the taking of straws. They set off with some provisions, each carrying a hunting horn. The rest set off in pursuit half an hour later. There were prescribed limits within which the hunt was contained, but it included Great Gable to the south and Scafell. Every so often the hares had to sound their horns which

to the ear and spoken into, amplified the speaker's voice considerably and greatly reduced the babble of conversation around him, as only one person at a time could thus speak to him. In any case, everyone around wanted to listen and hear his reply. Of course, he did it on purpose and found it amusing.

After the interval we, backstage, were asked to wait until everyone was seated. We could peep through the side curtains meanwhile. V.W. was among the last to be seated, and as he made to sit down, still talking to his neighbour, he suddenly disappeared from sight, having failed to put down his tip-up seat. The hunting horn flew into the air, descending several rows back and from the depths came a resounding 'Damn!'

Order restored and no harm evidently done, the Lark did eventually ascend gracefully. V.W. came backstage afterwards saying how much he'd enjoyed hearing it again; though one wondered how, for the hunting horn had vanished.

Some weeks later I was at his house in Regents Park and he confessed to a bruise or two but was otherwise quite unharmed. The hunting horn never turned up, but he had a spare.

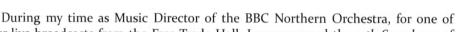

During my time as Music Director of the BBC Northern Orchestra, for one of our live broadcasts from the Free Trade Hall, I programmed the *13th Symphony* of Shostakovich, a major work for bass solo, men's voices and large orchestra. It is close to being a cantata with settings of poems by Yevtushenko, the first of which was *Babi Yar*, where there was a notorious massacre of Jews by Russian soldiers in Stalin's era.

For the first half of the programme, I thought Beethoven's *Emperor Concerto* would provide an upstanding, heroic prelude to the dramatic pessimism to come.

I asked Clifford Curzon, an old friend and colleague, to be our soloist and proposed an extra rehearsal devoted entirely to the concerto – something quite unusual and not altogether welcome with the orchestra. It was arranged for a Monday night, two days before the main rehearsals began, four before the concert.

Clifford was enthusiastic about it and glad to make the extra journey to Manchester from London it entailed. No, he didn't want to be met at the station. No, he didn't want to be taken from the Midland Hotel where he was staying and guided down the hill to the Milton Hall where the extra rehearsal was to take place – after all, how often had he played in Manchester?

---

magically echoed in the mountains.

It was said that in V.W.'s day they would stay out all night if the hares were particularly elusive, but in the years when I was a member we had an agreement to call it a day as dusk began. We would meet on the only road back to Seatoller where there was another house whose mistress dispensed tea, scones and brandy butter – greatly appreciated after a long day's pursuit.

V.W. must have hung on to his hunting horn and later found it useful.

The rehearsal began at 6:00 p.m. on a cold, dark, rainy night, something of a Mancunian specialty. No Clifford – tho' he must have arrived in Manchester, for someone had spoken to him by telephone at the hotel.

We took the long opening tutti to pieces, put it back together again and went on to the purely orchestral sections in the second and third movements – still no Clifford.

By now it was past 7:15 and I was just about to call for a break and send out scouts when the studio door was flung open and Clifford appeared, scarlet – he always went bright red when indignant, a sort of instant rage – and dripping wet.

He was a kind, considerate man and what, I'm sure, he intended to shout to me from the doorway over the players' heads was something like 'Dear Ray, everyone, I'm so very sorry but I lost my way'. What he actually said, eyes popping out of his red, sweaty face was: 'Ray! What a f-----g awful city this is'.

About eighty percent of the orchestra came from Manchester, a city of which they were very proud; that and the non-appearance added considerably to the atmosphere in the silence that followed.

I immediately called the break for which, luckily, I had ordered buns and cakes galore to go with their coffee or tea.

After that everything calmed down and we had a wonderfully concentrated second half of the rehearsal.

Four days later on the morning of the concert, after we had battled with *Babi Yar*, Clifford arrived on stage. Chorus, soloist and extra players had all left. We began the *Emperor* with the agreed intention of only playing a few bars here and there, remembering what we had particularly rehearsed the previous Monday.

The opening grand E flat chord had never sounded so well balanced – it has a rather strange, difficult scoring – and the intonation was perfect. Clifford's first cadenza was magical. We didn't stop.

There were only three people left sitting in the Free Trade Hall that morning after the big crowd for Shostakovich had left: the BBC Head of Music for the North, the librarian and his assistant.

Something took over and there followed one of the finest performances of that concerto I would ever hope to hear. No one said anything at the end. Silently the orchestra packed their instruments and went away. I didn't talk to Clifford or, indeed, anyone, and we all quietly left the Hall somewhat mystified and a little over-awed by what had happened.

Come the evening, I was early at the Hall. It was going to be packed, and backstage there was the continuous bustle of players and BBC engineers. As I was going up to my dressing room, I encountered Clifford, in tails of course, but waving his hands about, each one encompassed by a woolen glove with the frayed ends where the tips of the fingers had been clipped off – a common practice among players when the cold endangers mobility. It wasn't really cold, but those ragged gloves were a presage of what was to come.

Clifford, fussed and on the way to becoming red, said in a chain of indignant, disjointed sentences: 'Ray, I can't think why you asked me to do this.' 'They've only come for the Shostakovich.' 'It really isn't suitable that I'm here.' 'Perhaps I shouldn't go on.' 'It's really too bad'.

There were only about ten minutes before the broadcast was due to begin. We told him how wonderful he was – of course they'd all come to hear him! We reminded him how wonderfully he'd played the concerto, how we loved having him here, and we took his gloves off and got him ready in the wings to go on after the announcement was made.

He calmed down and with a look of one going to his execution, he went on to tumultuous applause. We settled down and I gave the downbeat for that first chord that had sounded so well that very morning. Not now. It was ill-balanced and out of tune. Clifford then started the first E-flat cadenza in E-major, a semitone higher, because his fingers slipped from the black keys to the white.

He corrected some of it somehow, and there followed perhaps the worst performance of the *Emperor* I've ever heard from both soloist and orchestra going from mistaken pillar to unfortunate post. It certainly seemed the longest concerto I'd ever had to do with.

We forgave each other, of course, and a few months later Clifford came with us on a European tour to Germany, Vienna and Salzburg, where there was one more moment of instant indignation. After a very good, well-received *Emperor* at Salzburg, Clifford rose, took a bow and went off stage, disappearing into a labyrinth of hanging curtains belonging to the sets of *Idomeneo* with which we shared the stage. After numerous, alarmed chasings into this fabric forest, Clifford appeared, bright red, as red as I'd ever seen him. He took another bow to a by now fairly hysterical audience. Then, with everyone in the wings shouting at him 'This way – no, not there', he disappeared into the curtains again, lost for good.

It was a wonderfully silly moment redolent of the earlier days in Manchester.

Great Court, Trinity

Anne Keynes at Trinity

Trinity: Neville's Court,
The Wren Library

Raymond Leppard and older
brother, Ronald

Princess Margaret and Raymond Leppard

Earnest Read conducting the school orchestra

Recording Handel's Samson at Abbey Road

Cavalieri—but are they *anima* or *corpo*?

Bob Dart at the keyboard

Raymond Leppard at flat in New York

Raymond Leppard and mezzo-sopran Frederica Von Stade

At 16 Hamilton Terrace
London

Park Avenue at 86th Street
New York

Janet Baker, Ileana Cotrubas, James Bowman, Jani Strasser, Raymond Leppard
recording *la Calisto*

Leeds piano competition jury, friends, administrators, including Marion Harewood,
Nadia Boulanger, Charles Groves, Nikita Magaloff, Yvonne Loriod, Raymond

ECO recording session

Cecil Aronwitz, Principal Viola, English Chamber Orchestra
at a Gramophone Award Ceremony

Memorial Plaque at Erin Arts Centre
Isle of Man

Window and plaque unveiled by HRH The Prince of Wales

I soon gave it up.

Elizabeth R

Elizabeth the Second, by the Grace of God of the United Kingdom of Great Britain and Northern Ireland and of Her other Realms and Territories Queen, Head of the Commonwealth, Defender of the Faith and Sovereign of the Most Excellent Order of the British Empire to Our trusty and well beloved Raymond John Leppard Esquire

Greeting

Whereas We have thought fit to nominate and appoint you to be an Ordinary Commander of the Civil Division of Our said Most Excellent Order of the British Empire.

We do by these presents grant unto you the Dignity of an Ordinary Commander of Our said Order and hereby authorise you to have hold and enjoy the said Dignity and Rank of an Ordinary Commander of Our aforesaid Order together with all and singular the privileges thereunto belonging or appertaining.

Given at Our Court at Saint James's under Our Sign Manual and the Seal of Our said Order this Eleventh day of June 1983 in the Thirty-second year of Our Reign.

By the Sovereign's Command.

Grand Master.

Grant of the Dignity of an Ordinary Commander of the Civil Division of the Order of the British Empire to Raymond John Leppard, Esq.

Made CBE

120

Gerontius maquette by Jeff Rouse

Raymond Leppard and Dame Janet Baker

Raymond Leppard at a party at Sandringham

Raymond Leppard and Marianne Tobias

Indianapolis home of Raymond Leppard

(Left to right) Leo de Rothschild, Raymond Leppard, Lady Penn

Raymond Leppard in Santa Fe, New Mexico

Lunch at a Shooting Lodge with HM Queen Elizabeth

Raymond Leppard and HM Queen Elizabeth at Sandringham

(Left to right) HRH The Prince of Wales, friend and Raymond Leppard

(Left to right) Lord Gowrie, Lady Cecilia McKenna, Raymond Leppard,
HM Queen Elizabeth, HRH The Prince of Wales, David McKenna,
Duchess and Duke of Grafton, Derek Hill

Fire destroys royal hideaway by the sea

Before: The beach hut where Prince Charles, inset top, entertained high-profile guests   After: The charred remains yesterday. Arson is suspected   *Pictures: ALBAN DONOHOE*

By Bill Mouland

ONE of the Royal Family's favourite holiday hideaways was found razed to the ground yesterday.

All that remained of the well-appointed beach hut on the North Norfolk coast was a crooked brick chimney stack and a few charred timbers.

Arsonists were thought to be to blame, although there was a theory that the fire started as intruders tried using a built-in barbecue on the verandah, which was particularly popular with Prince Philip.

The hut, which lies three-quarters of a mile down a dirt track on the Earl of Leicester's estate at Holkham, was a gift to the royals from the fifth earl in the 1930s. It had its own small kitchen, French windows and a flushing lavatory.

Fifteen miles from Sandringham, it was very much part of the royal scene in East Anglia. The Queen

had lunch there every year after the Sandringham Flower Show, a practice followed since her death by Prince Charles and Camilla Parker-Bowles.

Charles also holds picnics in the hut during his March visit to Norfolk, when he entertains high-profile guests such as Peter Mandelson, Stephen Fry, Emma Thompson and Joanna Lumley.

The Queen, however, is not thought to have visited the hut for some years – perhaps because the beach around the corner is designated for nudists.

The building was set among trees which afforded great privacy while gradually encroaching on the views of the sea. In recent years, however, a number of trees were cleared so the royals could gaze out on the glorious and lonely stretch of sand.

The hut caught fire nine years ago. Two passing nudists raised the alarm, beating the flames until the fire brigade arrived to put

them out. This time, however, six fire crews were unable to save it, despite drawing water from a nearby pond.

Leading fireman Steve Pope said: 'The hut was burning from one end to the other with flames reaching 60ft into the air when the first crews arrived. There was nothing we could do.'

Norfolk police spokesman Jon Austin said: 'We believe the fire was started deliberately and we are investigating.'

Vandals. Damn them!

MUSIC IN COUNTRY CHURCHES

Patron

His Royal Highness The Prince of Wales

music at

CASTLE ACRE

Thursday 27 and Friday 28 July 2000
The Church of St. James
Castle Acre
Nr Swaffham, Norfolk

The beginning at Indianapolis

Indianapolis Symphony Orchestra

On the way out

Mignon Dunn as Susan B. Anthony; recording session of
Mother of Us All at Santa Fe

Billy Budd at the Met

Portrait by Peter Egeli

Our beloved Debo, named after (and with permission of)
the Duchess of Devonshire

Raymond   Jack

Christel DeHaan in India

Portrait of Debo, commissioned by Leo de Rothschild

XXVI. Debo and Debo

I never knew about wanting a dog. There were red setters around when I was very small, but, by the time we'd moved from London to Bath, they had disappeared and I don't remember missing them or even knowing them very well to begin with.

The years, place, travel, and life passed dogless, but sixty years later with my appointment as Music Director of the Indianapolis Symphony came a certain stability, made more so by love, and with love came a beautiful German shepherd crossed with a chow, called Dusty.

So I learned to love a dog as well.

There were concerts in England with visits to Derbyshire, where an old friend of many years, Elizabeth Cavendish, lives in the village of Edensor, close by Chatsworth, home of her brother, the Duke of Devonshire.[4] His Duchess, one of the celebrated Mitford sisters, had done wonderful things to that great house, bringing it to a sort of life it hadn't seen for many years. The Duchess, beautiful and high-spirited, is known to her friends and family as Debo. There were dogs there too – quite a number.

Back in Indianapolis, Dusty was arriving at a certain age, which with dogs (unlike some humans I could name) comes often too soon. To encourage her to keep up her spirits, we went to the Humane Society of Indianapolis where a little round ball of fur unraveled itself and chose us to be looked after. She, like Dusty, was a mixture of chow and German shepherd, smaller and with a lovely face.

What to call her?

Just back from Derbyshire, there seemed very little question about it. So, with permission granted from the real Duchess, we found ourselves with another wonderful Debo as part of our family.

---

4   The Duke has since died and his son has inherited the title. The Duchess is now the Dowager Duchess of Devonshire and she is still Debo – our own Debo's namesake.

Of course she rules the house and gives us to understand how important she is – not that we doubted it for a moment. The word got out and for my 70th birthday, our dear friend, Leo de Rothschild, had the beautiful portrait of her facing this chapter done by a distinguished animal portraitist in London.

We don't show it to her very often in case she gets too uppity.

XXVII. This Side of the Iron Curtain

In February 1961, I played harpsichord continuo on one of Tom Goff's instruments at a memorable Festival Hall concert with the recently formed English Chamber Orchestra. The soloists were David and Igor Oistrakh, father and son, playing the Bach double-violin concerto and some Vivaldi.

Later that year, I directed a series of concerts with them and the ECO out of London, most notably in Oxford at the Sheldonian, that wonderful round building on Holywell designed by Christopher Wren.

The day before the concert we rehearsed in London at Tom Goff's house in Pont Street: the Oistrakhs; our principal cellist, Bernard Richards; someone from the orchestra to see to the music and the music stands; and Tom, in somewhat agitated attendance, anxious to know if his harpsichord would stand the pace.

The Oistrakhs were delivered in a Russian Embassy car whose chauffeur said he would return in two hours to pick them up. We all knew each other from the Festival Hall concert and the programme was much the same. It should have been a convivial meeting with coffee and 'play-time' biscuits (thin, rather dry, digestive biscuits with hard-sugar icing, not to be found in Russia, that David craved after his last visit). But then we noticed the extra person – a young man in a belted, light-coloured mackintosh with a brown hat, brim pulled down over his eyes. It wasn't clear how he got there, but he must have slipped in behind the violinists and chauffeur at the front door. When stopped by Tom's butler, he spoke in Russian to Oistrakh père who explained, rather apologetically, that he was an interpreter sent by the embassy to be of assistance. This was clearly a misnomer, for whenever he spoke it was either a grunt or a word or two in Russian addressed to one of the Oistrakhs, who clearly didn't like the young man at all.

He stuck to us like a limpet, following us up the dark stairs to the sitting room, eyeing Bernard Richard's cello case as if it might contain some lethal weapon.

David O. spoke sharply to him, directing him to wait in a corner out of the way, where he stood motionless for two hours without removing hat or mackintosh, declining coffee and 'playtime' biscuits with barely a grunt. The promise of a friendly morning's music-making showed signs of turning into a Casablanca-like drama. The English are good at not seeing what they don't want to see, unlike the Russians who were clearly embarrassed and discomfited. We did all notice that the young man's hands were permanently in the mackintosh pockets clenched as if ready with bomb or gun. As it turned out, we weren't far from the truth.

Otherwise the rehearsal went well and the Oistrakhs were, in due course, collected by the embassy car along with 'mackintosh.'

Tom then rang the embassy and made a fuss, saying the next time the 'interpreter' must stay outside. There wasn't to be a 'next time.' I don't suppose the under-secretary knew what he was talking about, but at least Tom felt the relief of protest.

The next day we made our separate ways to Oxford for a late morning rehearsal with the orchestra, more for seating, lighting and balance than serious musical revision. There was no sign of 'mackintosh' and we didn't ask.

The Oistrakhs and I had been invited to lunch with the distinguished Regius Professor of Modern History, Hugh Trevor-Roper, and his wife, Alexandra, in their attractive house on The High. We were to rest and change there for the concert. I hardly knew Hugh but his brother, a brilliant ophthalmologist and something of a scamp who lived near me in London, was a good friend.

Hugh was waiting in his car after the rehearsal and we bundled the Oistrakhs into it for the brief ride to his house where Alexandra had prepared a delicious lunch in the dining room a floor below the entrance hall and corridor.

Over drinks before lunch there was a certain amount of self-congratulation at having ditched 'mackintosh', who had indeed been at the rehearsal discreetly keeping his distance. But the celebration was premature for, halfway through a delectable cheese soufflé and an interesting revelation about Alexandra's grandfather, the first Earl Haig, the doorbell rang upstairs. Hugh excused himself and went up to see who it was. Of course it was 'mackintosh', whose entrance interrupted the Haig history, as we all listened to what clearly was becoming a heated exchange upstairs.

David Oistrakh put his napkin down and, appearing alarmed, went up the stairs rather rapidly for one of his rotund build. It was just as well for at that moment, having been denied entrance by the now enraged Hugh (he was known for his short fuse) 'mackintosh' had taken a gun out of his pocket. We had all followed up to the hallway and suddenly it was all rather dangerous.

Some explosive Russian phrases from father Oistrakh defused the situation and 'mackintosh' eventually sat quietly in the hall until we departed for the concert.

It was, of course, quite outrageous but, reflecting afterwards, you could only feel sorry for the young man scared to death that two of the most famous Russians of his time for whom he was responsible might, as Nureyev and several others had already done, defect to the West. Come to think of it, it was rather bright of him, without benefit of language and in the space of a cheese soufflé, to have found out where we were. At least he would be able to tell his grandchildren he had nearly shot an august Professor of History in Oxford.

XXVIII. Glyndebourne

Glyndebourne is a house in Sussex whose eccentric owner, John Christie, formerly a master at Eton, married in the early 1930s a young singer who had been making a modest career for herself with the traveling Carl Rosa Opera Company.

It was for her that Mr. Christie built an opera house, scoured Europe for the best musical and theatrical talent and started a summer season largely devoted to the operas of Mozart, not then so frequently performed as now.

Audrey Mildmay, Mrs. Christie's professional name, made a very creditable Susanna and Zerlina, but it was the skills of Carl Ebert and Fritz Busch backed up by meticulous musical preparation under Jani Strasser that soon earned Glyndebourne Opera a world-wide reputation for excellence.

A major conditioning contribution to this excellence lay in the fact that opera was produced there under the Festival (*stagione*) rather than the Repertory system which obtained principally in Germany and in most large opera houses. A new opera production may be given adequate, not to say excellent, preparation and rehearsal. After the première it would be unusual for it to be heard more than twice in one week. There isn't the public even in large cities to sustain more closely-placed performances. Supposing a total of twelve performances is envisaged in the first season with four weeks of preparation before the first night, the new opera's appearances will occupy the performers over a period of ten weeks. A lot can be forgotten and blunted in that length of time, with other engagements claiming their attention.

In between those performances other operas already rehearsed and in repertory will be given. Supposing the new opera was Weber's *Oberon*, a week of shows in Repertory opera may read as follows: Monday *Oberon*; Tuesday *Fledermaus*; Wednesday matinée *Magic Flute*, evening *Carmen*; Thursday *Fledermaus*; Friday *Oberon*; Saturday matinée *Carmen*, evening *Magic Flute*.

Four different operas in one week of eight shows, even allowing for a little exaggeration, is bound to take its toll on standards. Small wonder that chorus members arriving in their dressing rooms and seeing their costumes laid out by wardrobe for that evening might say, 'Oh, bandanas – so it's *Carmen* tonight'.

A drop in standards may hardly be noticed in the first season but in the next, the 'new' opera, now not so new, will be given only two weeks' rehearsal. Inevitably, there will be changes in cast who have to pick up their positions and reactions in double-quick time, let alone survive the perils of curtailed music calls.

Moral to prospective opera goers: Always try to go to a new production in Repertory opera during the first weeks of performances. On the other hand, if the opera you are eager to hear is not in its first season, it may be as well to go to one of the last shows when the new people have made their way and settled into their new rôles.

No such reservations apply to performances in the Festival system at Glyndebourne where, after the five or six weeks of rehearsal (the usual prep, even if the opera is not 'new' that season), the performances are placed close together so that, if anything, they tend to mature with regular repetition.

Glyndebourne has the added good fortune of being situated in beautiful country amid the downs of Sussex. Cast members and many connected with the running and production of the operas live in houses rented for the season within a ten-mile radius of Glyndebourne itself. In this way there grows up an almost familial relationship among cast, chorus and the company in general.

While the first opera is in its last stages of rehearsal, the second is begun and their opening performances mingle with the concluding ones of the first. This pattern is repeated and the sequence goes on from late spring to late summer and usually allows for five operas; some of which are repeated from previous years, but always allowed the same amount of preparation.

I believe Glyndebourne does it better than any other place in the world, and after two early years as répétiteur, I conducted there for ten seasons and enjoyed it all greatly.

Of course there were incidents and I thought it might be of interest and amuse if I recounted some – in no particular order.

XXIX. THE SAGA OF MILES MALLESON AND HIS WIGS

In 1954, my first year as répétiteur at Glyndebourne, Strauss's *Ariadne auf Naxos* was given with the composed, operatic prologue. It had been performed at the Edinburgh Festival by the Glyndebourne Company in 1950 preceded by the original Molière play instead of the composed prologue. Sir Thomas Beecham conducted.

In 1953 it was produced at Glyndebourne without the play and Sir Thomas, but with the delightful but fairly brief operatic prologue.

It was realised that a thirty-minute beginning, however delightful, would make for a rather short evening before an audience most of whom had come all the way from London, dressed up in evening attire, having paid a good deal of money for their seats. It was decided to first play in concert on stage all the incidental music that Strauss had written for the play without any acting. It was hoped that this would adequately fill out the first part of the evening before a picnic dinner on the lawns or something more formal in the restaurant. It didn't.

So, in 1954 when I began there, Busoni's rather arid one-act opera *Arlecchino* was given before the composed prologue to *Ariadne*. That didn't work either so it was dropped altogether, in any version, for a while.

In 1962 when I came back for the production of my realisation of *L'Incoronazione de Poppea*, the General Manager, Moran Caplat, decided to revive the opera in its original version and precede it, before the dinner interval, with Molière's play, casting Miles Malleson once more as M. Jourdain. (He had played it with great success in the Edinburgh Festival production of 1950).

Miles Malleson was more of a 'character' than a great actor, but given the right part, which this most certainly was, he could be hilariously funny. Something of an introverted, chinless wonder with an infectious gurgling chuckle, he became the personification of the nouveau riche, vulgar bourgeois gentilhomme of Molière's play. Miles himself, we were told, was completely bald but always wore a wig. That much was fairly evident we thought.

During the play M. Jourdain decides to give a grand dinner at which both a tragedy and a comedy will be played, if necessary both at the same time. To further impress his guests he sports a full-bottom wig and, in changing from his everyday one, reveals that he, too, is completely bald. Audiences loved all that.

Both *Poppea* and *Ariadne* were in rehearsal at the same time, so the casts met frequently about the theatre, most often in the artists' canteen. First there were rumours about it; then it was confirmed that in the play when M. Jourdain removes his everyday wig and is seen to be bald, Miles insisted on wearing a bald wig over his own hair – if it was his own.

There was much discussion about it, and his neat hair style became the object of extraordinary scrutiny as we all drank coffee together in the canteen.

It was there that we noticed a gradual change. After a week of rehearsal the hair seemed distinctly longer. Speculation was rife and we began to wonder if we had been mistaken. After two weeks there was no doubt about it. His hair seemed much more luxuriant and some said it had changed colour a little. Some also said they could detect a slight lifting at the edges.

Of course he said nothing. Rehearsals were going well and he told us that in his free time he was enjoying the countryside around the opera even venturing to the coast from time to time. 'Salt air is very good for the hair', he said. Everyone nodded; a few weaker people showed signs of convulsion and had to pretend it was over something else.

At the end of three weeks, during a coffee break, he patted his head saying, 'Oh dear, it really is getting too untidy. I must make an appointment with my hairdresser'. We didn't ask which of the local barbers he would patronise, but the next day he appeared with neat, noticeably shorter hair. We all tried not to look, but as if taking part in some weird charade, Miles carried on as usual, perhaps preening himself more and was more than usual full of gurgling bonhomie.

All was eventually revealed when an actor friend of his came to see the performance and, in the interval, told someone that Miles had a series of wigs made that differed only in length of hair. As a young man he had become completely bald and thereafter had invented this sequence of events to bolster his own confidence and, this friend suggested, to see if any of his colleagues would notice.

Before the end of the second hair-style cycle, our performances had begun. We hardly saw him except onstage coping well with M. Jourdain's wigs as part of a stunningly funny representation of Molière's character. Miles was a lonely man, and that added pathos to his and the playwright's character.

XXX. Stormy Weather

Vittorio Gui, who led the Rossini revival at Glyndebourne, was a delightful man, a little *pomposo* perhaps, but a genuine and careful musician, well read, widely experienced, with a particular flair for Italian opera of the early nineteenth century.

He came to Glyndebourne in 1954, my first year as a répétiteur, as the unspoken successor to Fritz Bush who had died the previous year. He was virtually unknown in England tho' celebrated in Italy where he had been a rival to Toscanini, whom he in no way resembled and greatly disliked.

In his first year at Glyndebourne he conducted *Cenerentola*, *Macbeth* and *Così*, of which the outstanding success was the Rossini. That and the *Barber of Seville* two years later established a new vein for the house that had made its reputation on Mozart.

It wasn't at first a conscious new direction, but the public reaction to this way of performing Rossini was as enthusiastic as their reaction to *Figaro* or *Così*. Musically the two composers are not so far apart where the methods of composition are concerned, but their styles couldn't be more different. It was Gui's natural affinity for, as well as his scholarly research into, the original texts that defined the revival at Glyndebourne.

Gui revealed the width of his interests and knowledge quite slowly. I was somewhat surprised when one day after rehearsal he told me he had only lately come across some of Purcell's odes and theatre music and had been deeply impressed by them. I was touched that he should have asked me, as a young beginner in the profession, questions about seventeenth-century English music even if he did know my academic background. I doubt Toscanini would have admitted gaps in his knowledge or would have been in the least interested in Purcell, if he had even heard of him.

I found in a catalogue a volume of the Purcell Society (I think it was *King Arthur*) and gave it to him. He wrote me a wonderful letter not only thanking me but wishing every sort of good to come from the work he had already seen me do. It vanished in the Hamilton Terrace fire but the memory and impressions of it have remained.

Rossini's music after he died has been at the mercy of every soprano, mezzo, tenor, baritone, and bass who thought, because of the splendour of their voices, they could improve on it to their advantage. You only have to think of the many versions of Figaro's first aria in the *Barber of Seville*, with squeaks here, falsetto there and a frequent flagrant disregard for the original notes. The same goes for soprano versions of Rosina's first aria '*Una voce poco fa*', which was intended to display first innocent charm and then a fiery little spitfire. The license for agility, extremes of range, pausing on high notes and the like, reduce a beautiful aria to cheap, shoddy vulgarity.

Gui would have none of this, or rather only as much as he thought Rossini would have countenanced. He was that wonderful thing, a purist with an impure mind; I've always tried to follow his example.

So, in the *Barber* at Glyndebourne, Bruscantini as Figaro and Graziella Sciutti as Rosina had such an exciting, controlled freedom that the spirit of Rossini's masterpiece was revealed with unerring directness, which the Sussex audience recognised. In Gui's hands, Rossini was never common and never academic; rather, it was always sophisticated, elegant and humanly beautiful in comedy as in tragedy.

Gui liked to speak English with occasional lapses into Italian. Describing his own anger at some customs holdup, he said, 'It was horrible. I went red like a *pomo d'oro* (tomato)'; which indeed was his custom if things weren't going well. As with powdered coffee he had a nice line in instant indignation, which became a catch phrase that first year.

One time in the organ room, I had occasion to introduce a newly appointed associate stage director to him for the first time. He put out his hand and said his name, 'Vittorio Gui' as is the custom in Europe. In return the young man took the outstretched hand saying 'Richard Day'. There was a moment's silence and Vittorio, glancing out the window said, 'Yes, isn't it!' That was a lovely moment.

XXXI. *Calisto* and the Bird Seed

Ursa Minor, the little bear in the night sky's constellation, appears as Calisto in Ovid and several other classical texts. She is also the subject and title of one of Cavalli's best operas which, in the 1970s, I prepared for Glyndebourne. The librettist, Giovanni Faustino, devised clever variants on the classical legend so that it became a comedy of sexual ambivalence with serious, touching undertones.

As the opera opens, Calisto is an innocent, virginal nymph in the Goddess Diana's train, a group of devoted ladies whose behaviour is supervised by a crabby, aging virgin, Linfea. She, in an amusing solo scene, tells the audience she has always been curious about the opposite sex, but whenever in a weak moment she was tempted to say 'yes', the sterner voice of duty always said 'no!' Before the end of the opera, however, she is whisked off by some of Pan's lusty satyrs to find out all about it and, one hopes, some resolution to her doubts.

In the production at Glyndebourne Hugh Cuenod, the Swiss tenor, played Linfea in travesty, reflecting the ambivalent character of the whole opera. Hugh, who even now as I write is approaching the age of 106, was in his performing days one of the most brilliant portrayers of secondary, somewhat eccentric characters, such as Sellem in *The Rake's Progress* and Monsieur Triquet in *Eugene Onegin*, usually stealing the scenes in which he appeared.

Tall and thin, his costume for Linfea was a parody of the one her Goddess wore, breasts and all. These, rather sagging but shapely as befits a stalwart, well-preserved virgin of advancing years, were made of muslin stuffed with bird seed, strapped to Hugh's chest and covered by the costume.

After a few performances, Hugh complained that his 'breasts' were getting smaller. I could see from the orchestra pit that, after Hugh's scenes, there were some specks scattered about the stage. Clearly they were leaking.

It transpired that, under the hot stage lights and in an exceptionally hot summer, Hugh had been sweating a lot, which meant that his 'breasts' had to be washed after every performance and hung up to dry in the courtyard behind the opera house. The public weren't allowed there so that the artists could sit and relax between scenes, their dressing rooms overlooking the court's quadrangle, open to the skies.

Once washed, the breasts were hung up in the least conspicuous corner of the quadrangle where they, for a time unnoticed, became a major attraction to local bird life.

By the third or fourth performance the birds had not only consumed a large amount of bird seed in each breast, but also made several holes in the muslin wide enough to allow further depletions onto the stage when Hugh was wearing them.

Some bird-proof material was found and thereafter they kept their shape without leakage. Of course, they became the focus of much ribald comment, even some indecent molestation from the rest of the cast. Hugh loved it.

XXXII. RELUCTANT SOPRANOS

Everything is so well rehearsed at Glyndebourne that almost nothing ever goes awry in performance. An occasional stumble is corrected without the audience ever knowing or feeling anxious. There was, however, one alarming moment that very nearly caused a breakdown. I was conducting and remember it well.

It was the first night of Cavalli's *L'Ormindo*. We'd already had a major crisis at the beginning of rehearsals when, at a first musical reading in London, the singer who had been cast as Erisbe, the lovely young princess heroine whose amorous adventures thread through the opera, turned out to be a senior, rather plain Italian lady with a hard, unsupple voice. She had slipped through the casting net by virtue of the similarity of her name to that of the composer.

The crisis was eventually dealt with tactfully at Glyndebourne; the lady behaved with decorum and left Sussex quietly with a large packet in her handbag. In her place the beautiful young English singer, Anne Howells, who was to have sung the part of the princess's maidservant, took it over, rose superbly in the social scale, made the part her own, and had a great success.

The French soprano who took Anne's place as the maidservant, Miranda, was Jane Berbié, a delightful, pretty soubrette who shone brightly in all the rehearsals. She omitted to tell anyone that she suffered from stage fright. It is a condition well known to many actors, like John Gielgud and Edith Evans who took a variety of precautions to overcome the sudden terror of going on stage.

On the first night of *L'Ormindo* all was going extremely well. You could sense the excitement of not only the audience, but also the performers playing an opera for the first time in over three hundred years.

All went forward splendidly until the fourth scene in Act One where Miranda had a charming, comic solo scene where she comments on the tangles in which the lovers have already been embroiled. Not for her: no one would ever persuade her to take a husband. These solo scenes drawing amusing conclusions about the action so far were a popular feature of early seventeenth-century Venetian opera.

In this case there was a pretty, lively *sinfonia* that precedes her entrance. We played it. No Miranda. It seemed that no one could persuade her to go on stage.

The orchestra was very quick on the uptake and we started all over again with hardly a pause. Still no Miranda.

On the fourth time 'round, there was a rustling and bustling in the wings and Miranda flew on, hat askew, spilling things out of a basket she was clinging to for dear life. Roars of laughter from the house, signs of relief down below.

Of course she was, at that very moment, over her fright and gave a lovely performance of her scene, with great applause at the end. She brought the house down, as she had nearly done for me before it began.

XXXIII. Head Coach

Jani Strasser had been Audrey Mildmay's singing teacher and, vetted by Fritz Busch, Jani was more or less hijacked from Vienna, with his wife Irene and son, to become head of music studies at Glyndebourne's first season in the 1930s.

He wasn't a great musician, but he had an amazing heart and a stubborn tenacity for detail. He brought a degree of accuracy and ensemble that raised the standards way above those found in the general world of opera in England at that time.

He was shrewd and quick and loved to be teased, so his music staff adored him and admired the way he stood up to even the most celebrated of singers. We used to give him morning reports of the previous day's coaching and playing for rehearsals. It didn't matter if you were Birgit Nilsson or Miss Blogs in the chorus hoping to understudy her, the corrections were just as direct and uncompromising. They all respected him.

He was just as demanding of his music staff. I've certainly never worked such long, hard hours as in those two years as répétiteur. Even when you rose to the exalted rank of conductor, his strictures wherever he saw error were just as direct, if a little more respectful.

There were so many stories about him, some, doubtless, apocryphal, most of them somehow reflecting his strengths and weaknesses.

There was one about his offstage playing of the flute-like cuckoo instrument in *Hansel and Gretel* at the Vienna Opera where, in earlier days, he was occasionally hired. Its bird song plays a major part in the scene where the children in the woods pick strawberries and then imitate and mock the bird while they play. Gradually the darkening forest becomes more and more sinister as do the cuckoo's two repeated notes. Finally it becomes a ghostly echo as Hansel calls out its two notes singing 'Who's there?'.

The instrument is not at all difficult to blow but it behooves the player to play with rapt concentration or it can easily go wrong. Unfortunately, Jani's playing of the last and most sinister echoes did go wrong. Instead of 'cuckoo' the bird song became 'oo cuck' at least a dozen times, causing general hysteria on stage and eventually in the audience. It seemed to us only Jani could have managed it.

On another occasion Jani was prompting and was superb at it as long as all was going well. In the most complicated ensembles, he would point at the singer from within the prompt box by the footlights and whisper the words of his or her next entrance with consummate virtuosity. The trouble began if somebody got out of turn. If that happened, Jani's skill as a coach and intolerance of error took over and a pained look appeared on his face. With hands clasped to his face, head shaking, the cry 'Falsch, Falsch' would come from the box, often quite audible in the house and certainly of not much use to the singers on stage.

There was another delightful story Jani himself used to tell about a rare occasion when he was baritone soloist in a performance of the Brahms *Requiem* with the local Lewes amateur choral society. Adrian Boult had been hired to conduct the last rehearsal and concert.

Jani suddenly realised that, as the soloist standing in front, he was blocking the view of a diminutive, elderly soprano. 'Oh! I'm so sorry, I'll move to one side; you can't see the conductor'. 'No, No!' the little lady replied, flattered by the notice taken. 'Please don't. It's quite all right, I saw him last year'.

At the end, like most of us, he outstayed his abilities and was asked to hand over control to a younger man. He didn't live long in his retirement.

Dear Jani, his devotion to his beloved Glyndebourne and his sense of standards will certainly never be forgotten. It's very touching that one of the Christie grandchildren is named after him.

XXXIV. LETTER TO THETIS

Thetis Blacker, famous for her batiks that now hang in several cathedrals and public places, was, earlier, an important part of Glyndebourne's social tapestry. She sang in the chorus when I first knew her and took small parts but, realizing her limitations, abandoned singing for her other enthusiasm in which she had great success. She was much-loved and died only a short while ago. This is by way of an affectionate remembrance.

Dear Thetis,

You are gone now – probably teaching the angels about mushrooms or how to make batiks. I don't suppose sloe gin or Roman snails would come into it, tho' you never know. I'm told Heaven is very broad-minded.

We began at Glyndebourne in 1955. I was in my first year as a répétiteur and you were a member of the chorus. That, in case people don't understand, was already a major feather in any young professional singer's cap. You used to say you wouldn't have been accepted were it not for Moran Caplat's (General Manager) approval. I doubt it but, if true, it showed Moran's undoubted flair for backing winners.

Those two seasons fostered a friendship that I've valued all my life. I only regret that your change of career and my change of country made, lately, a long lacuna in it. It changed nothing of the value of those earlier days or the awareness of those wonderful achievements of yours which the world, if it looks at St. George's Chapel at Windsor or Durham Cathedral or Glyndebourne will acknowledge.

I heard a recording at Glyndebourne of your inspired tribute to Moran Caplat whose death preceded yours only by a few years. Altogether it was an event I very much regret missing, the more so as I listened to your voice with George and Mary who went on to describe the occasion, worthy of both of you.

I wrote to you about it not quite certain that a lacuna that big could be encompassed by a letter, but I shouldn't have doubted for, by return, there came a typically loving reply which exonerated us both and restored that warmth of friendship that had never gone away.

18 Nov 2003

Dear Raymond,

What a joy to get your letter! The years rolled away as I recognised your writing on the envelope. Thank you so much. I am such a bad letter writer, and all those years of silence signify nothing ... (several pages)

Too many of our old friends have died. And as they go, one regrets not seeing more of them while one could. So, please...

I am so exceedingly glad you wrote to me. Many benedictions and much, much love.

Thetis

We saw quite a lot of each other in those two early seasons at Glyndebourne and in between and after in London. I had left Cambridge for the first time two years earlier. My father, in spite of grave disapproval of my doing so in mid-Ph.D., nevertheless bought me a small, second-hand Morris 8 (my first car) so that I could get about and, perhaps, visit the parental home in Bath where the error of my ways could be remonstrated. He gave it to me without explaining the significance of the insurance he took out for one driver only. The purpose, presumably, was to make it not available for group outings with artistic scallywags, which might lead to interchangeable drivers and, therefore, accidents.

One morning, hurrying into rehearsal at Glyndebourne, a good friend, Anthony Besch, also in his first year there as an assistant director, asked to borrow it for an urgent errand in Lewes a mile or two away. Of course I agreed and threw him the keys as I went into the theatre.

Anthony, sadly another one who can now only be fondly remembered, had a propensity for accidents and awkward situations. Once in Lewes, he had difficulty finding a parking place, but fortunately came across one between two 'No Parking' signs outside the Law Courts at the top of the hill. To improve matters it was Quarter Assizes day. When Anthony returned from his errand he found an irate policeman who gave him a summons. The law then found out that the poor little car was insured only for the owner to drive and gave me a summons, too.

Anthony said he knew just the lawyer in London who'd get us out of the scrape, but when the case came up a month or two later, in the very building whose front had been so affronted, we lost – quite reasonably, for there was no possible defence. I lost the use of the car for a year and, in addition, incurred a small fine. The lawyer's fee was £80, which Anthony didn't have just then. Altogether a rather expensive day.

All this, dear Thetis, to explain why I came to ask you if you would like use of the car for a year (properly insured this time), and you said you'd be glad to have it. The car's registration, and therefore its nickname, were CUK. When you took it over and drove down to the family home at Shamley Green, [5] it started to rain. The windscreen wipers ceased to function and you had a problematic journey, which you described in a wonderful letter. You said you weren't a bit surprised that CU(c)K(oo) was upset and wept all the way to Kent, but now it was quickly recovered and responding well to a diet of grade-A petrol and some new windscreen wipers. I've lost the letter – burnt most probably at Hamilton Terrace – but the memory and the fun of it linger on.

During those visits various enthusiasms appeared and passed like white summer clouds across the blue skies of your vivid imagination.

First, you'll remember, there were mushrooms. We scoured the countryside and found more varieties than I would have thought possible. You knew them all, especially exulting in the discovery of the ones that would cook well. Young puffballs sautéed in butter were particularly good but there were others still more rare. We weren't poisoned once, tho' the possibility did occasionally cross my mind – those bright yellow ones growing out from a tree.

Cooking was a particular bond between us, especially in London where we used to exchange dinners and vie with one another in the search for unusual dishes, occasionally with queasy results. They were brilliantly original meals on your part, less so on mine; tho' there was a smoked-fish soufflé that turned out surprisingly well. As I recall, Elizabeth David was a good friend of yours and an admired influence.

Then there were the Roman snails – the ones that are called escargots in smart, Frenchified restaurants, larger and marginally more appetising than the smaller, rather slimy English garden snails. You were very keen

---

5   I was a fairly frequent visitor to Shamley Green where the Blackers had a large house in the Tudor style fashionable in the 1930s. Thetis' father was a well-known psychiatrist, a brusque, handsome man who was inclined to burst into your guest bedroom at 6:30 a.m. suggesting a run or at least a walk before breakfast. Her mother was a gentle, rather frail lady, the perfect foil for her husband and an admiring mother to her three children; John who was much abroad, I think in the Civil Service; an older sister, Carmen a very distinguished Japanese scholar, a Fellow of Clare Hall, Cambridge; and, of course, there was Thetis.

to breed them with a view to selling them at a considerable profit to those smart restaurants.

There were two large, wire-meshed cages you had built with some shrubs planted inside for habitat and a plentiful supply of, I think, mulberry leaves, their favourite food.

They prospered. I even think there was another cage built to give them sufficient lebensraum. I also think you hadn't taken into consideration your own sensibilities and love for all creatures in creation for, as I recall, when it came to the point of a Roman snail holocaust, you couldn't let it happen. It was just too much carnage of the animals you had come to admire. You unleashed the cages and the snails, thousands of them, ravaged every garden within several miles before expiring, presumably from natural causes. There were several lawsuits threatened, but I don't believe anything serious materialized. Although the snails became a no-talk topic, I sensed in you a certain feeling of satisfaction at having saved so many from an ignominious death.

One weekend at Shamley, I remember a project to make sloe gin. A sizeable number of canisters were prepared and put down in the cellar to mature. A few weeks later they exploded and made a terrible mess. That cloud passed quite rapidly.

Because other friends may read this, I can't omit retelling your own story of the night watch during your father's last illness.

He was bed-bound and not much enjoying it, but you were all so good seeing that someone was always in the house and could be summoned, if needed, by a series of bells that would ring from his bed to all parts of the house. You told of one particular day when the bell hadn't stopped ringing until the evening. Things calmed down a little and eventually you managed to get to bed, only to be awakened at three o'clock by recurrent bells. Putting on a dressing gown, you went along to your father's room and, going in, said, 'Oh! Daddy, what is it now?' A protracted silence and 'Mind your own business' snapped out from beneath the bed clothes. Question answered, I suppose.

Mushrooms, Roman snails, cookery – the zest with which you pursued your enthusiasms delighted, inspired and was admired by all your friends. Of course, at first, singing predominated and endured the longest then, to the extent of taking lessons from Elena Gerhardt, succeeded to the extent of playing a small part in Glyndebourne's production of The Rake's Progress and a bigger part in the same opera at Sadler's Wells.

Nevertheless it became clear to you that you weren't ever going to move up into some of the major roles, and all the time you were beginning your life's work by making those amazing batiks for which you became so famous. From the early days, when your flat in Chelsea was full of various pieces of fabric in various stages of being waxed and dyed, you developed your skills traveling extensively in the Middle East. There, the ancient techniques in this art form and the degree of mystery in the images of their cultures fired your imagination and fulfilled the purpose of your life. The genius that had been battling with singing, sloe gin and snails burst out and produced wonderful things.

I'm so glad to have known you and thank you for all you contributed to my life's enjoyment.

Much, much love - Raymond

I can't leave this letter of affectionate remembrance to dear Thetis without a smile and the recalling of something she wouldn't altogether have wished to be recalled. Yet for all those who were there it was unforgettable.

There was a party during the season at Glyndebourne. I can't remember who hosted it but everyone – chorus, music staff, principal singers, managers, directors, conductors – was there, including this character made up by Thetis, in some ways a caricature of herself, which probably explains why it was so successful.

She dressed up as one of the local, wealthy county ladies who (ungenerous of us now to mock) did so much at the beginning of Glyndebourne to make it succeed.

Mrs. Payley-Paget was her name. She was about as tall as Thetis, wore a cloche hat (which never came off), a cocktail dress worthy of Chanel (perhaps it was Chanel), shoes to match and a quantity of jet beads and some other jewelry redolent of the 1920s. It was an amazing transformation and an amazing performance. If anyone dare mention the name Thetis, whom Mrs. Payley-Paget only superficially resembled, there was a look that would have stopped the devil in his tracks. Even Carl Ebert, not known for his sense of humour, was completely bamboozled when she asked some leading questions about losing his temper in rehearsal (which he frequently did). He dared not offend this grand lady who might well be of considerable influence with those who employed him. Everyone enjoyed that.

In her last letter to me Thetis said that Mrs. Payley-Paget could be no more. She was wrong. Mrs. Payley-Paget would always command a little smile-lit corner in the hearts of those remembering our much-loved Thetis.

XXXV. Joan of Art

'Joan of Art' was the nickname given to John Drummond by John Betjeman. It showed a perceptive understanding of a complex crusader for the Arts. Drummond was ruthless with Philistines, many of whom were prominent in the English establishment, just as the original Joan herself defied and insulted those in the established Mediaeval Catholic Church. After all, she, too, had heard her angels. John's crusade against mediocre standards in the arts seemed sometimes to have been guided by a Superior Being, too.

As if seeking suitable epitaphs for his opponents, he produced with Joan Bakewell a wonderful survey of tombstones called *A Fine and Private Place*.

He was among the most intelligent people I've ever met, and his intelligence was supported by a phenomenal memory. As to manners, there was a good deal lacking, tho' it must be said that the higher the social standing of a likely recipient of an ill-mannered rebuke, the more was it ameliorated down to a gentle tease. Below these standards or sources of influence, he could annihilate and, as a result, by the end of his life he had created an army of antagonists that would have daunted David and the Israelites.

He once asked me if I would act as go-between with John Crosby in New York. There was a thought of the BBC broadcasting some performances from the Santa Fe opera that Crosby had founded. I knew him well, having conducted there for five or six seasons. 'Joan' by this time was head of Radio Three and the Promenade concerts, which he programmed brilliantly for ten years and was deservedly knighted for his work. It didn't improve his manners.

I arranged an evening meeting with John Crosby, who had a fine townhouse near the Pan Am Building, where we were warmly welcomed.

John, unlike 'Joan', was not a great talker and, after a few polite enquiries as to health, duration of stay and general well-being, became silent. Just as well, for 'Joan' began talking and barely drew breath for the next two hours, at which point I said firmly that we must go.

We walked together up Lexington Avenue towards my apartment on Park and 86th, at first in silence. Then 'Joan' exploded saying, 'Ray, I don't know why you took me there' (nothing about my acting as a go-between). 'We had absolutely nothing to say to one another. He doesn't like me – he really doesn't like me and, what's more, I couldn't get a word in edgeways. The man never stops – quite impossible to deal with'.

So much for any link between Santa Fe Opera and the BBC.

The harangue continued until we parted at 86th Street. We never spoke of it again.

John Crosby telephoned the next day. 'What a strange person, Raymond, do you have any idea what he wanted?'

XXXVI. THE WAY TO A GRAMMY

One morning in New York I was telephoned by a rather potent sounding lady from CBS, asking if I was free on such and such a date.

There's a tone of voice, a certain degree of emphasis when a simple question can sound like a command or a comment on one's underwear. Nannies used to use it before taking you out: 'You never know when you mightn't have an accident'.

Her call had a sort of authoritarian sound that always makes me react in a way similar to an occasion when I received a tiresome call from an agent asking me to telephone a tenor who was anxious to be considered for an engagement. I said (perhaps rather arrogantly), 'I'm sorry, but I don't ring tenors, tenors ring me'. There comes a time when seniority must count for something.

So, to the potent lady in New York, I answered, she must ring Ann Colbert, my agent, if the call was about a professional engagement, and I put the telephone down.

She rang again, later that day, asking in a slightly more conciliatory manner if I might possibly be interested in making a recording of a trumpet concerto with a brilliant young, black trumpeter from New Orleans. I didn't need the work and accompanying a child prodigy, black or white, in the concertos of Haydn and Hummel didn't seem the most appealing of ideas. I declined.

Before I could escape, she asked if I could at least spare the time to hear the young man and help him with the style of this eighteenth-century music. Someone must have told her of my background of teaching for I find such appeals for help difficult to resist; they are quite different from stern enquiries as to the condition of my underwear. So I agreed to meet with him at one of the Carnegie Hall rehearsal rooms a week later.

I duly turned up, not in the best of moods; promises about such arrangements have a habit of looming larger as they get closer and become an out-of-scale burden. At the rehearsal room I was seized by the potent lady and introduced first to the accompanist, then to some CBS people, and finally to a nice, modest-looking young man holding a trumpet, who barely spoke a word and seemed very shy. His name was Wynton Marsalis.

Not so shy when he began to play the Haydn concerto. On first impact, in a confined space, trumpets always sound like trumpets, and it must have been so at Jericho as well as at Carnegie Hall, the sheer volume of noise strikes one first. A few bars in and one can begin to notice things and differentiate.

What struck me then was the purity of intonation. So many trumpeters play sharp when they get louder or play in different registers – not this young man. So many coarsen the quality of sound in the lower and upper registers – not this young man. Then he could do what many can't: stay in the same dynamic over the whole range of the instrument, or such of it as was covered by Haydn's exploration of the key trumpet, newly invented in his day.

Technical matters apart, what struck me most was the sheer vitality of his music-making. It's true Haydn had on this occasion made his journey to Carnegie Hall via New Orleans, but that was to be easily remedied for Wynton took to musical ideas of phrasing, ornament and style like ink to blotting paper. I undertook to help him – tho' remarkably little help was needed – and to conduct the projected recording of the Haydn and Hummel concertos, together with one by Leopold Mozart for good measure.

CBS had banked up considerable funds behind the Iron Curtain and this, it appeared, was a splendid way of using some of them. So we all went to Prague in early December. It may have been economical for CBS; it was nearly fatal for Wynton and the projected recording.

Still under the shadow of Eastern powers, this once beautiful city, beloved of Mozart where *Don Giovanni* and much else of value saw the light of day, now was a sad, sorry sight. Prague had escaped damage from air raids; the wonderful series of bridges over the Moldau were intact, if shabby, but there was nothing in the shops. We were followed everywhere by shady-looking characters sent to keep a watch on us and, in the grey December light, everything was depressingly drab. So was the orchestra and not very good, either.

The first session was spent mostly in attempting to establish an A from which to tune everything. They were used to a considerably sharper A than we play to in America, and both Wynton and I suffered. Our ears had the greatest difficulty in adjusting. For me it was a matter of grumbling and wincing. Wynton tried to play at the higher pitch and was driven to distraction. A lower pitch was tried, but it only drove the orchestra crazy and made them worse. The whole thing, it was clear, was a failure.

Here the potent lady came into her own. 'We obviously cannot make the record in Prague. Any ideas?' I said, 'Why don't you ring Ursula Jones in London to see if the English Chamber Orchestra is available. You might also ask about the Abbey Road studios. It may well be there's less going on so close to Christmas'.

The potent lady was successful on all accounts, and the next day we packed up and flew to London.

We held a brief rehearsal with the orchestra. Not everyone of the ECO was free in those few days before Christmas so, because of substitutes, it was decided to change the orchestra's name for the recording to 'the National Philharmonic Orchestra'. The substitutes were fine and a wonderful spirit grew behind it all, enhanced by Wynton's superb playing now that he was at a pitch he knew.

I found out afterwards that in the evening after the first rehearsal he had been in touch with some New Orleans friends who happened to be in London. They had gone out to a club, playing jazz until three o'clock in the morning. The first session was at 10:00 a.m. that morning. At that period in his life he could switch from one style to the other, classical or jazz, each needing a different embouchure, let alone the musical differences, without blinking an eye. However, Wynton's sort of exuberant innocence couldn't last forever, and he doesn't mix the two styles now. With us, it was a brief trip into never-never land and much valued on that account. It's rare to have come across such talent.

We made two more classical CDs with the English Chamber Orchestra playing under their own name. And we did win Grammys in 1984 and 1985 for the first two CDs. On one of the CD visits, I got him to play for the Queen at a charity concert in St. James's Palace. She was very impressed and I rather think he was, too.

XXXVII. Ruth Fermoy

This is but one person remembering a most remarkable lady: beautiful, complex, attractive and powerful, she achieved remarkable things, and led a remarkable life. I was lucky enough to have become involved in some of it.

Friendship with Ruth was a gradual process. The formal politenesses were, of course, observed from the first meeting, in my case the King's Lynn Festival of 1963 when I brought the English Chamber Orchestra for a programme of Bach in St. Nicholas Chapel. Thereafter it was like Ibsen's onion in *Peer Gynt*, the layers gradually peeled off until, by the time she left this planet, I counted her among my closest friends and believe she would have said nearly the same about me, tho' there would always have been some element of reserve – that was her nature.

She was at once so very private and so very public. The public aspect was determined, consistent and extremely effective. She achieved most of the many projects she undertook. The private was hers to dispense as she saw fit.

As a young woman she had studied piano seriously and would, doubtless, have begun a successful professional career had she not been wooed by and then married to Lord Fermoy, a wealthy American who inherited the title and became part of the Norfolk social and political life. They came to live in Park House on the Sandringham Estate and so began a long enduring friendship with the Royal Family, culminating in Ruth's appointment as Lady in Waiting to The Queen Mother. She had three children, none of whom gave her great happiness. Her son killed himself; one daughter married into the Spencer family[6] and lived, ironically, in Park House until she was divorced; the third offspring sought intellectual stimulation which she frequently confused with another sort. Even her most celebrated granddaughter, Diana, was a disappointment, refusing much sound advice from her grandmother, carefully but despairingly given. Ruth had already alienated Diana's mother by testifying against her in her divorce because Ruth knew she was in the wrong.

So the division between Ruth's private and public lives deepened and she saw to it that the two were kept as far apart as possible. I think I was one of the few who, to some extent only, was allowed to bridge the gap.

6   Viscount and Viscountess Althorp (later Earl Spencer) were the parents of Lady Diana Spencer, who married His Royal Highness The Prince of Wales in 1981.

Her closest friend of long standing was a Dutch medico coming from a distinguished political family in Holland. I met her rarely and it may be that she predeceased Ruth, another secret department of her life. They shared, for a time, a house in France at St. Paul de Vence where I once visited briefly. Some weeks before my visit, they had to stay the Scottish painter, Anne Redpath, whom I used to meet often when Glyndebourne was in Edinburgh, her home city. A few years later I bought – how could I not – a lovely painting of St. Paul she had done in that visit to Ruth and Jane.

Ruth was the doyenne of King's Lynn and the annual festival became a celebration of the good things she had brought to the city. She used her royal connections to put people on its board who could help her maintain it and its standards. She founded the festival in 1950, and from the first it had a particular character of its own and soon took its place in the hierarchy of its grander, international fellows.

After the war, summer festivals sprang up all over Europe, but none had the qualities of the one in Norfolk. Bayreuth saw the renaissance of Wagner; Glyndebourne and Salzburg were reclaiming Mozart; Edinburgh, starting in 1947, was on a very grand, hybrid scale; and in the next year the Aldeburgh Festival began with its focus on Ben Britten. Two years later, on a much smaller, more domestically intimate scale but with wide aesthetic purpose, came Ruth's plan for Lynn, reflecting the varied interests of her friends and the people who lived there. Music was an important element, but literature, theatre and the visual arts were made of equal importance and she persuaded an amazingly distinguished list of people to come and take part. Frequent visitors included John Barbirolli and his wife, Evelyn (he brought the Hallé Orchestra several times and, on one occasion, Ruth gave a most creditable performance of the Schumann concerto with them), Humphrey Lyttleton, Hugh Casson, John Betjeman, Julian Bream, Anthony Craxton, Prunella Scales, Janet Baker, Heather Harper, Osbert Lancaster, Cleo Laine, Johnny Dankworth, and so many more. At the same time, the local arts organisations performed alongside their more celebrated fellows, tho' they tended not to perform in the premier sites – The King's Lynn Players, the Art Club, West Norfolk Needle-workers, Morris dancers, the King's Lynn Festival Chorus – and there were trips to some of the great houses – Oxburgh, Blickling, Holkham and Houghton. Geoffrey Agnew arranged the first of many exhibitions. There was a wonderful one of works by Van Dyck in the new Fermoy Art Gallery, a large warehouse backing on to the river behind St. George's Guildhall that Ruth converted in memory of her husband.

Geoffrey Agnew wrote about Ruth in the preface to the 21st Festival book: 'She planted the tree but it rooted and nourished in local soil and, although many may come from all over England and from abroad to enjoy the fruits, she has kept it, above everything else, a Festival for King's Lynn'.

I would add, by way of further explaining the character of it all, that the local soil was well educated, well-heeled and generous; exactly the right humus for dear Ruth's sort of festival to grow and flourish.

She soon asked me to become a member of the festival committee. Gradually I became more involved in the planning of it, with meetings as often in London as in Norfolk where I became increasingly fond of the coast, the city, the countryside, the houses, the architecture, and, most of all, the people who lived there. I liked Norfolk so much that I made plans to build a studio house on a plot of land by the church opposite Ruth's house, a lovely eighteenth-century vicarage at Hillington. I often stayed at that house and one summer, when she was going to spend time in France, she lent it to me knowing I was in the middle of preparing my edition of Monteverdi's *Orfeo* for Sadler's Wells and was much tested to find quiet space. It was a wonderful summer. I hired a cook and kept on the cleaning lady, worked hard during the week, and on weekends had friends to stay. One of the weekend activities I shall always remember was the reading of Milton's *Paradise Lost* after a good dinner, sitting in Ruth's drawing room, each guest with a copy and taking turns to read it aloud. If people have never done it, they should try. It's magic the way that great poem comes alive with both sight and sound at the same time.

Sadly, the studio plan came to nothing; the church decided it needed more burial ground. Later I was offered a couple of acres at the edge of the Houghton estate by Sybil Cholmondeley, but that, too, was refused planning permission, largely, I believe, for socialist us-against-them reasons. I suppose it wasn't to be and my removal to America decided the matter.

Ruth was failing, too, and as her health declined, the world she had created at Lynn began to crumble. The festival management was taken out of her hands; familial disappointments and poor unwarranted publicity added to it all.

Her court appointment became increasingly important and her 'boss' never wavered in her support. She was buried next to her son in Sandringham churchyard. There was no visit there that did not contain a walk behind the church to pay respects to a most remarkable woman.

XXXVIII. About Jan

She was involved in one of the first recordings either of us made. Together with April Cantelo, Gerald English, various members of the Dolmetsch family – rather few were still left – and some others, part of that 'knit-your-own-violin school' who valiantly kept the world of the late Arnold Dolmetsch professionally alive at Haselmere in Surrey (shame on me for mocking). One day a proper evaluation will be made of their devoted endeavors in the cause of early music; music composed before the piano was invented or Rachmaninoff even heard of. The music we were involved with was by John Dowland, the seventeenth-century lutenist and songwriter. We were hired by EMI as part of a plan devised by Diana Poulton and designed to take this lovely music out to a wider public. It cost EMI very little, for the Dolmetschs didn't care much for money and we young professionals were glad of the work. John Dowland, too, was in need of promulgation, deserving more than we were able to give him on that occasion.

She is Janet Baker.

My deep affection, regard and admiration for Jan (as she is sometimes called by her friends) began at this time and has only increased in the succeeding decades. Then, quite lately, at the very height of her career, she courageously decided to stop, giving herself, I don't doubt, a great deal of anguish over it. But she left stellar memories and, next best to the real thing, a large collection of superb recordings that must serve for us as reminders; and we must be grateful for them.

In the days of that early recording she was still living in Yorkshire, the county of her origin, where her husband, Keith Shelley, was successfully involved in the world of automobiles.

Janet, at that time, was doing a great deal of traveling between Yorkshire and London for singing lessons with Mrs. Isepp and the occasional engagement that helped to pay for them. It was a way of life that couldn't be sustained indefinitely and, as the singing took precedence, Keith valiantly sacrificed his own career. When they moved to London, he became her second manager and travel companion, always cheerful, wonderfully practical, and so very proud of his wife. Now, in his declining years, the rôles are reversed, and it seems to work as well that way as the other – only the music is missing. Even Jan's subsequent splendid work over five years as Chancellor of the University of York; the committed participation in the Munster Trust; her national honours of DBE and, more significant still, the Companion of Honour, couldn't make up for not performing any more, at least I wouldn't think so. She is a stoic, tho', and it's another thing to admire about this extraordinary musician-singer.

Jan has written her own biography, *Full Circle*, and described in it, with touching honesty, the responsibilities she undertook as she realised what a God-given voice she had. Her career demanded of her a deeply committed study of vocal techniques and of the music she would use it for. That necessary gravitas was evident in all the performances with which I was involved. Not that laughter and humour were lacking.

There was a morning recital in the Edinburgh Festival for which, as an encore, she said she would sing Arne's charming setting of Shakespeare's lyric from the *Tempest*: 'where the bee sucks, there suck I'. In rehearsal she found the key a little low. Could I play it a semitone higher? Of course, there was no problem about that, until, that is, when we came to the end of the actual recital. Responding to vociferous applause, after two encores, as a third she thought it was time for 'where the bee sucks'.

I played the opening phrase as an introduction in the higher key as planned. After a moment's hesitation, Janet began in the old, lower key. Naturally, I came down with her but it sounded bizarre, then even more so when the last section, 'merrily, merrily shall I live now', she had a shot at restoring the higher key. The bee sounded as if it had taken more pot than pollen. Bizarre was no longer the word for it, and I don't know how we finished it. Everyone was laughing or at least mystified, and we behaved like two school children giggling at some social mishap.

Accidents apart, Jan had a real gift for comedy. Her Dorabella for Scottish opera was famous, and her throw-away line at the end of Purcell's cabaret song, 'Ah, cruel, bloody Fate', when the miserable Phyllis closed her eyes and died was masterly. Fortunately, it's on a recording of a recital we later gave at Aldeburgh.

Indignation was a rare but striking characteristic, very impressive when the cause moved her. I'm hopeless at it and tend to shrug my shoulders when faced with bad behaviour – say nothing and move on. Not Janet.

We were once, in fairly early days, asked to give a recital at a very grand house in the west of England. It was to be in aid of a most worthy children's hospital, and of course we agreed without hesitation or fee.

We motored down in the late morning and, after a brief rehearsal in the Grand Hall, wonderfully decorated for the occasion, we were given a rather scratch lunch in the butler's pantry – the butler was very welcoming, rather as he would be to new members of the staff. Then we were shown to some servants' bedrooms to rest and change. Perhaps our hosts, whom we had hardly met, had a house full of guests who were staying the night – perhaps not.

It was suggested that we stand with our hosts to greet the guests, which we declined. There was then a grand dinner for more than two hundred people, which we also declined. At something after 9:30 p.m., we gave the recital, which went extremely well. The well-lit audience were in an approving mood and seemed to be having a very good time. We didn't hear much about the charity, but there was no doubt about the enthusiasm and the air of extravagance that permeated the whole evening redounding to the glory of the house.

Back in London Janet asked Emmie Tillett (we shared the same agent, a wonderful lady to whom we both owed a great deal) to find out how much was raised for the children's hospital.

'So sad', was our hostess's reply. The cost of the dinner, the decorations, the lighting, the chairs and extra staff meant there was little or nothing left for the hospital.

Janet did one of her best indignations. We gave many similar recitals and raised large sums of money for many charities after that, but only if a sum was agreed on beforehand that would be sent to the charity concerned, come what may.

To think of Jan is to remember how often through her artistry, combined with the composer's vision, a moment would suddenly open the mind's eye, the heart, the being to reveal a glimpse of what Gerontius's Angel was leading him forward out of this world to see.

Immediately as I write this, a short list of such moments comes to a grateful mind that had the luck to be traveling the same road at the same time:

Elgar:	*The Dream of Gerontius* the bars when the Angel sings to reassure his failing spirit: 'Yes, for one moment, thou shalt see thy Lord'.
Monteverdi:	*Il Ritorno d'Ulisse in Patria* the final duet (with Ben Luxon), more a hymn to loving constancy than to earthly love itself.
Schubert:	*Ständchen* a light-hearted, touching serenade to an easily awakened, sleeping beloved.
Cavalli:	*La Calisto* 'Ardo, sospiro' – the anguished Diana, Virgin Goddess, when she admits to herself the love she feels for Endymion (James Bowman).
Gluck:	*Orfeo ed Euridice* 'che faro' – a tragic song of loss.
Handel:	*Ariodante* 'Dopo notte' – expressing the sheer joy of a life freed from adversity, refreshed and begun again.
Handel:	*Xerxes* 'Ombra mai fu' – perhaps the most beautiful melodic line ever written.

There were, of course, many more.

XXXIX. L.F.

Probably the most difficult to describe of all the people with whom I've had a long and valued friendship was 'L.F.,' which stands for 'Little Friend'. L.F. was a title that somehow came to be used by most of her friends so that we could talk about her, ask after her, convey messages to and from her without people within earshot looking 'round at you – as they most certainly would have done if you'd said, 'Princess Margaret rang and wanted to know if . . .'. It was bad enough if people got to know you knew her. L.F. telephoned to a house I was renting during rehearsals at Glyndebourne and, since I was out, my housekeeper, Mrs. Ovary, answered and was thunderstruck when she realised to whom she was speaking. L.F. never let me forget she knew the housekeeper's name and what was I getting up to? Mrs. Ovary was thereafter bursting to ask questions and, doubtless, told all her friends. It could all have been avoided had L.F. known she was L.F.

We met in 1958 at lunch with 'good' Simon – Simon Phipps, the Chaplain of Trinity and later Bishop of Lincoln. (There was also a 'wicked' Simon in college at the same time with many friends in common, so the epithet became sufficient for identification in conversation.) 'Good' is, sadly, no longer with us, but it's pleasant to think of him having jolly lunch parties *al fresco* on the Elysian Fields with Little Friend a frequent guest.

I had the set of rooms under Simon's in Bishop's Hostel, a group of buildings just off Trinity Great Court along past the Buttery. Our friendship began soon after 1948 when he, not yet ordained, was one of the brightest sparks in the Footlights Club that put on the May Week revues at the Arts Theatre and met regularly during the year for conviviality and the trying out of new material. It was not clear at that time whether he would go into the theatre or the priesthood. God won. I'm still not quite convinced that he made the right decision, though meeting him several times in his last, retired years, he clearly thought it had been. His commitment to the memory of his wife who had been a mainstay and lately died was very moving. He was lost without her and didn't linger. Yet his work in the fading Anglican Church was not (if we were to believe Harry Williams, who was his Dean of Chapel at Trinity) as brilliant as the theatrical promise shown in those earlier years. All the same, he was good and a dear man.

The lunch in Bishops Hostel was the first of many such occasions and the beginning of a much-valued friendship with the Queen's sister that lasted 'til she died in 2002, though at that awful, lingering end she shut herself away. Only a very few of her women friends, like Prue Penn, saw her, nearly blind and unutterably miserable in her bedroom in Kensington Palace, not even answering the telephone; a truly sad decline of such potential brilliance, a loveable unachiever.

She was wonderful but, it's true, she could be willful, contrary, bad-tempered, rarely reasonable, occasionally ill-mannered – and often 'difficult'. I believe a lot of those 'difficult' moments harked back to her younger years when she was the apple of her father's eye and spoiled not only by him (certainly not by her mother) but, later on, by those sycophantic courtiers and ill-chosen friends with whom she surrounded herself from time to time. Thank heaven for those good souls who really loved her and whom she trusted, like Elizabeth Cavendish and Prue Penn. She would have stumbled so much more without them.

The day she died I was conducting in Stuttgart. Back in the hotel after rehearsals and some sad phone calls, I saw a lengthy programme about her on German TV. Clearly it had been prepared in anticipation, mostly from old newsreels. It showed how radiantly beautiful she had been in her youth –quite outclassing in style and glamour her more recent successor as the people's Princess.

I doubt she was ever that; indeed she would have thought it rather common and redolent of Walt Disney, but a star she certainly was and those who were allowed rather closer loved her.

After the war, society changed and there was a great leveling of classes. She resisted all that, perhaps misguidedly. She lost the struggle and isolated herself in the process. From the frustration came the quixotic behaviour which so often obscured a truly warm-hearted person underneath. Certainly there was never a more loyal friend.

Apart from the changing society, she had to face an appalling obstacle imposed on her by her lack of education. L.F. was formidably intelligent, doubtless inherited from her mother who, apart from having had the benefit of a good Scottish schooling, was fortunate enough to have had a life filled with responsibilities and calls to action that few women could have survived and which exercised her mind always. Her daughter had no such call but the inner driving force was as strong if not stronger without the intellect to implement it.

She was amazingly quick with a memory that would have startled Methuselah. She would tackle any problem, any philosophical argument, any artistic controversy without hesitation or the intellectual background to support her often quite accurate perceptions and intuitions. As a result she would change the subject whenever she came to a dead end in any discussion and become tetchy or dismissive when people tried to stick to the point.

One of her major successes was as Patron of the Royal Ballet where her beauty, poise and enthusiasm for the dance rang all sorts of bells all over the world and, guided by people like Freddie Ashton and Dame Ninette, she supported all the right things and was a major factor in the company's success. Their reputation in her time surpassed even that of their initially more celebrated Russian contemporaries at the Bolshoi. They even picked up a Russian star or two like Nureyev who then teamed up with Margot Fonteyn to head perhaps the finest company of its kind, and L.F. shone with them.

An immediate result of lunch with 'good' was an invitation to *West Side Story* which had just arrived in London. There followed invitations for weekends at Royal Lodge in Windsor, the first in June 1959. The first of many. Those were wonderfully quiet days in that small, beautifully proportioned Georgian house.

Queen Elizabeth (The Queen Mother) loved it and was prone, when you were alone with her, to reminisce about her early married days there with a rather frail husband whom she guarded so well and the two young girls who, as we did thirty years later, found there an unobserved freedom with very few formalities, beautiful gardens and a protected countryside of gently sloping green hills surrounding it all. It was truly an idyllic place.

Queen Elizabeth came back there to die, so tactfully it seemed to avoid overshadowing a great anniversary of her elder daughter's reign and so gently that the moment of her going went almost unnoticed save for a universal sadness and gratitude for a life so well lived, showing always the joy she found in living which she shared with everyone around her.

We went for a second time to *West Side Story*, that brilliant reworking of Shakespeare's *Romeo and Juliet* with rival gangs in New York instead of rival families in Verona. L.F. had never read or seen the play though, of course, she knew the implications of the two names and identified with the fate of the two lovers.

Later, during a weekend at Royal Lodge, when everyone else had retired for the night, she began to talk of the bitterness she felt towards certain of the courtiers who had conspired to take her away from her great love. She told me she had written a lament, both words and tune, and would I write it down for her as she sang it, then harmonise it for piano. By now it was after 3:00 a.m. (she always stayed up terribly late even in weekday evenings in London when her guests' eyelids were drooping and thoughts of work the next morning were hazily depressing).

Taking down the tune with the words presented no problem. They showed their Scottish ancestry but for all their derivative phrases it was a distressingly sad true song of lovers forced to part and very moving indeed at that hour. The harmonisations improvised at the piano proved rather more difficult – 'no, not that', 'yes, that's it – no, it isn't' etc., etc. But, finally, we got there and retired to bed at 4:30 a.m.

The next week I went to Kensington Palace with a neatly written copy for final approval. After listening to it, she said she wanted to have it in print, not for general circulation, but to make it a more definite statement. There was to be no name or ascription beyond the title, 'A Lament'.

I talked with Martin Kingsbury, a friend at Faber and Faber who published my realisations of Monteverdi and Cavalli for Glyndebourne and elsewhere. He was discretion itself and kindly had four copies made as if they were proofs for some future publication. No one else knew of them.

L.F. let me keep a copy for myself and until now almost no one else has seen or heard it. Playing it through brings back the image of that sad L.F., haunted for all the rest of her life by a lost love. Perhaps she haunted herself but for her it was real enough.

> *'Love of my life and love of my heart,*
>
> *We never dreamt that we'd ever part.*
>
> *Lover, my darling far over the sea*
>
> *What is my life without your love for me?*
>
> *We met we loved and the years rolled by*
>
> *But love is no secret and you had to fly.*
>
> *But darling, my darling, they'll never know*
>
> *How deep the love we had to forego,*
>
> *For our love was dearest love, faithful and true;*
>
> *What is my life without my love for you'.*

The years did indeed roll by. She married and had two extraordinarily gifted, handsome children. Then a divorce, and a return to the questing life as before.

There were lovely summer weeks hosted by her mother at Sandringham where, through Ruth Fermoy and the King's Lynn Festival, I had many friends. L.F. came to most of them but somehow she never seemed very happy there and took sometimes to being difficult, though there were jolly times, too; swimming parties with Prue at a neighbour's pool, picnics with wasps, Cole Porter after dinner, the annual Sandringham Show (which she rarely visited) and a few concerts at the Festival.

The decline began when, on a Caribbean island where she had been given a house, she put both feet into a bath of scaldingly hot water and burnt them very badly. For months she could barely hobble about and felt very badly done by. Then a stroke and the physical decline was rapid, though to her I know it felt endless.

That image at the end of the Stuttgart film of an unaccompanied hearse making its lonely way down a road to the crematorium after the funeral service must rank among the saddest I've ever seen.

XL. Queen Elizabeth, The Queen Mother

The first time I met Queen Elizabeth was a few days after the Baedeker raids on Bath in the 1940s.

Living in Bath we were used to air-raid sirens as the German night bombers flew over to bomb Avonmouth Docks where ships unloaded supplies of all sorts to our sorely deprived country. Occasionally, they would drop a bomb on their way back, possibly to lighten the load if they were being chased, or perhaps it was an example of German humour. They did very little damage.

Not so the raids Hitler ordered after we had done such great damage to Germany. Coventry with its Cathedral was one target; Bath, a largely eighteenth-century city, was another. For two nights the accustomed sirens brought no passing traffic but a storm of destruction killing more than four hundred people and destroying many lovely buildings, including the Assembly Rooms where Jane Austen's characters met and played out their dramas. Somehow the Abbey escaped serious damage. For the next few days, everyone was helping everyone else to recover and the spirits were amazingly high. Schools were closed. Mine turned itself into a soup kitchen for those who didn't have one any more. After about four days, the morale began to sink and the horrors of the bombing were remembered and brought chills.

At that crucial time, King George and Queen Elizabeth motored down from London and spent the day relatively unattended except for the Mayor and a few members of the royal household. There was, certainly, no obvious police presence. They went everywhere, talking to everyone, climbing over rubble, even taking a plastic cup of our soup which, with a piece of bread, we were told, was all they had for lunch. The soup was pronounced 'delicious' – which it wasn't – but it was the thought that counted and, by the time they left, Bath felt quite restored and proud of itself.

The King smiled often, I recall, but spoke very little. He was a shy man and inclined to stutter. The Queen laughed and carried on with everybody around her. She had a particular smile, a little impish and very knowing but always with a warmth that inspired an affectionate response from those smiled upon.

She never lost that smile even past her centennial year.

It was many years after the air raids that I met her again. I had grown up (sort of), been in the RAF for three years (called up at the end of the War), gone to Cambridge and returned as a Fellow of Trinity to lecture and teach while carrying on another life as a professional musician in London. Through Simon Phipps I met Princess Margaret and was invited to Royal Lodge for a weekend. There was quite a small number of guests: Elizabeth Cavendish; Prue and Eric Penn; John Betjeman, whom I already knew; the Droghedas whom I didn't; and Tony Armstrong-Jones, who had been a contemporary of mine as an undergraduate. I drove Tony down from London. He was bringing plans for an aviary that was to be built in the garden by the pool. I think he had other matters in his mind, too, which didn't come to fruition until much later.

Royal Lodge was, next to her Scottish castle, Queen Elizabeth's favourite place for quiet times with friends. Eventually she came there to die.

It is a beautiful eighteenth-century country house in rolling countryside, quite near but not within sight of Windsor Castle.

I should say here that I certainly have no background that would suggest royal connections of any sort and cannot explain the friendship with L.F. and her mother, but it began that first weekend and persisted for well over forty years. Once Queen Elizabeth suddenly asked, 'Raymond, how long have we known you?' I couldn't answer accurately so I said, 'I hope not too long, Ma'am', and gained one of her impish smiles.

It was all so wonderfully relaxed and informal that first weekend. However, there was always that sense of respect due to the Royal Family for, although they are attractively themselves, they represent England; thus, no matter how long and firm the friendship, they have to respect it themselves even in private and we have to acknowledge that, too. In practice, there's no great sense of barrier, at least with the members of the Royal Family I knew. There were endless ways in which they displayed their attachment and confidence or sincerity of friendship.

I remember one of those weekends at Royal Lodge, sitting in the library at dusk on a balmy summer evening alone with Queen Elizabeth, the French windows open to the lawns at the back and side of the house. We were talking about my family, my harpsichord, and of Tom Goff and his love for ghost stories. She said quietly, 'You know, Raymond, I sometimes sit here by myself in the evening and I can hear Bertie [George] and Harry talking out there, and then I see them coming together towards the windows'. It made me realise how alone she must often have felt, a widow for so long, one daughter very busy and successful as Queen and the other rather turbulent and sometimes difficult, scarcely a homebody.

In London there were occasional concerts, dinner parties and theatre, sometimes with L.F. alone or with friends; sometimes Queen Elizabeth came too, as on this particular occasion to a revival of *Show Boat* that had had excellent notices. The date was fixed a month or so in advance. As it happened this was four days after my house in Hamilton Terrace burned down.

There hadn't been time to get fussed (and, oddly, I never really did), given a lunch-time broadcast concert the next day at St. John's Smith Square and, two days later, a Cavalli Mass at Westminster Abbey. Then, on the evening of *Show Boat* there was a late-afternoon flute and harpsichord recital with Richard Adeney, also at St. John's Smith Square, which left very little time to change and get to the theatre in the Strand ahead of the royal party.

My wonderful secretary, as she was then, friend as she is now, Una Marchetti, had seen to the cleaning of my dinner jacket and trousers which, with my evening shoes, had amazingly escaped incineration in a wall cupboard, but were severely smoked.

Three times through the cleaners and they were pronounced not only well-pressed, but also smoke-free. The recital over, I changed rapidly into a new shirt, black tie, clarified tuxedo and shoes, dashed into a waiting cab and arrived just as the cars from Kensington Palace were drawing up. I joined the party as they were being greeted by the theatre manager, and then we were shown to excellent front-row seats in the balcony. The rest of the party knew of the fire, were glad to see me alive and said nice things about the house. 'Thank you for the thought but just let's enjoy the evening', I said, which we did. We were enjoying all those wonderful old tunes beautifully staged and sung when, in the middle of 'Old Man River', L.F. nudged me: 'Raymond, do you smell burning? I think the theatre's on fire'. Of course, it was me as my warmth and that of the theatre released the remains of the singeing smell that had escaped the cleaners. It penetrated two or three seats along to Queen Elizabeth who leaned forward, anxious. 'It's all right, Mummy,' L.F. said. 'It's Raymond. He'll take his coat off' (which I did) 'and maybe his trousers' (which I didn't). There can't have been many royal escorts to leave a theatre in such déshabille with amused comments from passersby.

After a while, the weekend country venue changed to Sandringham in Norfolk. Perhaps some part of the family took up residence in Royal Lodge, perhaps it changed because of the link with Ruth Fermoy (who became Queen Elizabeth's favourite Lady in Waiting) and her ties to King's Lynn, which is just down the road. Ruth had started a summer festival in Lynn with which I, too, had become involved. The Sandringham weeks were timed to coincide with the festival and the Sandringham show. Queen Elizabeth, as patron of both, came often and quite informally to concerts or readings in one or other of the Lynn churches or the mediaeval guildhall, behind which was the flourishing Fermoy Art Gallery. That led down to the Great Ouse, a wide river slowly moving out to the Washes and the North Sea, which with its wharfs and warehouses, some now derelict, made you realise what an important city King's Lynn had once been.

Sandringham was built for King Edward VII, mostly for the shooting, but it became a much-loved retreat from the affairs of state by generations of royals. Queen Alexandra lived there, mostly alone, until her death in the mid-1920s. It is a mammoth house and had been still bigger until it was reduced and renovated, becoming the warm, friendly country house it is now. The gardens, owing much to Queen Elizabeth, have great lawns stretching down behind the house to a lake, and off to the north side, there are two double avenues of pleached limes, alongside of which there is a chain of box hedges that make small spaces where you could and often did assemble for drinks. 'A little more martini, Ma'am?' 'Well, just up to there', as a small, plump Queenly index finger slowly mounts the glass.

Queen Elizabeth was careful but not overly careful for her guests' country pleasures. The men breakfasted downstairs, as did the Queen when she was staying in the house, the only lady to be seen at that hour. After the papers and a good deal of conversation, guests dispersed to meet again a little later in the long saloon, a lovely open room that, to judge from earlier photographs, had once been almost submerged in dense, maze-like Edwardian clutter, the despair of any maid equipped with purpose and a duster.

All that is now changed, tho' I saw an echo of it the first time I was in the drawing room which gives out from the saloon and leads to the dining room. There were then two large, elaborate cabinets with shelf upon shelf of fabulously valuable Fabergé eggs and knick-knacks – a vestige, apparently, of a much earlier Christmas tradition of the giving of gifts between royal personages spending Christmas at Sandringham. The ideal gift for someone who has everything. The delicate gifts have now been removed, presumably for safekeeping.

The gathering after breakfast was to decide what anyone wanted to do that morning – long or short walks, quiet reading, letters, shopping in Lynn, perhaps a trip to see one of the grand Norfolk houses or churches.

Everyone gathered again at one o'clock for drinks before usually setting out for a picnic. The Royals are very keen about punctuality and fairly ruthless about those who are not. David McKenna's wife, Lady Cecilia, was prone to be tardy and frequently found herself left behind having to catch up under her own or David's steam.

A favourite for picnics was a little wooden house that Lord Leicester had built for Queen Elizabeth many years before. It was perched high up in the dunes of the beaches that extended from Holkham Hall, Lord Leicester's magnificent home that we sometimes visited socially. When we arrived, usually in three cars at a spiffing pace (royal chauffeurs are famously speedy and those following are hard put to it to keep up), hampers of delicious food, delivered earlier, were opened. 'Just something simple, and we help ourselves' said our hostess. A warm, chatty, gluttonous scene ensued. No staff. After lunch some of us swam or just walked down to the sea. It was easy to overdo the gluttony and some took a nap under a neighbouring tree. We once left Derek Hill fast asleep behind a thicket. When a chauffeur was sent back to find and collect him, he was a good deal put out that no one had noticed he was missing.

There was one potential hazard at that lovely spot. Being so remote, the beach below was known as a nudist beach. The police, warned ahead, did what they could to gently persuade the naked enthusiasts to be discreet and avoid any embarrassing moments.

Once I was walking after lunch alone with Queen Elizabeth down to the beach when a rather straggly-looking couple with a young child, all stark naked, got up from amid some tall sea grasses and began to walk towards us, presumably making for their car and clothes. As we passed them Queen Elizabeth, not batting an eyelid or changing pace said, 'Good afternoon. What a beautiful day it is'. They began to reply and then stopped abruptly as they realised who was speaking to them. We proceeded on and Queen Elizabeth said, 'Raymond, I've always thought people look rather better with a little something on'. I said, 'Certainly, Ma'am, in this case', and got one of her impish smiles in return.

Sadly, a few years ago, vandals set light to the little wooden house and it is no more. Neither is Her Majesty, so perhaps there was some higher coincidence at work; but it doesn't vindicate the vandals, damn them.

The main event of the week was the Sandringham show. Most English villages have an annual function where everyone brings something they've made, spun, baked or knitted, and the local industries set up their stalls to demonstrate their wares.

The one at Sandringham naturally attracts large crowds. After a long night, by midmorning the tents were up, the stalls arranged, the St. John Ambulance and the local veterans all ready. Queen Elizabeth, coming in one of Queen Alexandra's horse-drawn landaus, accompanied as often as not by Prince Charles, would drive around in state to open the day. House guests walked down earlier past the lake and listened to the brass band playing variously well, sometimes very, and we all awaited the National Anthem as HM Queen Elizabeth drove up.

There followed a slow tour around the show – basket makers, cake and jam competitions, roses from the local growers, honey from the beekeepers, soap makers, all to be admired and praised. Queen Elizabeth in earlier days walked about, visiting every stall, knowing so many people on the estate, remembering their names (a particular royal talent). Lately she got on and off a converted open golf cart with a driver, but she never missed a tent or forgot a name. A lady in waiting followed behind stacking dozens of bunches of flowers presented by dozens of curtseying little girls. The flowers would all be sent to the local hospitals, but each one was received as if it was just the bouquet the Queen had been looking for.

Prince Charles usually followed at a distance, and behind him the house guests buying dishcloths and baskets galore, jars of Norfolk honey and scones for distribution to friends. The gifts were bundled into cars before the walk uphill back to the house and Pimms No. 1.

Present overall was the love for this little figure in pale blue with a hat the shape of a blue crescent moon. It was palpable and, tho' on such a small scale, you got a glimpse of the part she had played in keeping England together during the worst years of the war, as she had done in Bath. Today in Norfolk, she was theirs and they were hers. 'Absolutely', as she frequently said. Wonderful as that was, for private memories, it was the evenings at Sandringham that remain most vividly in the memory.

Back from a picnic there was usually a do-little time until at about 6:00 p.m. People gathered in the saloon for drinks before dinner, usually without our hostess. There was talk, some vetting of the day so far, or the latest news from the world outside, and always a large, complex jigsaw puzzle set out on a side table. The Queen was particularly good at them but didn't mind a bit if other guests joined in. No one, however, was allowed to look at the box cover.

Derek Hill and I secreted for fun a piece in the handbag of a member of the household we wanted to tease; she was rather bossy and had a big nose. It all worked a treat. The puzzle was nearly completed by the Queen who then complained about the missing piece just at the moment Lady Grossbeak discovered it in her bag. 'Oh!, I'm so sorry, Ma'am'. 'So I should think' was the Queen Mother's rather testy response, as the puzzle was finally completed. It was rather cruel of us but everyone was amused, even Lady G. herself, who for the rest of the evening was a good deal less bossy.

After drinks at 6:00 p.m., we drifted off to our bedrooms to bathe and dress. There aren't many houses now where everyone puts on a black tie for dinner and where it seems perfectly natural to do so, all part, I dare say, of the respect and recognition of our hostess and the House of Windsor she represented.

We reassembled refreshed and somewhat smarter in the drawing room just before 8:00 p.m., joining the house party and possibly a few local guests. Our hostess, with that sure, simple sense of theatre, arrived last looking wonderful. She usually wore spectacular jewelry, different every evening and each with a fascinating history, which she was happy to talk about if you sat next to her and asked. Queen Victoria married off her children to all the courts in Europe, and that, it seemed, was the source of many of those dazzling creations.

The seating plan at dinner was different each evening and since the house party was much the same each year, you tended to find yourself sitting next to someone with whom you were glad to play catch-up.

Whenever I found myself sitting either side of HM, I reveled in her wit and wisdom. I never heard her say a cruel word about anyone. The closest was when she asked about a stained-glass window (for which we had all contributed) at the Arts Center, Port Erin, Isle of Man, in memory of Ruth Fermoy. She asked if Ruth's two daughters had given anything towards it. On being told that they had not and had positively, quite rudely declined, she looked shocked and said rather emphatically, 'Silly girls'. That was about as critical an observation about anyone that I heard her utter.

Nothing shocked her. If you asked her advice it was always given with the best results in mind and least harm to all, never dogmatic but with an understanding of every aspect of the problem – as I am sure her favourite grandson knew very well. They were very close.

Her laughter was contagious. I remember during that conversation about the Fermoy window, telling her of another famous large window in the main Presbyterian Church in Douglas also on the Isle of Man, on which is boldly inscribed:

> *Given by John Anelay*
>
> *of Blackburn*
>
> *June 1893*
>
> *To the Glory of God*
>
> *and in loving memory of his wife Alice*

She began to laugh and set the whole table going. 'There! I always knew God was a good family man'.

This lady was held in such deep affection by all of those about her, never sad when not alone. She was a wise person who saw things with such a clarity worthy of one of the great philosophers. Yet nothing seemed to hinder her pleasure in life and her possessions.

One year we had a fire alarm in the middle of the night – a real one. We were awakened by staff knocking on doors and were told to come downstairs in our dressing gowns. My bedroom that year was quite close to the landing outside Her Majesty's and we met there wondering if we really need go any further. Everything seemed all right and there was no smell of burning, one I knew very well. Soon several other guests arrived and, as we stood there talking, I noticed HM was wearing a large string of pearls (I supposed she'd just taken them as she seized her rather elegant, fluffy dressing gown). I couldn't resist saying, 'Ma'am, I see you've dressed for the occasion'. 'Oh', she replied, 'I couldn't possibly have left without them', and then there was one of those self-mocking impish smiles. You couldn't help but love such a person.

XLI. Love Will Find Out The Way

Dear Raymond,

Queen Elizabeth, The Queen Mother, bids me write to invite you to stay at Sandringham in the summer. If your plans allow, Her Majesty hopes you will arrive on Tuesday the 28th July and stay until the following Monday, 3rd August.

Yours ever,

Alastair
Comptroller to Queen Elizabeth, The Queen Mother

Over many years, with occasional variants, this semiformal invitation announced Queen Elizabeth's annual summer visit to Sandringham. It was always timed to end the day before Queen Elizabeth's birthday on August 4th, for which she returned to London and received her Londoners outside Clarence House. She was a lady of regular habits and constant friendships.

The week in Norfolk was planned to coincide with the Sandringham show and the King's Lynn Festival. There were occasional visits to nearby houses like Houghton and Holkham, to some of the lovely Norfolk churches and, coincidentally, to some delightful picnics at shooting lodges or at the little beach house that Lord Leicester had built, discussed earlier.

It was a week full of good things savoured in a leisurely manner with lots of time for conversation in between. No one was ever in a hurry, but punctuality in arrangements reflected Royal practise and to be late for an expedition could result in being left behind – which occasionally happened to a laggardly guest.

The whole was imbued with that tranquil enjoyment that characterised our hostess. I've never known anyone greet advancing years with such gentle elegance and enthusiasm, with such eager curiosity and quiet wisdom, with the obvious handicaps of old age ignored to extinction.

The guest list was nearly always the same tho' in later years it shortened a little due to natural attrition. The age-induced handicaps became plainer to all, but there was no lessening of enjoyment on that account – it was not possible with such an example to follow.

At this time the Festival at King's Lynn, a few miles down the road, was going great guns and, depending on the programme, the Sandringham party of an evening motored into the city for a little culture. Queen Elizabeth, a knowledgeable music-lover, was Patron of the Festival. As often as not I was involved in one or other of the concerts and that entailed some high-speed dashing in to Lynn for rehearsals and back for a picnic or some other expedition.

At one of the last of these wonderfully enjoyable weeks, Queen Elizabeth was close to celebrating her 100th birthday. Guests were expressly forbidden to bring gifts, but I had a minor brainwave – inexpensive but, as it turned out, not trouble-free.

In the two weeks before coming across the Atlantic, I had been conducting the Indianapolis Symphony Orchestra (of which I was Music Director) in a concert that included an orchestration I had just made of Beethoven's piano variations on *God Save the King*. It seemed to me that, in no disrespectful way, it might make a suitable expression of loyalty and affection for the pre-centennial celebration in Norfolk. There was only one lyrical variation in the minor – nothing to give offence. All the rest were cheerfully upbeat and lively, casting no shadows upon the monarchy. What's more, while orchestrating the scurrying last variation, there had come suddenly into my mind a lovely Scottish folksong which, I was delighted to discover, fitted exactly as a counterpoint to the busy semiquavers in the passages leading to the grand restatement of the National Anthem melody. The words, too, seemed apt. There was something of Queen Elizabeth's life in their sentiment, as well as a personal connection associated with my life partner, Jack, with whom I would be traveling to London in two weeks.

> *Over the mountain and over the waves,*
>
> *Under the fountains and under the graves;*
>
> *Under floods that are deepest which Neptune obey*
>
> *Over rocks that are steepest*
>
> *Love will find out the way.*

(I don't think Beethoven would have minded, but I did wonder if our hostess would know the song. She did, and the words, too.)

After the concert in Indianapolis Doug Dillon, our brilliant sound engineer, prepared a compact disc with an attractive jacket and a card suitably inscribed with birthday wishes from all the orchestra, all of whom enthusiastically agreed to the breaking of all manner of union rules to allow the disc to be made.

Some days later, with the time factor as our excuse for the extravagance, Jack and I boarded the Concorde for its amazing three-hour flight to Heathrow.

We'd barely taken off when the Fates began their mischief. Jack, thinking that we should check that all was in order, handed down the royal parcel. To our horror, we discovered there was no CD in the whole packet. We searched all the carry-on luggage – no disc anywhere. The flight attendants became involved; explanations were made and the interest spread to the cockpit from whence the captain kindly volunteered to send a message to the symphony back in Indianapolis.

Dick Hoffert, the orchestra's CEO, was, fortunately, in his office, We were assured that, somehow, by the time we landed in London, a copy of the CD playing Beethoven's variations with 'Love will find out the way' would arrive at Sandringham before me – and it did. I've no idea how it was done.

I parceled it, wrote some more on the card and presented it to Queen Elizabeth that evening before dinner. I explained to her not only how it came about, but also something of its adventures en route, along with the little added folk song. She was delighted and intrigued and recited the poem, for she knew the song. Her memory was incredible.

All the guests were assembled, including Princess Margaret, who was unwell and not in the most cheerful of moods. So, when her mother said she wanted everyone to hear it, L.F. declared she'd heard it already (she hadn't of course), knew it and didn't particularly want to hear it again. Her mother pointed out that it was her birthday and she wanted it played – which it was, twice. In between I played the intrusive folk song on the piano and that even amused L.F., who then wanted to hear it again so as to spot the tune. So all ended happily.

The CD is surely still at Sandringham and will give future royal historians something to puzzle over. This is how it got there.

XLII. Norfolk Churches

From mediaeval times until the eighteenth century, Norfolk was a hub of trade between England and northern Europe. It prospered mightily. Testifying to its success and, accrediting their maker for at least some of it, the people of Norfolk, over three centuries, built a large number of beautiful churches, some modest, some rather grand. When trade waned and the county reverted to less prosperous farmland, they were left unattended and, now, many of them are in danger of falling down.

Sandringham, the Royal Family's country estate, sits within a few miles of all of them. Small wonder then, that such a caring person as HRH Prince Charles should have taken a lead in the campaign to mend, restore and refurbish these beautiful buildings. If they aren't filled each day with devout parishioners, at least they can be visited and admired as a unique part of England's heritage.

As I had been a frequent summer visitor to Sandringham and having had the privilege of knowing HRH in his Trinity days, it was only natural for him to ask me to help, and for me gladly to respond. His close connection with the English Chamber Orchestra made their involvement inevitable, and they most willingly joined the campaign.

All we needed was to get people to notice and see for themselves what must be done to mend matters. There's no better way to get people inside a church, apart from births, deaths and marriages, than to give them a concert.

Sitting down, mostly in hired chairs (for often the pews, if they ever existed, have crumbled), they can look about as they listen and see what a deal of devoted skill and architectural endeavour had been involved and notice how good their forbears were at it. The need to mend, repair and restore then becomes a reality far more potent than any appeal leaflet arriving through their home letter box. The price of tickets apart, a modest reception in a tent afterwards can reap quite some rewards and, of course, the Royal presence is a draw in itself.

A series of concerts over quite a long period has resulted in quite an amount of repair work. A number of stellar soloists have given their services and proven a major attraction – the cream, so to speak, on the pastry.

Both cream and pastry had to be driven from London, resulting in some quite amusing episodes. It's easy to get lost in the highways and byways of Norfolk. Thank heaven for the portable telephone and the short distance between one mistaken market town for another.

Once you've arrived, the churches themselves presented their own problems. Oboes can play in choir stalls; horns cannot. Violins don't do well in a pulpit, and stone floors don't work for cello spikes. It was nothing to find that, after rehearsal, mice or rabbits or squirrels had discovered the vestry where the musicians had left their instrument cases and the occasional ham sandwich purchased against temporary starvation.

Piano concertos were a proven attraction for the public and a headache for the musicians' seating plan. A nine-foot Steinway in the chancel will probably just fit, with only a glimpse possible between pulpit and choir stalls, making for a certain amount of guesswork between conductor and soloist.

All obstacles overcome, those Norfolk church concerts were a joy, giving performers as well as audiences a lovely sense of being part of something very worthwhile.

One of our regular soloists was Slava Rostropovich, among the greatest cellists of our time; he lived a life with an infectious exuberance that sometimes bubbled over.

Occasionally, if the church was within manageable distance, after a concert there was a reception back at Sandringham for specially invited guests. At lunch before going off to rehearsal, I heard Prince Charles ask his grandmother, the Queen Mother, if Slava had been invited to the party afterwards. 'Of course', she said. 'Well, Granny, be careful when he gets here and you have to greet him that he doesn't come and kiss you; he does me and I find it very embarrassing'. A moment's pause and 'Granny' gave one of her particular smiles but said nothing.

It was a very good concert with a lengthy interval reception for the generality to enjoy so that the particularity could get to Sandringham in good time afterwards.

Slava was one of the last to arrive there and was applauded again as he moved down the corridor of guests to be greeted by Queen Elizabeth. You may be sure that those of us who had been at lunch were transfixed. Bubbling with excitement and enthusiasm, Slava came closer with arms at the ready for an embrace. At the last minute (some said it was until she saw the whites of his eyes), with a winning, broad smile, she stretched out her arms rigidly in front of her in such a way that Slava could do nothing but take her hands in his. Her arms did not bend and she kept him at arms' length – he couldn't get nearer. It was masterly and warranted smiles of delight among those who knew. I'm not sure if Prince Charles got any tips from it in case of further encounters.

Kiss or no, I think we made quite a lot of money that night towards a new roof on one of the Norfolk churches.

XLIII. Sleep in Peace

Lullabies in music go a long way back. No matter when in history or at whatever social level, it has always been natural for a nursing mother to lull her progeny to sleep with a song. The world's repertoire of folksong has been the richer for it.

Christmas, clearly, has provided a more specialised incentive. The Christ Child, tho' naturally peaceful, had a rocky journey both in the womb and after. Moreover, shepherds, oxen and three wise kings from abroad can be very noisy. The mediaeval church, when music began to be decipherably written down, inserted at Christmas time phrases like 'Hodie Christus natus est' into the Mass and often set them in triple time, both to introduce a certain lightheartedness and possibly reflect the rocking rhythms of a mother's arms.

The lullaby soon became a regular subject for composers, from William Byrd's 'Lullaby, my sweet little baby' in his collection of *Psalms, Sonnets and Songs* of 1588 to Benjamin Britten's *Charm of Lullabies* in 1948; more, surely, have followed since.

It is, however, unusual to find a lullaby with a social message, and I confess to being partly instrumental in creating one.

One of our closest friends whom Jack and I hold most dear is Christel DeHaan. She has used the fruits of an immensely successful life (yet to be chronicled) to establish charter-like schools, each known as Christel House, in Mexico City, Bangalore in India, Caracas in Venezuela, Capetown in South Africa, and Indianapolis. This began more than ten years ago, and the schools have given education, health, and vision to thousands of deprived children who never could have made their way with their background of poverty and ignorance. The results are staggering and inspiring. Christel pays as much attention to the working of each of her schools as she used to in matters concerning the big business world. (Christel's schools haven't as yet produced a composer, but they will.)

Concerts have been frequently given to help towards their funding, but I felt we should also give something of a more spiritual nature as well, since music can lift up the heart as well as raise money. My partner, Jack, came up with the initial inspiration.

We had been listening to a new recording of Mendelssohn's *Octet*, a favorite of ours and a marvel, for he wrote it when he was only sixteen. It was beautifully played by a group, several of whom used to play with the English Chamber Orchestra in my London days.

As a filler, they had come across another octet, this time by Joachim Raff. Not being an admirer of Raff, I didn't listen to it. Raff was not the most gifted of composers. He wrote a lot and, as a sort of musical jobber, did a lot of orchestration for Liszt. I was, perhaps, overly censorious to Jack about him. But then I was surprised and a little ashamed when, a few days later, he made me listen to Raff's slow movement – an inspired, lyrical andante that held me spellbound. One or other of us, possibly both at the same time, saw it would make a wonderful present for Christel if I could orchestrate it in time for the annual Classical Christmas concert by the Indianapolis Symphony that she sponsored.

I did, we did, and it came about. Christel was delighted. We called it *Lullaby for the Children of Christel House*.

A year or so later, when we were to have a young, professional choir from Bloomington, Indiana to sing in some other works at that same annual concert, I reset it for soprano solo, women's (or children's) voices and orchestra. I even had the temerity to write a poem describing how the young lives of children, if cherished and cared for with love, can find fulfillment, happiness and peace, no matter how little there was to hope for when they were born.

We recorded it on a Christmas CD and everyone seemed pleased. I think even the children like it and claim it as theirs – which indeed it is.

XLIV. Theatre and Directors, 1 – John Dexter and *Billy Budd*

I had come into contact with John Dexter while writing music for a production by Tony Richardson of a Middleton play at the Royal Court Theatre, in which the remarkable, somewhat ill-fated Mary Ure played a leading part. I felt uneasy there, not being much in accord with the pervading politics of Sloane Square and John Osborne's *Look Back in Anger*. The place seemed exclusive and rather forbidding. John Dexter was known for his extreme behaviour, and the occasional social gatherings in that leftish, partly gay atmosphere with all the 'in' jokes did nothing much to dispel my apprehension.

Years later when I came to care nothing for such stupidly jarring inhibitions, I was delighted to be invited to conduct *Billy Budd* at the Met in a new production with John Dexter directing.

In the past John had successfully directed a number of 'original' experimental plays, but I was much relieved at our first meeting to discover he wanted a realistic, direct approach to *Budd*, reflecting the intent of E. M. Forster and Ben Britten in their re-creation of Melville's great novel. The result was one of Ben's finest achievements, second only to *Peter Grimes*.

John found the simple truth of it and let it guide him throughout. There were wonderful sets that with superb engineering could narrow the stage's focus, from the decks of *H.M.S. Indomitable* stretching high to the back of the stage, to Captain Vere's cramped cabin whose claustrophobic atmosphere made the tragic drama played out there all the more powerful.

We had a superb cast led by Peter Pears as Vere. The part was written for him, and

I believe his appearances in the two seasons we played *Budd* were his last in opera.

During the rehearsal weeks, I saw a great deal of Peter. Ben had recently died, and Peter was a vulnerable, lonely man. Often he would come to my apartment high up on Park and 86th for late-night company after a frequent hamburger (which, unexpectedly, became a favourite food) at a former speak-easy on Madison. He had been invited to stay with the original Billy, Theodor Uppman and his wife who, understandably, grumbled that Theodor hadn't been offered the part.

Her discontent distressed Peter, but he could do nothing about it had he wanted to. I was the nearest old friend with whom he could spend comfortable time in the evenings after rehearsal until he could return to his lodgings and retire peaceably to bed. In those evenings, we talked a lot about his earlier life with Ben. It would be hard to recall it all in detail – and I wouldn't attempt it if I could – but some phrases linger in that rather high-pitched speaking voice: 'You've no idea, Ray, how difficult it was for us to live together in London before the war'. I think they took up with Isherwood and Auden on that account, whose friends were bolder and sheltered each other from damaging comment and behaviour, let alone the illegality question as it was then. They followed Isherwood and Auden to America and there were some fruitful collaborations. But Ben and Peter were too private for Auden's carelessly public manifestations of the gay lifestyle; they returned to England during the war, settling in Aldeburgh.

Peter gave a most moving portrait of Vere, especially in the epilogue where, as an old man, he expresses the harrowing doubts about allowing Billy to be hanged for the implicit mutiny in killing the villainous Claggart. And yet Billy blessed 'Starry Vere' as he died, and Vere senses the spirit of forgiveness in this and finds peace as he comes to the end of his life. It seemed, in some way, to sum up the lifetime of Peter's relationship with Ben, and the great B-flat major climax comes as a reassurance that, after all the stresses and strains of their life together, they had at the end found a quietus.

In earlier years Peter was widely regarded as the *eminence grise* at Aldeburgh, something of a threat to those who had anything critical to say or appeared in any way disloyal to the Red House. The sycophants around Ben and Peter were only too ready to ingratiate themselves by passing on suggestive snippets of information, so that, at times, Aldeburgh became a town of whisperers.

In New York, I came to realize that Peter had been bending over backwards all the time to protect Ben, defend him from being hurt and, in the process, sometimes appeared overbearing and disagreeable, whereas it was Ben who was the dangerous one, easily offended and often unforgiving for an imagined slight. The words 'in favour' and 'out of favour' were frequently heard in that East Anglian town.

Glyndebourne was especially disliked and out of Ben's favour. It was a regrettable prejudice since his first two chamber operas, *Lucretia* and *Herring* began their successful careers there under the Christie aegis.

It may be there were more substantive reasons for the subsequent split, but there is an amusing story, possibly apocryphal, of Ben sitting on a bench in the covered way while *Lucretia* was being rehearsed within. Old John Christie, Glyndebourne's founder, comes by with several pugs, having taken them for a walk. He sits down next to Ben and they exchange 'Good mornings'. John C. looks at Ben and says, 'Who are you?' (He knew perfectly well but was an inveterate teaser.) Ben, astonished, 'Well ...I'm Benjamin Britten'. 'Oh, and what do you do?' Ben, nursing an incipient huff, said, 'Mr. Christie, I composed the opera they're rehearsing now in the theatre!' (Pause) 'Oh, dear! You shouldn't've, you know'. John then gets up and leaves with pugs, chuckling.

It may not have happened quite that way (or at all), but it represents the sort of misunderstood criticism that Ben couldn't bear and would always resent.

I'm grateful to him because it was he who invited me to prepare an edition of Monteverdi's *Il Ballo delle Ingrate* for Aldeburgh in 1958, my first professional venture into the world of seventeenth-century Italian opera, something that was going to occupy quite a few years thereafter.

Johnny Cranko directed, John Piper designed the sets and the cast was excellent. Tho' the style of that music was at that time strange and new to many people, it was voted a success.

When Glyndebourne invited me to prepare an edition of *L'Incoronazione di Poppea*' in 1962, I was considered to have abandoned Aldeburgh for the enemy camp and so I became 'out of favour' for a few years. Yet Ben, probably at Peter's suggestion, was one of the first to get in touch when my house in Hamilton Terrace burned down, offering his own microfilm of Monteverdi's *Ulisse*, which he knew I was preparing for Glyndebourne.

This extraordinary genius could be the most delightful company. But often, I believe, he was disguising a torrent of hurt, offense and anger which would probably burst out when he was alone with Peter, who then had to disguise an implacable ruthlessness towards people he felt had injured him.

Our Billy was Richard Stilwell, tall, handsome with a lovely baritone voice and a vulnerably eager figure on stage. His descent from the highest point on the ship's prow to the main deck, front of stage, in a matter of seconds in response to Captain Vere's call for volunteers was one of the most spectacular moments in a great production. One of the most moving was the contemplation of his own death and how, eventually he accepted his fate: 'they'll . . .drop me deep, fathoms down, fathoms down how I'll dream fast asleep'. All the while the piccolo sounding like a distant bosun's pipe summoning him away.

James Morris played Claggart, the evil one whose lust for power over Billy, perhaps for Billy himself, results in his own death. James had a fine, dark bass-baritone voice and was a very good-natured person who was very good at playing not-very-nice people. His soliloquy about his obsession with Billy and the desire to annihilate him was alarmingly convincing. He was also an excellent Nick Shadow in *The Rakes Progress*, which I later conducted for Santa Fe. He redeemed this Satanic image, however, with a moving portrayal of Mendelssohn's *Elijah* that he came to sing with me at Indianapolis.

I so much enjoyed those two seasons of *Billy Budd* at the Met and certainly owe much of it to John Dexter, sadly no longer with us.

XLV. THEATRE AND DIRECTORS, 2 – LAVELLI AND PARIS OPERA

The two seasons I've least enjoyed were spent at the Paris Opera, *le Palais Garnier*, one of the most beautiful theatres in Europe, now superseded by a modern, characterless building that works better.

I was invited to prepare Rameau's *Dardanus* for a new production to be directed by Georg Lavelli and was delighted at the prospect. Rameau, in my view, is the last undiscovered master of the eighteenth century and very few of his operas had, at that time, been revived.

His highly ornamented style is difficult to put into fluent performance and the extravagant demands of production have further hindered matters.

Some years earlier, I had recorded for Phillips with the ECO two LPs of his music to the ballet/fête, *Le Temple de la Gloire*, a strange work with text by Voltaire; part opera, part dance, which came to life most vividly. With that in mind, I set to work on *Dardanus*.

I already owned the complete edition of Rameau's works, published originally in the first years of the twentieth century under the somewhat surprising aegis of Camille Saint-Saens. Then I was fortunate enough to come across a copy of a contemporary edition of the *nouvelle tragédie* of *Dardanus* represented *pour le première fois* by the Académie Royale de Musique on the 7th of April, 1744.

In fact it had been first performed in 1739 and was revived, republished and revised more than six times in his lifetime, but the 1744 edition represented the more-or-less final version. The supplement of the complete, twentieth-century edition contained all the later variants in case they were needed.

I had worked with Lavelli some years earlier at Aix where Handel's *Alcina* had come to wonderful stage life through his vision of the great sorceress who, when she tired of her lovers, turned them into wild animals. They became her adoring slaves, guarding her from harm, never threatening those who took their place or seeking retribution for their own rejection. The splendidly bizarre look of her court and its eventual dissolution made a successful whole background of the opera into which the subplots fitted convincingly.

Remembering this, I was excited at the prospect of working with him on *Dardanus* and all the more disappointed when it turned out so badly due, largely, to his lack of an overall concept as to how it should be; how the larger theme could be played out.

I met with him more than a year before rehearsals began and found him vague and uncommitted. Later, when everyone was assembled, it was clear he was no closer to being sure what it was all about than before. The lack of purpose in his direction affected every aspect of the production. The actors moved without conviction, the sets by Max Bignens were laughably inappropriate, and the sheer mechanics were never well-executed. It was a slow process towards disaster, which with such extraordinary music and a superb cast seemed then and seems now so very sad.

One of the sets was a huge velvet box with a myriad of electric bulbs inserted in the walls and ceiling. Of course, many of them fused during performances and were only spasmodically replaced by a lax stage staff. Occasionally they exploded, which added a certain percussive effect to the score and scared the singers.

Another more ludicrous manifestation of a willful designer's 'originality' was the sea monster that Dardanus must slay to save a maiden and win his prize. It comprised a huge, seamless black plastic sheet covering most of the backstage floor. It was blown up by wind machines as the monster rose from the sea. After Dardanus slashed it with his sword, the sea monster – punctured and with wind machines turned off – sank to the floor defeated. The first time 'round it was rather impressive but, of course, the slashes had to be repaired before the monster could be blown up from the sea again. The repair tapes were visible, so it seemed to have had a nasty accident on its way up from the depths, which caused ribald comment from the audience.

Then there were the *songes* (dreams) that play an important part in the plot. It seemed perfectly reasonable that, being of the air, they should fly, an effect commonly used in the eighteenth century. The four dreams were put into harnesses and uplifted. Unfortunately, no one was able to control the separate wires so that, from the first dress-rehearsals to the last performance, the *songes* kept on bumping into each other. Worse, the blissfully peaceful dream music would be interrupted by a '*merde*' or a shriek and then more ribald comments from the house.

It would be kinder to pass by the orchestra, who were more interested in recipes for onion soup than any focusing on a relatively unknown great composer of their own country. From one rehearsal or performance to the next, it was never certain who would be playing. For most of the time, it was an orchestra of deputies.

The music staff, like the orchestra, was union-ridden, protected from all censure by the threat of that favourite French pastime, the *grève* (strike).

As the memories of this sadly trying time gradually recede, one amusing episode remains to leaven the lump.

There was one particularly untalented répétiteur (the lover, I later discovered, of the female head of the music-staff union) who found a simple chamber-organ accompaniment to a lovely ariette sung by Frederika von Stade ('Flicka' to her close friends). It was quite beyond his capabilities. He wrecked it every time and I asked that he be replaced. 'Impossible' was the union manager's response.

We came to the final dress rehearsal and the same muddle occurred again. I lost my temper and yelled at him, 'Monsieur, vous êtes un c.....' – a vulgar word I was rather surprised I knew. There followed a complete silence and everything stopped until one of the double-bass continuo players leaned over saying to Jean Mallandaine, who was playing harpsichord, in a perfectly audible, quiet voice, '*Ah! C'est vrai çe qu'il a dit*' (It's quite true, what he says). Of course everyone collapsed laughing, and I dare say a *grève* was thus avoided.

Every performance brought the same débâcle, and I could sense the orchestra looking forward to another explosion like the one they had so enjoyed. It never happened. We all went back the next season, of course for the money, and partly with a sense of revenge, partly in the hope things might improve and, to some degree, they did.

Musicians sometimes need their heads examined.

XLVI. THEATRE AND DIRECTORS, 3 – PETER HALL, STRATFORD AND GLYNDEBOURNE

There's a place in the last act of *Twelfth Night* as the tangle of false identities begins to unravel: Olivia has mistaken Viola (dressed as a young man) for her twin brother, Sebastian, whom she has just married. When Sebastian appears, she looks at them both and says, 'most wonderful'.

In Peter Hall's magical production at Stratford in 1960, this became an unforgettable moment. Those two words were enshrined in silence, focused upon by everyone on stage, each of whom would clearly interpret them differently:

- *The wonder of the twins, each of whom had feared the other was drowned in a shipwreck;*

- *The wondering relief of Antonio, the ship's captain, that both are alive. He loves Sebastian and says so;*

- *The wonder of Sir Andrew and the fearful wonder of Sir Toby having just taken a beating from Sebastian;*

- *The wondering, cynical amusement of Feste the clown;*

- *The wondering dawn of the Duke's love for Viola, now declared a woman;*

- *And, finally, the wondering, libidinous implications of Olivia's reaction to seeing two Sebastians: What could be better than one lover? Two, of course. Even if one were a woman? Perhaps. – said with such good humour.*

It was all there, and it made for one of those moments in the theatre that stays forever in the memory, and all made from two words – 'most wonderful'.

Somehow it symbolized, as on a much larger scale did the whole production, the best of Peter Hall.

It had lovingly embracing sets by Lila de Nobili, one of the greatest theatre designers, who did extraordinary work for Peter's early days at Stratford in *Midsummer Night's Dream*, *Two Gentlemen of Verona*, *Cymbeline*, and then vanished from the scene. Before Peter took over the company in 1960, there was *Love's Labour's Lost* transported from Cambridge. I had a great time writing the music and was, coincidentally, appointed Music Advisor. Music apart, my main contribution was to act with Peter in getting rid of the little café-sounding ensemble that played in the pit for tea trays in the entr'actes and made occasional subterranean accompaniments to the songs whenever they turned up in the plays. We appointed a group of eighteen players made up only of such instruments as were called for in the texts and who would all appear on stage when necessary. The old pit was built over to give a fourteen-foot apron to the existing stage, providing a much closer actor presence to the audience.

There was another memorable theatre collaboration that year at the Aldwych over Giraudoux's *Ondine*, a tragi-comedy about a water nymph who loves a human and is doomed to stay young as her lover grows old. Peter's wife, Leslie Caron, was the star, and perhaps the allegory fitted because their marriage began to break up at that time.

Rewarding as my connection with Peter Hall at Stratford and the Aldwych had been, it couldn't compare with the collaboration over four operas at Glyndebourne.

There had already been *Poppea* with a fine production by Günther Rennert, followed by the first Cavalli revival, *L'Ormindo*, again directed by Rennert.

Moran Caplat and George Christie had long wanted to involve Peter at Glyndebourne, and the second Cavalli, *La Calisto*, seemed a heaven-sent opportunity. The seventeenth-century Venetian operas became potential successors to the remarkable sequence of Rossini operas that had flourished under Vittorio Gui. A new team might develop something worthy to follow them and take their place alongside Mozart and other more contemporary pieces.

Peter and John Bury, the stage designer, faced the problem of realising the look and the setting of those operas in exactly the sense with which I had approached their music. It was not a matter of copying exactly the staging of those seventeenth-century Venetian theatres, tho' this could have been more easily done.

We knew, for example, that Drottningholm in Sweden boasted such an authentic theatre built in the mid-eighteenth century but modeled after its Venetian forbears. (There are several such scattered about Europe). But, fascinating as the old decors and mechanics were (I had conducted Sacchini's *Oedipus at Colonus* there), they had little or no relevance to the present day.

You can replicate virtually everything about those operas. but you can't recreate a seventeenth-century audience with its backgrounds and expectations. Present day audiences in those authentic places observe something historical, no matter how well performed, and they may like the opera for many good reasons, but it will still be an observation, not an involvement.

We tried to recreate the spirit of the work we performed, tho' using modern instruments in the orchestra and modern techniques of stage craft. We had a wonderful cast: Janet Baker, Ileana Cotrubas, James Bowman, Hugh Cuenod and Ugo Trama, and it was voted a success.

At one point, however, it was close to disaster. In the original manuscript, which consists of two musical staves, one for the voice and the other for the continuo, the line for Jove is in the bass clef. However, when he transforms himself into Diana in order to seduce little Calisto, one of the Goddess's most devoted nymphs, the musical line changes to soprano clef.

As it happened, Ugo Trama, who had already been at Glyndebourne for several seasons, often warmed up his fine bass voice by singing falsetto in the soprano range. Of course I knew this, and it was an added reason for casting him in the part. Rehearsals began well except that the scenes with Jove as Diana were always hysterically funny – worryingly so.

Early on we had a rough run-through on stage with anyone in the company welcome as audience. In the theatre, the guffaws, smirks, giggles and applause during those same scenes were so loud that the sense of it all vanished and the music was hardly audible.

We crept to our various homes that evening in something close to despair. Very early the next morning, telephones rang off the hook. Peter, Moran and I came to the conclusion that the only possible solution was for Janet to sing both parts: the Goddess Diana she had already prepared and that of Jove disguised as her.

We met before breakfast at Glyndebourne, rang Janet, who had driven, worried, back home to Harrow for the night, and asked her if she would do it. I can only think the idea had already occurred to her for, begging a further half hour to think about it, she rang back and said she would. In doing so she saved the day and took on one of the most memorable performances of her career.

It meant there was a good deal of new music for Janet to learn. Further, she had to play Jove in disguise, the only difference in costume being a large, silver-capped walking stick that Jove always carried, a symbol of authority. She did it brilliantly and was extremely funny as the lascivious Jove in drag, and heartrending as the Virgin Goddess struggling with her love for Endymion.

Ileana, with her ravishingly pure voice was perfect as the innocent nymph, Calisto. Ugo Trama took the cut in his part extremely well and was a grandly masculine Jove. Hugh Cuenod (See XXXI) in drag played the spinster nymph Linfea, weighing her libidinous temptations in the balance of possibility only to find the question taken completely out of her hands. James Bowman was a touching, handsome Endymion, and the rest of the cast maintained the standard of it all.

In its final format the piece became a comedy with a warm, amused, friendly focus on sexual ambivalence – who was what and where and how – elegantly portrayed with some very beautiful music to bear it along.

Our next essay was on a much grander scale: Monteverdi's *Il Ritorno d'Ulisse in Patria*.

The seventeenth-century librettist, Badoardo, portrayed this last stage of the hero's journey home against a background of a war between the gods. Ulysses has angered Neptune, who enlists the assistance of Jove to prevent his return. Only Minerva protects Ulysses and shepherds him through the slaughter of the suitors intent on seizing Penelope and his island to the joy of their final reunion.

All this tested the skills of John Bury much further than with *Calisto*. He had to create Jove's world above, Neptune's below the sea, and Ithaca, its shore and palace in between. Moreover, Neptune had to rise from the sea, Jove descend from the skies, and Minerva appear to Ulysses on Earth, then fly to Sparta to bring Telemachus home to help his father.

Apart from the miracle of engineering and the managing of it, the main concern of everyone was the representation of the human condition: the three suitors; the old shepherd helping his beloved master to regain his palace; the son bringing a ray of hope to the beleaguered, constant Penelope; and the most human moment of all, her reluctance to believe the man she now sees and who has saved her is indeed Ulysses. They have been apart for so long and she has become accustomed to her solitude. Ulysses, in a scene that is almost unbearably moving, has to woo her all over again.

Gluck's *Orfeo* was chosen as Janet Baker's farewell to the operatic stage. There were faint echoes in the choice of Kathleen Ferrier, whose mantle had fallen on Janet from the beginning and whose skill in singing she far surpassed. Peter seemed to have given Janet, increasingly through the two previous operas, a controlled fluency on stage which somehow liberated an ever-widening range of vocal expression. It was a great performance, and the fact that it was her last in opera made Orfeo's failure to release Euridice from death's hold all the more poignant. It was also a great production with memorable images like the Gates of Hell and the inspired concept of the Elysian Fields, where in a blue haze the blessed spirits, half naked, moved always in slow motion so beautifully reflecting the gentle peace of Gluck's music.

Two years after *Orfeo*, we revived *Poppea* in a new production. There was no question of involving Janet and I am glad of that. She had sung *Poppea* with me in a rather poor production at the Coliseum – sang beautifully, of course, but she didn't seem happy portraying the courtesan's overriding ambition to become Empress. It didn't relate to her own character and, rather like Edith Evans playing Cleopatra, it didn't quite suit. Ottavia would have been better.

At Glyndebourne Maria Ewing played the part superbly. I've rarely seen anyone identify themselves so completely with a rôle they were playing. It was quite frightening at times.

I had conducted *La Cenerentola* with her in Houston some years earlier, where again she showed this gift of being able to identify herself with the character – this time the poor waif who wins her prince and charms everyone with her simple good humour and a considerable amount of fine coloratura singing.

It was reassuring to find the same opera still working as well as it had twenty-two years earlier.

There was one rather amusing incident involving an understudy.

In an early scene, Poppea expresses her ambitions to her nurse, Arnalta, whom she loves and trusts. Where better, Peter thought, than in the intimacy of a bath house where confidences can be exchanged privily. Maria played it naked with Arnalta decorously ushering her into and out of the bath behind a large towel. The rim of the tub was judged exactly so that, even from high up in the balcony, only Maria's head and shoulders were visible, tho' with backlighting her silhouette showing through the towel was, for some, worth the price of the ticket.

Maria is a temperamental lady, and about the fourth performance, out of sorts, unwell or for some other reason, she cancelled.

The Glyndebourne practise of carefully prepared understudies meant that, with an afternoon brush-up call, the second Poppea was ready. We were all rather excited at the chance it gave to the young soprano who sang superbly, and everyone was delighted with her performance afterwards.

There was, however, one miscalculation. When it came to the bathroom scene, the towels, the silhouette looked fine. But someone had overlooked the fact that the new, well-endowed Poppea was six inches taller than Maria; thus, standing in the bath, she revealed considerably more than had originally been planned. There was a gasp of surprise behind me in the audience, but we all carried on and I don't believe the young understudy realised what had come about, at least not until her betoweled exit, with Arnalta giggling into its folds.

Soon after that I came to America and the link with Peter was broken.

XLVII. The Trouble with Flying

In 1972 Glyndebourne staged Monteverdi's *Il Ritorno d'Ulisse*. I had re-worked the score of the realisation in time after the fiery débâcle at Hamilton Terrace.

In the previous autumn of 1971, there was a series of urgent meetings with Peter Hall, John Bury, Moran Caplat, George Christie and myself. All had read the libretto, of course, and all realised there were horrendous technical problems ahead. Music, timing and cost vitally affected what was going to be possible. Five heads were thought to be better than one – very much in the way Glyndebourne usually functioned.

Predominant at first was the problem of flying – where to, where from, how much, how many, and how did the music fit. It was obvious that comparatively simple flying, the kind you see in *Peter Pan*, wouldn't do.

Apart from the earthly conflicts Ulysses has to face once deposited asleep on Ithaca's shore, there is a war going on in Heaven and Monteverdi's gods function either high up or rise from the depths of the sea. What's more, they have to interact with each other and sometimes with the humans on Earth.

Neptune, supported by Jove, is intent on Ulysses' destruction. His son, Polyphemus, had an eye put out by Ulysses while escaping from Sicily (being a Cyclops, he only had one to begin with).

Minerva, supported by Juno, is intent on helping Ulysses return to his homeland. She even goes off to Sparta to bring back Ulysses' son, Telemachus, who has seen the beautiful Helen (she whom all the row was about at Troy) and is in a position to bring comfort to his mother, Penelope, and help his father reclaim the island.

After coming down to Earth dressed as a shepherd in order to talk to Ulysses, Minerva must fly away and then, in due course, return in her aerial *Carro* (chariot) carrying Telemachus with her:

Telemachus sings:	*Lieto cammino, dolce viaggio,*	Joyous journey, sweet voyage,
	Passa il carro divino	The divine chariot flies
	Come che fosse un ragio.	Onward like a beam of light
Then, together,	*Gli Dei possente*	The powerful Gods
Minerva and	*Navigam l'aure*	Navigate as we furrow
Telemachus:	*Navigam l'aure*	Through the winds.

You can't ignore that, so John Bury devised a sort of overhead railway, strong enough to carry two bodies in a splendid chariot. Dressed up and lit, it made a tremendous impression. There was another complication that had to be incorporated and cost a great deal more money. Minerva had to come down to Earth to deliver Telemachus and eventually rise out of sight into the top of the fly tower. It's quite unnerving up there, and we were lucky that our 'gods' didn't suffer from a fear of heights.

Then there was Neptune, who had to rise from a turbulent sea and, in his anger, capsize the Phoeacian ship that had carried Ulysses back to the shores of Ithaca. Not content with sinking it, he then turns it into a rock.

Turbulent seas are not difficult. We know how the seventeenth-century Italian opera houses did it and that can't be improved upon. Two horizontal poles, covered in canvas shaped like corkscrews and painted blue-green with white peaks, are rotated in clock and counterclockwise motion. The effect is delightfully convincing and, of course, the more poles the more sea and room for Neptune to rise and sink the model ship, which, upturned, becomes a rock.

Neptune, however, can't just rise up at the back of the stage. He has to move forward in order to discuss matters of vengeance with Jove in the heavens. This means another track at ground (sea) level, the inverse of the heavenly one. Anne Howells, who sang the part of Minerva, called the opera 'Monteverdi's Flying Circus'.

All this John Bury designed with a wonderfully simple vision, combining superb twentieth-century engineering with lovely stylised versions of seventeenth-century decor and costumes. It all worked superbly well, making a splendid vehicle for this difficult but wonderful opera.

There remained one impossibly difficult problem: the slaughter of the three villainous suitors and their sycophantic crews.

Penelope, inspired by Minerva watching from above, decrees that whosoever can draw Ulysses' great bow and shoot an arrow from it shall have her hand in marriage and so rule the island.

Drawing Ulysses' bow after all three suitors have failed was no problem for the hero, who was disguised as a beggar. How to kill them with his arrows was another matter.

The description in the libretto is ludicrously unhelpful: '*cosi l'arco saetta, seguono le didascalie*'. 'So is the bow fired, follow the stage directions'. (There are none).

We discussed the problem endlessly, suggesting impossible solutions: The arrow might fly on wires (which would be seen in the stage lighting); no arrows, just a clasping of hands to hearts (which would look like sudden, multiple heart attacks); arrows fitted to costumes that would pop up when released (this works very well in a William Tell situation, but for fifteen or more people to kill, it would look like a busy railway station with the signals going off all over the place, or a group of porcupines).

At the end of a long day at the Bury house, Peter suddenly said, 'There's nothing for it; Ben (Luxon) has to have archery lessons. He must use real arrows to begin the slaughter. We can plot the rest'.

And so it came about. Ben was sent to archery school and proved himself a very apt pupil, an excellent bowman; an echo perhaps of his ancestors in Cornwall, bowmen who served King Arthur. Or was it King Henry V later at Agincourt?

Our troubles were not quite over. We realised there would have to be much diplomacy to persuade the cast there was no danger in it, especially when quite clearly there was. Curiosity about it was rife, but it was all kept secret until Ben was trained and ready.

His skills were first publically displayed at the end of a long morning rehearsal on the rehearsal stage at Glyndebourne. It was the least formal place to display what was a dangerous solution to a dangerous moment in the plot. The three suitors and their followers were just about to wish each other a good day and disband for lunch when Peter, who had ordered the line of axes to be put up, said, 'Come and take a look'.

Ben drew his bow and the arrow whizzed through the line of arrowheads plonk into the target set up at the end. All the onlookers knew where Peter had placed them in the scene during the rehearsal just ended and how close the flight of the arrow would come to each of them.

A general 'Oh!' and everyone glanced at his neighbour. A certain pallidity came over faces otherwise tanned by the Sussex sun. Some began to mutter something about consulting their union as to the legality of it; some just shook their heads; some said, 'That won't work'; some said it in Italian *'non è possibile'*.

Then Ben shot another and another with exactly the same flight through the axe heads, and the same plonk each within inches of the other. It merited and received general applause.

Gradually courage returned and eventually, with highly detailed planning and rehearsal, it turned into an amazing scene of slaughter so carefully choreographed that no one was in danger except for the stage hands in the wings, which area had to be cleared for that scene at every performance. Arrows thudded into upturned tables and criss-crossed the stage.

In the middle of it all stood Penelope, motionless, lit from above while the arrows appeared to flash past her in all directions. Janet must have been nervous about it but never showed the least tremor. She was an example to everyone in this as in so many other ways, a truly exceptional artist and person.

When the noble story of constancy, love and endurance came together with virtually all the problems of its presentation resolved and a cast that couldn't have been bettered, there happened in the lives of most people involved in it a sort of blessing of experience and enrichment. It was one of those gifts that come only occasionally in life, that contribute to an accumulation of riches that makes living an increasingly wonderful activity.

It was indeed a gift from the gods.

XLVIII. On Mozart
and Figaro

Among the best of Mozart's operas, *Figaro* is, perhaps, the most perfect; and it appears again and again in whole or in part throughout most musicians' professional lives.

My first experiences were a few student performances, but the first professional ones in public were at Covent Garden and on one of their provincial tours. I suppose they were try outs of the in-and-out sort that are, regrettably, part of an extended repertory season in most large opera houses. I remember very little of them except that casts changed at every performance – try outs there, too, no doubt. There was virtually no rehearsal. After all, who needs to rehearse *Figaro* when we all know it?

Of course, everyone gets through it. That's what Beverly Sills admiringly called 'professionalism', and, in a sense, it is to be admired. But there is a difference between skilled performers 'getting through' and an integrated representation of a masterpiece by a cast and orchestra well-rehearsed under a conductor and director who share a single view of the way it should be when presented before an audience.

During the in-and-out 'professional' performances, you occasionally get a glimpse of that other standard. A member of the cast will sing an aria in such a way that, for the moment, it transcends the rest and a higher interpretative level is revealed.

I remember one evening, in the midst of one of those early Garden Figaros many years ago, Kiri Te Kanawa singing '*Porgi Amor*' with a sad, truthful beauty that made me suddenly realise how wonderfully Mozart had identified, in musical terms, with that woman's heartbreaking reflection on a love that seemed to be no more. Her performance went way past the skill of singing (which often becomes the main criterion for critics and audiences alike) and showed a world of experience that was not present during the rest of the evening, 'professional' as it was.

That level of artistic truth can only be achieved throughout an entire opera in houses that adopt the festival pattern: several weeks of rehearsal, followed by performances scheduled close enough together (and with no changes in cast) so there is room for further development as the purpose and vision grow with the interrelation of the characters in performances.

Such houses as Glyndebourne and Santa Fe enable this to happen, and once you have worked at either of them, anything less seems indeed less.

Of course the great repertory opera houses devote an equal time, artistic skill and devotion to the preparation of a new production, but the performances, after the first few, tend to be quite far apart. The casts, often doing something in between, lose the initial concentration and it all becomes 'professional'.

There is an even less attractive, faulted way of presenting opera, regrettably prevalent in America. A few days together for the music and the moves on stage, hired scenery and costumes (sometimes bring your own), a few orchestral rehearsals and a local, amateur chorus equipped with more enthusiasm than voice, and that will do it. It's a sort of instant opera but, like that sort of coffee, there's no substitute for the real thing.

Not 'instant', but flawed was a *Figaro* I undertook with Scottish Opera. There was adequate time for musical and production rehearsal with an excellent cast. I wasn't told about the sets.

They turned out to belong to an earlier production that Scottish Opera, short of funds as usual, had to resuscitate to make ends meet. They were the hopelessly 'original' work of an inexperienced, 'thoroughly modern Millie' of a designer just out of design school who can't have read a synopsis of the plot. There weren't enough exits or entrances to accommodate the end of Act II, with gardeners bearing broken flower pots, Counts coming in and out in a rage about locked doors, people jumping out of a window and the arrival of two boisterous figures waving marriage contracts accompanied by their lawyer, while the Countess and Susanna lock and unlock doors to escape discovery. At one point the gardener had to take refuge in the Countess's bedroom, which didn't seem at all right. There was also a mysterious, immovable staircase that pointed up into the stage-left flies. We could only suppose the 'Millie' thought countesses always go upstairs to bed – not so. For our purposes it was an unusable and ever-present menace.

Another Figaro I conducted some years before that was in Oslo with Joan Cross in theatrical charge. She had been a celebrated Countess in her earlier days, and with conventional sets without 'originality'. She reproduced what she remembered of it all, but with great conviction and enthusiasm. It was late autumn or winter, and I mostly recall the welcoming, somewhat formal kindness of the Norwegians and that spectacular, snow-covered road running straight through town and on up to the Royal Palace. Halfway up on the right, there was a remarkable concert hall with murals by Edward Munch, more famous for his 'Scream'.

The opera house had been and, in between operas, still was a cinema. There was very little room backstage, and the pit below stretched narrowly and widely on either side of the conductor, making it difficult to control the extremities. As to the qualities of the performances I can only remember the *Brillup of Figaro* was very well-received and we had to give several extra performances.

Mozart's *Figaro* – his masterpiece – will survive in some measure almost any attempt to modernise, newly interpret or otherwise make it a vehicle for a director's originality.

The finest version I have so far seen was at Glyndebourne under Peter Hall's direction with sets by John Bury. The cast was unexceptionable, and I only wish I had had the good fortune to conduct it. From everyone concerned it seemed to manifest a sort of deeply considered search for the simple truth to be found in each situation as it arose.

A remarkable example of the vivid illumination this approach gave to the text came at the beginning of Act II.

Set in the Countess's dressing room, the scene opens with a long, beautiful orchestral introduction before she sings the famous aria *Porgi Amor*. This has proved a major problem for many directors. Sometimes it is ignored altogether, relegated to being a sort of entr'acte with the curtain rising only a bar or so before the Countess sings. Sometimes, beautifully dressed, she sits patiently through it in front of a mirror, eventually posing the question of lost love to her own reflection. Sometimes the curtain rises at the beginning and Figaro is there putting the finishing touches to an already immaculate wig and is dismissed just before the aria. Sometimes the Countess will act it out alone, picking things up and putting them down, looking out of the window, then turning back to sing. In one production I remember at Sadler's Wells, you saw as the curtain rose a painter looking like Franz Liszt sitting at his easel, a half-finished portrait before him, which he packed up, taking his leave just before the aria began. Several distracting thoughts came to mind: Would he have finished the portrait by the end of the run? Did he leave because the light at 7:00 a.m. (for da Ponte makes it perfectly clear this is the beginning of the day) was insufficient? Why, if the Countess was dressed for an early sitting, would she need Figaro and Susanna after it and not before? Tho' of course they may have come to her at 5:00 a.m. before the Act began.

At Glyndebourne the curtain rose on an empty dressing room as the music began. Through the dim, shafted light of early morning, you gradually noticed another room within, the bedroom, of course. On the bed was a single, forlorn figure who, in that lovely instrumental prelude, came slowly, disheveled from her bedroom where she has spent the night alone. Of course, she will need Figaro (the Barber of Seville, one remembers) to put her hair in order and, soon, Susanna to help her dress. Before that she asks the question that has been with her all night long: 'Where is Almaviva? What has happened to the love we shared in the days of Dr. Bartolo?'

Kiri's fine singing on that repertoire evening back in the days of Covent Garden on tour – for it was the same Countess, the same aria – was transformed and became really great in that place, in that setting. Unforgettable.

XLIX. Music and Directors – Peter Wood and *The Beggar's Opera*

The two directors whose work I've most admired and with whom I've most enjoyed working in opera as well as theatre are Peter Wood and Peter Hall. We began to know each other in early Cambridge days, but there were only a few collaborations at that time. I was more concerned with musical affairs and they with straight theatre.

They are very different people. P.W. has an extraordinary ability for flair when he is taken with an idea and responds directly and vividly to the vision the flair conjures up. P.H. takes more time. There's a tenacious hold on a concept, a vision, but there's a lot of considering to do before the truth and practicability of it all can be turned into action. Once the ground plan is complete, it becomes a matter of putting the relevant things in place during rehearsal.

P.W. gets impatient with himself and others as he tries to work out the realisation of his vision in rehearsal and it sometimes founders. P.H. is patience personified, and while P.W. creates as he directs, P.H. persuades everyone calmly to come 'round to his already determined point of view.

They are both highly intelligent, likeable, self-aware men of immense talent; P.W. less ambitious than P.H., who likes power. They both served the National Theatre extremely well in their different ways, setting standards that have never been surpassed. Collaborating with them was a joy.

There were four operas at Santa Fe with P.W. – *Così*, *Magic Flute*, *Mother of Us All*, Cavalli's *L'Orione* – and a memorable *Beggar's Opera* at the Aldwych. With P.H. there were four operas at Glyndebourne – Cavalli's *La Calisto*, Monteverdi's *Poppea* and *Ulisse*, Gluck's *Orfeo* – as well as many collaborations at Stratford and the Aldwych.

Santa Fe is the closest thing to Glyndebourne in America, tho' Brian Dickie's Chicago Opera Theatre now runs them close. Early planning and putting together early the three people in charge of music, production and decor are critical, so that, together, they may assemble ideas and come up with a single plan. The man who coordinates all this, the General Manager, has to steer the whole thing, supervise the casting and keep a wary eye on finance. At Glyndebourne there was Moran Caplat, John Crosby at Santa Fe, and Brian Dickie in Chicago. To be successful, there have to be about four or five weeks of rehearsal, adequate orchestral time and, finally, performances close enough together to allow for growth during the run. There must also be a carefully prepared apprentice/understudy system so that they can act as chorus and yet be able to step into a major rôle in an emergency.

Just why P.W. took on *The Mother of Us All* at Santa Fe isn't clear. It's a strange opera about a heroine of women's lib in America, Susan B. Anthony, with a libretto by Gertrude Stein and music by Virgil Thompson. The improbability of the subject, excellent cast, and my cajoling may all have contributed, but the result was a brilliant production that made up for the work's deficiencies, turning them into a dazzling piece of stagecraft.

It was fortunate that Virgil Thompson, famously difficult, was confined to a sickbed in New York. I had occasion to telephone him to ask permission to compile a brief overture. P.W. wanted to start the opera with a patriotic parade instead of its original, rather limp beginning. 'Go ahead, you can't ruin it', was Mr. Thompson's curt response, followed by 'Can't think why Crosby should hire two Englishmen to put on an opera about America'. I was irritated by this and said, 'You forget, Mr. Thompson, that without Englishmen there would never have been an America to write an opera about'. Grunt at the other end and the conversation was over. We neither saw nor heard from him again.

P.W.'s focusing on the showman's side of the piece left Susan B. Anthony as a lone, sometimes forlorn figure, and the last soliloquy, beautifully sung and understood by Mignon Dunn, 'A long life . . .', became all the more moving because of it.

P.W.'s *Magic Flute* was less successful and I was equally responsible for it. We changed the order of some scenes to make clear how bad is the Queen of the Night or how good is Sarastro. It didn't work but nobody much noticed the difference. There was one very funny moment when the Queen of the Night's elevator, bringing her up from subterranean depths, stuck just as her head appeared. So her second coloratura aria was sung literally at floor level, evoking strange resonances with Salome and the improbable image of John the Baptist's head singing high Fs. The Queen herself was not amused.

Così, on the other hand, was the best-conceived version in my experience. Of course it's still a comedy, but an increase in the sense of theatrical veracity has made us all question unreal situations. What on earth are those two silly girls doing alone in what is a rather grand house attended only by a pert, flighty girl who sometimes seems to rival her mistresses in her flirtations with an old, lecherous Don Alfonso? In that situation, only the two good-time boys have a reality.

We decided to make Despina a much older, matronly woman who, of course, could be safely left to look after these two girls while the family (their parents?) were away. It makes sense, too, of her relationship with Don Alfonso. They have the sort of conversations and actions that belie a long-standing sexual intimacy, now, probably, a matter of amused memory.

We were able to persuade Patricia Kern to undertake this unusual Despina, and she reveled in it, making a wonderfully lovable, wise older woman devoted to her girls and to having a bit of fun on the side. Don Alfonso was converted to a close family friend, perhaps a cousin of their parents or an estate manager – certainly not the 'dirty old man' who pinches Despina's bottom whenever he sees her. He doesn't need to.

With any production of *Così* there's the problem of the ending, and neither Da Ponte nor Mozart gives us any indication as to how it should be. Do the young men stay with their new-found loves even though found by counterfeit measures; or do they return somewhat shame-facedly to their former loves? Neither solution seems particularly satisfactory. The latter would entail a great deal of explaining and apologizing. The former has the element of deceit, which could undermine future trust. P.W. made each of the men pass by each of the girls, lingering long enough to show an equal attraction, but there was no definite commitment. The opera ended thus, with all four apart from each other. Wiser? Sadder? Who knows? The audience must decide. Several interesting modern possibilities came to mind as the curtain fell. It was a touching picture of lovely, unsure youth.

The quintessential Peter Wood production occurred at the Aldwych with the *Beggar's Opera*, that racy, mid-eighteenth-century play with songs that virtually put pay to Handel's Italian opera world.

The story of Polly, Lucy, the Peachams and Macheath grabbed every eighteenth-century imagination in London. The witty lyrics were set to any available tune, some rather cheekily taken from Italian opera. They were soon hummed everywhere.

The nineteenth-century found the *Beggar's Opera* vulgar and licentious (which it is). The era after the First World War, however, found it delightful and returned it to the London stage.

At first it was presented as an opera with spoken dialogue. There was an orchestra in the pit and every tune was attractively harmonised and orchestrated. Each song had to have an orchestral introduction so that the singer could find his or her note. Some versions had quite elaborate choruses and extended entr'actes. All these gave an irritating stop and start effect, which spoilt the dramatic flow.

Discussing it with P.W., we decided to follow the example we had set for ourselves over Shakespeare at Stratford on Avon; that is, everything had to happen on stage. With typical flair, P.W. made all the beggars convicted felons awaiting transportation to Australia. How better to pass the time in their collective dungeon than to reenact the history of the highwayman, Macheath, his escapades with the law, and his devious love affairs with Polly and Lucy. Beggars play lots of street instruments (they make money that way), so we used concertina, flute, penny-whistle, trumpet, percussion, bassoon and horn, as well as a barbershop male-voice quartet – villains all, consisting of two tenors, baritone and bass. We even had a rickety harmonium to give a faintly pious note to the more noble sentiments offered by the more deceitful beggars.

What looked like huge cardboard boxes and partitions were made to represent a thieves' den, a magistrate's court, Mr. Peacham's house and, at the end, most wonderful of all, the prow of the ship which was to take the beggars off to Australia. This, just as their opera was coming to Macheath's last moment on the gallows. It surpassed Gay's original ending and made one of the most striking final curtains I have ever seen.

It should have been a major success, but it wasn't. Our two leading ladies, Dorothy Tutin and Virginia Mckenna, were perfectly cast as Polly and Lucy. However neither was a professional singer and body-carried amplification had not at that time reached the sophistication it has now, so that their singing sounded weak.

All the same, I still remember those beggarly days with great affection. Were I troubled by nostalgia, there would be regrets; but the idea was so good, the musical settings worked and P.W. directed so brilliantly that I'm only grateful for having been involved. The memory of those days is quite unsullied by its comparative failings.

L. And So, Indianapolis

When finally, in 1976, I decided to come and live in America, I was lucky enough to be taken on for management by Ann Colbert. She was a formidable lady, a 'Berliner' like President Kennedy (one wonders how he would have made out if he'd come to Hamburg), only she was born there and proud of it. She had been a highly successful journalist but left Germany for reasons of Jewish persecution and became one of the most respected agents in New York, direct, honest and a good listener. She understood that I needed time to explore the musical world of America and, even more, to know for sure that I had been right to leave England, with those stifling arguments about 'authenticity', and extend my musical horizons in this new culture.

She sent me hither and thither to virtually all the major orchestras and quite a few lesser ones, too.

After a while, in 1984, Leonard Slatkin invited me to become Principal Guest Conductor with his symphony in St. Louis, a post I enjoyed greatly. It was my first extended experience of America's Midwest where, I now believe, the best of American values are to be found.

In 1985 I accepted a guest week at nearby Indianapolis, Indiana, famous for its annual 500-mile car race, but otherwise a mysteriously unsung city. (St. Louis, on the other hand, had its Arch, beer, Westend, Great Exhibition Park, Mississippi River, Mark Twain and Huckleberry Finn).

The centre of Indianapolis is marked by what's called Monument Circle, in the middle of which there is indeed a monument rather in the shape of Cleopatra's needle, with a lady on top wearing a hat with a bird. It commemorates some rather obscure battles but serves well as a focal point for the city.

Encompassed within the Circle is one of the smallest cathedrals in the world and the Indianapolis Symphony's home in the Circle Theatre – later the Hilbert Circle Theatre. It started life as a swanky cinema, modeled on one of the smartest cinemas in New York (long since demolished). In its heyday, it put on stage shows alternating with projected films and a resident orchestra to fill the gaps. Ghosts of Fred Astaire, Ginger Rogers, Tommy Dorsey, who had all performed there, added to the atmosphere. It was redesigned for the orchestra with the proscenium arch set back to allow full vision of the players.

The renovation wasn't finished when I first came to Indianapolis. At that time, the symphony's concert series was given in a hall at Butler University built especially for both the symphony and university by the Clowes family, after whom it was named. Unfortunately, their generosity and good intentions came apart at the seams.

The university's activities far outweighed the symphony's claim for the use of the hall, so the orchestra could rarely rehearse in it. Even the concert dates clashed occasionally with university functions.

Just before my first visit, the possibility of the orchestra taking over the downtown cinema became a probability. I was taken to see the somewhat derelict building and sensed the potential.

Back in Clowes Hall we gave a reasonably good concert. I greatly enjoyed working with the orchestra in spite of some rather shakily-held positions. There was a lot of love and care in their music and the orchestra only needed guidance and improvement in skills for them to prosper.

I did not, on that visit, much enjoy Indianapolis itself. I was put in a hotel on the Circle, which hardly passed muster. Then, following a practice I'd undertaken in all the cities I visited for the first time, I set out at about six o'clock in the evening to walk the surrounding streets so as to get a sense of the place. It was deserted. The streets were empty – clean but empty. There was neither a drunk nor a dog. Worse, everything was shut, nothing open, no public transport, only a few cars that gave the impression of getting out of town as fast as possible: All most discouraging.

Back in New York, Ann Colbert telephoned me saying, 'You made quite a hit with the Indianapolis Symphony Orchestra and they want you to be Music Director when the present one, John Nelson, leaves next season. I think you should decline; there are several other likelihoods in the offing'. I agreed, tho', apart from the dead city, I had greatly enjoyed the orchestra, warts and all. Personalities apart, there's always been a streak of the magister in me – fostered by Cambridge, no doubt – and clearly there was some magistering to do in Indy.

Against Ann's advice, I accepted a return visit the following season after the orchestra had moved into the Circle Theatre, which, refurbished without losing anything of its period looks, had a wonderful atmosphere of its own.

The rehearsals went even further than before, all on the theatre's stage where we were to perform – an essential factor in the development of dynamics, ensemble and tone quality for any orchestra. It seemed to me this one was set fair for a great future.

I understood later that my predecessor wanted to increase the size of the orchestra. As it stood with only eighty-seven players, it was the smallest full-time symphony (that is by year-round contracts) in America.

This must have been at the root of the somewhat anxious question asked by the chairman of the symphony's board, Rae Humke (the best we ever had), at a one-to-one luncheon, ostensibly a social occasion but which I later assumed to have had something of a vetting in it. Pleasantries finished, Rae asked me if I was happy about the size of the orchestra. Did I have any thoughts about adding desks of strings and extra winds to bring it up to the size of the other full-time orchestras in the States?

I replied emphatically in the negative. The numbers presented a golden opportunity to build the character of a classical orchestra with a particular style and sound of its own. The numbers were admirably suited to the music of Haydn, Mozart, Beethoven, the earlier Romantics, Brahms, Schubert, Mendelssohn and Schumann – until you come to the late nineteenth century when a sort of *follie de grandeur* seems to have overtaken the European music world and Mahler could write a symphony for a thousand performers. Things quieted down after the First World War when money was short. The Indianapolis orchestra, skipping the monster-sized pieces, could take up the repertoire since then. If people wanted to hear a Mahler symphony, Scriabine's *Poème d'Extase* or Wagner's *Ring*, they could go up the road to another great orchestra in Chicago whose size is suited to such music. Played with smaller forces, it just doesn't sound right.

I had not at that point been asked about taking over the music directorship, tho' I was pointedly given reassuring details of a recent financial drive that had put twenty million dollars into the orchestra's endowment fund. When I left fourteen years later, we had increased that to more than one hundred twenty million dollars – a symbol, I hope, of our general development.

I would here digress a little to describe the economic structure that sustains the Indianapolis Symphony Orchestra (and virtually all other orchestras in the country). It is a structure that is uniquely American which, when it works, works better than any other from the point of view of an orchestra in its society.

Each major city, no matter how large, has only one symphony orchestra – unlike London and most major European cities, which each have several of them struggling and squabbling over public monies for survival. In America there is so little government money that virtually all support must come from the home base, which focuses things wonderfully. If a city can't afford it, there will be no symphony to be found there. Even New York finds there is only enough money for one.

Remarkable, then, that Indianapolis, a medium-sized city when the orchestra was founded more than seventy-five years ago, should have made it survive and prosper. It certainly would not have done so were it not for the initial generosity of Eli Lilly, grandson of the founder of the pharmaceutical firm. He and his descendants realised that to develop his drugs they needed to attract the most brilliant scientists in the world to a city that could show an intellectual climate for them to inhabit with their families.

Schools, theatres, churches, museums and a symphony were essential parts of his scheme of things. For all his wealth and success, Eli Lilly was a modest man, shunning publicity, a characteristic of the men in charge of that company during my fourteen years with the symphony – like Dick Wood, Randy Tobias, and Sydney Taurel. They continued the company's and community's support of the orchestra, and have acted as advisors when necessary with the discretion characteristic of the firm.

Under their aegis and that of a sequence of excellent ISO board chairmen, we have seen the endowment fund grow until now it provides approximately one-third of the income needed to sustain the orchestra. Another third comes from ticket sales and the last one-third from our annual fund to which the public contributes.

After my second visit to Indianapolis, I still hesitated, tho' clearly something was happening to the city. Its centre was full of life; people milled about downtown 'til after midnight. Plans were afoot to develop downtown as a place to live as well as work and shop (and all this has come wonderfully to pass). It all added up to something very encouraging so, when later I was asked again to accept the directorship of the symphony, I agreed, much to Ann's displeasure. 'You'll regret it. They're like the town; they're Indianoplace'. With considerable restraint, I replied that the place was perceptibly undergoing a great change and the orchestra showed every sign of being ready to do the same – and I was going to see to it.

And so it turned out, tho' a good friendship was severely strained.

The next fourteen years were among the happiest and, in some ways, the most fruitful of my life. Everything grew: the city; the number of wonderful people in it who wanted the orchestra to prosper. I found the love of my life or, rather, love found us. And the orchestra, so full of talent, set out to develop its own style and character, as I knew it would.

The object of it all was to develop the music-making skills and to establish the image of a distinguished classical orchestra. Towards that end I scheduled a lot of Beethoven in my first full season; for the second a great deal of Haydn and Brahms; for the third, a bias towards Mozart and Schubert. Of course, it had to be planned discreetly, with many 'lollipops' in between the serious stuff. No one likes to be preached at, especially in a nonreligious setting, so there was a certain slyness in the planning. Nevertheless, like a good vaccination, the classical agenda seemed to take. After a while, people noticed that the way we came to play Tchaikovsky's *Manfred* Symphony was quite different from the classical clarity with which we played Beethoven's *7th Symphony*.

Eventually, we made two European tours and another one to the American South. We were broadcast each week locally and started a series of thirteen hour-long programmes each year with commentary that went to more than 200 radio stations all over the country. We made nine commercial recordings which sold well and, very important, we stayed in the black and increased our endowment fund.

Throughout, we sought to involve the minds as well as the hearts of our audiences and, out of their interest, to enlarge their numbers and improve our cultural ratings in a city overly dominated by sports. Music education in the public schools was spotty and, on the whole, poor. We established our own education department and appointed a splendidly committed, original-minded person, Beth Outland, who has revolutionised our contact with the schools. The orchestra's musicians, many of whom have young children, joined in and willingly gave of their skills to great effect. We instigated a new sort of programme note, wittily written by Marianne Tobias, that instruct and amuse, to quote Addison's ideals of the eighteenth-century Spectator. She is one of the mainstays of life in Indianapolis music and a dear friend, pianist, author; altogether a superb person. We added lights, projections, and analyses with illustrations into the performances. There were meetings before, meetings after, parties here, parties there, a veritable social centre.

As candidate Barack Obama said, perhaps rather too many times, change is necessary in all things. So, after fourteen years, I left the main job at the orchestra to have a little more time to write, undertake the occasional opera and generally reflect how wonderful it has all been – and still is; how much I've enjoyed it all – still do; how lucky I've been – still am.